Praise for *A Song for Wildcats*

This collection is lush, haunting, and touches on many themes that are incredibly tough, yet Caitlin handles them with an expert touch. Along with her riveting prose and breathtaking attention to detail, the way Caitlin's writing approaches discussions of mental illness and trauma makes me feel utterly seen. With a dreamlike (or nightmare-ish?) quality that makes the reader feel as though they are walking through mist in some liminal space, *A Song for Wildcats* authentically exhibits what it's like to live with mental illness. Caitlin is a writer to watch, without a doubt. Pure talent.

— K.J. AIELLO, author of *The Monster and the Mirror*

Exquisite as a noose fashioned from lace, as violent as arsenic served in a painted teacup. With each story, Caitlin Galway crafts a delicious, gothic world informed by the morbid fascinations of its characters. Galway examines love with a microscope and uncovers its unspeakable qualities: the darkness of loyalty, the recklessness of devotion. The writing is suspenseful and gorgeous. A cross between Mavis Gallant and Shirley Jackson, between Patricia Highsmith and Louisa May Alcott. I loved it.

— HEATHER O'NEILL, author of *The Capital of Dreams*

Moving deftly between the real and surreal, *A Song for Wildcats* manifests the achingly familiar wounds from trauma, grief, family, and mental health into strange realms. These stories, full of doppelgangers, malevolent spirits, and fairy wisps, speak in the language of wildcats: urgent, otherworldly, and impossible to ignore.

— PAOLA FERRANTE, author of *Her Body Among Animals*

There's a lot to admire about these stories — exquisite language, nuanced characterizations, and sophisticated insights into desire, longing, and identity. But what might be most striking is the unwavering authority of Caitlin Galway's storytelling, which recalls some of the great short fiction writers in the English language, particularly Grace Paley and Mavis Gallant. *A Song for Wildcats* is an outstanding collection by a writer to watch.

— PASHA MALLA, author of *All You Can Kill*

Caitlin Galway's swooning prose breaks like waves through this sharply observed world tour of indelible characters tossed through time, rugged with loss, and fraught with longing, where violence is often a whisper, sometimes a roar, and desire burrows like roots into their intimate histories.

— ELAN MASTAI, author of *All Our Wrong Todays*

A Song for Wildcats is a remarkable collection of five stories that move seamlessly through historical time periods and settings with a touch of the surreal. Whether it's ghosts in Northern Ireland during the Troubles or doppelgangers in 1980s Las Vegas, Caitlin Galway's striking and elegant prose transports you into the rich inner worlds of her raw but fiery characters. These urgent stories of desire, secrets, unconditional love, resistance, and survival are intimate, dreamlike, and profoundly affecting.

— KATHRYN MOCKLER, author of *Anecdotes*

Caitlin Galway's *A Song for Wildcats* is a haunting collection of stories that span the world, the 20th century, and the human heart. A truly huge achievement, but it's the small details of Galway's characters that will stay with readers long after the book is back on the shelf.

— REBECCA ROSENBLUM, author of *So Much Love*

Full of longing and desire, *A Song for Wildcats* weaves together love stories, ghost stories, and stories that reach for the magic at the edges of our world. With writing that is visceral, lyrical, and sensual, Galway's stories are haunting and transportive — perfectly capturing the wildness of the human heart. A book to devour and an author to watch!

— ANUJA VARGHESE, author of *Chrysalis*

Every self is a world and every sentence is a song in this collection of lush, delirious fiction. The book's cast of glorious eccentrics — philosophers and doppelgangers, amateur occultists and enigmatic animals, queer Romantics and aspiring revolutionaries — stand in trembling but wholehearted defiance of the myriad banalities and cruelties that confront them. Profound as a swan song and mesmerizing as a siren song, *A Song for Wildcats* reminds us that a vivid imagination can bend space-time, and that each human action is imbued with a tender and merciless gravity. What absolute luck to be alive and reading books at the same time Caitlin Galway is writing them.

— JADE WALLACE, author of *Anomia*

A Song for Wildcats

A Song for Wildcats

stories

Caitlin Galway

Copyright © Caitlin Galway, 2025

All rights reserved. No part of this publication may be reproduced, stored in a retrieval system, or transmitted in any form or by any means, electronic, mechanical, photocopying, recording, or otherwise (except for brief passages for purpose of review) without the prior permission of Dundurn Press. Permission to photocopy should be requested from Access Copyright.

All characters in this work are fictitious. Any resemblance to real persons, living or dead, is purely coincidental.

Publisher: Meghan Macdonald | Acquiring editor: Megan Beadle | Editor: Russell Smith
Cover designer: Laura Boyle
Cover image: frame and rower: istock/francescoch (modified by Karen Alexiou and Laura Boyle); Lynx constellation: istock/Allexxandar

Library and Archives Canada Cataloguing in Publication

Title: A song for wildcats : stories / Caitlin Galway.
Names: Galway, Caitlin, author
Identifiers: Canadiana (print) 2024048147X | Canadiana (ebook) 20240481488 | ISBN 9781459755161 (softcover) | ISBN 9781459755178 (PDF) | ISBN 9781459755185 (EPUB)
Subjects: LCGFT: Short stories.
Classification: LCC PS8613.A45993 S56 2025 | DDC C813/.6—dc23

We acknowledge the support of the Canada Council for the Arts and the Ontario Arts Council for our publishing program. We also acknowledge the financial support of the Government of Ontario, through the Ontario Book Publishing Tax Credit and Ontario Creates, and the Government of Canada.

Care has been taken to trace the ownership of copyright material used in this book. The author and the publisher welcome any information enabling them to rectify any references or credits in subsequent editions.

The publisher is not responsible for websites or their content unless they are owned by the publisher.

Printed and bound in Canada.

Rare Machines, an imprint of Dundurn Press
1382 Queen Street East
Toronto, Ontario, Canada M4L 1C9
dundurn.com, @dundurnpress

"Where can we hide in fair weather, we orphans of the storm?"

— EVELYN WAUGH, *Brideshead Revisited*

To-day, I will seek not the shadowy region;
    Its unsustaining vastness waxes drear;
And visions rising, legion after legion,
    Bring the unreal world too strangely near.

— EMILY BRONTË, "Often rebuked, yet always back returning"

Contents

A Song for Wildcats	1
Heatstroke	43
The Islanders	61
The Wisp	121
The Lyrebird's Bell	157
Acknowledgements	223
About the Author	225

A Song for Wildcats

I lived within a glass casket, off which the world glanced and glided away. Before me, sailboats lazed along the harbour. The occasional motor trailed a veil of foam across the sea's unblemished blue. The air was thick with the sweat and dust of foot traffic and the smoky chestnut flour, mountain mint, and wild figs of the market stalls. And I was there, loitering in the piazza, yet I was not. The glassy remoteness that had long encased me, and intensified the past year at school, had followed me to Ajaccio.

It was still my first week in the small commune on the west coast of Corsica, a mountainous island whose country seemed on the brink of war. My mother had imbued my travels with a sense of academic urgency. Here was a chance to prepare for the rigorous fall semester, without disruption, and maintain my scholarship after months of medical leave — a leave I did not want, or need.

Colour it as she liked, it was an exile. And I welcomed it. I could afford it with the money earned working weekends at a thatched-roof pub back home in Fulbourn, and leaving meant reprieve from my mother's choked respectability, the drab misery of dwelling under her pinched-lipped, suburban disgust.

Don't look at me like that, Alfie. You were both told in no uncertain terms to keep away from each other, and you didn't listen. Do you have any idea what could happen to this family? It'd be me they'd blame, you know, for never remarrying. Pacing the sitting room, she would twist the plastic rosebud in her ear while I sighed and buried my face in my hands. *Oh, none of that, yeah?* Flinging up her hands. *And a cabinet minister's son — really, Alfred. Do you mortify me on purpose? The lad's father is intervening — he says there has to be some distance between you. He practically threatened me.* She would thus end the daily tirade with her hand on her chest, panting daintily from the exertion of it all.

Nonetheless, Ajaccio seemed a wise choice to both of us: rich with rare biodiversity — I was studying the natural sciences — and detached from the political upheaval across mainland France. It followed the old English logic of coastal climate clearing the body and mind of illness. And my mother believed it was an illness, a sort of perversion of the psyche, at the root of my recent melancholy.

For years I, too, had feared such perversion in myself. Now I did not see my nature as abnormal; rather, lust itself was a wild, precarious instinct I had not carefully considered. Throughout the affair with the cabinet minister's son, a classmate at Cambridge, I had failed in that most natural of functions: to identify what was good for me, and what was not.

In fact, I had held so little control within the year-long affair that I hardly understood my choices as they happened, nor my *vacancies* — those moments absent of choice, lowering over me like a cage. From nearly the start of the affair, even at its most tranquil — waking to the misty green court through his room's old, mullioned windows, meeting at the elms at night, or gazing across the oak-panelled dining hall — I felt as though I had been pushed from a high peak, rolling backward with a sack cinched over my head.

A Song for Wildcats

I had not, when imagining love, accounted for whatever quality in me veered toward destruction, or provoked it in others. But here, alone, I would learn the art of self-preservation. I would never allow myself to fall into such destructiveness again.

I leaned against the gate behind me, which encircled the piazza's isolated garden. Daggered leaves broke through, prickling my skin. The burn of the iron seeped through my shirt, and the sun's razored heat cut into my skin. But it was some other body being touched, some faraway soul, while I received only blunted, second-hand nerve impulses. I had just sunk my nails into my cheek, into the tender sting of a sunburn, when a small commotion broke out at the centre of the market square.

First came a violent squeak, then a voice through a bullhorn. American, bold, arrestingly clear. I followed it, making my way through the crowd toward a group of young demonstrators. They were lambasting de Gaulle's resistance to reform, to tearing down social facades and letting burn what needed to burn. Their signs protested, in strikes of red paint, imperialism and the war in Vietnam.

"Revolution isn't pyrophoric," said the voice, first in French and again in English, for tourists like me. "Sparks of change build between wars and revolts. The human condition isn't to stagnate. Every point of reform and enlightenment that we reach as a society must be the beginning, not the end."

The voice came from a young man with windblown blond hair and wearing a blinding white T-shirt half-tucked into torn jeans. I was surprised to see how many people stopped to listen as the group handed out newspaper pages and pamphlets. He was inviting. He spoke seriously, yet his voice leaped over the idling crowd like a clear-flowing spring. Whenever someone approached him, he offered a wide smile, its corners sharp and piercing. It vanished and reappeared, again and again, as he drew the breezy hair from his face.

3

I believed in the eruption of global unrest. Though in London we had marched against the war, I admired the fervour sweeping across France. The world was in flux, as it had always been. Societies looking inward, seeking outward. I told myself that this was the reason I drew closer to the demonstrators, but in truth, something in the rhythm of my breath propelled me forward, rowing me like a vessel through open space. I did not realize how close I had gotten until the man's eyes met mine.

"*Salut*," he said, handing the bullhorn to his colleague.

A drop of warmth fell through me. His eyes were a lucent undersea blue, and a small freckle sat low on his cheek, like a fake beauty mark.

"Hi," I said.

He held up a pamphlet, casually as a bottle of beer. "Want one?"

It alarmed me that he could see me in any real sense. Lately I had felt like I was not wearing my own face; when I looked in the mirror, my reflection disordered itself into a jeering derangement of features.

"What?" I said. "No. No, thanks."

A puzzled look, then the corner of his mouth sparked up. "Why not?"

"I just …" The moment stretched. He was looking too plainly at me, and soon I could barely see beyond the burn of embarrassment. "I just have to go."

I turned and walked away. Head down, rubbing my chest, breath straining through a tightening channel. I disappeared along Rue des Anciens Fossés, in the opposite direction of my hostel, and dipped into a shaded alleyway of cold, scuffed stone.

His smile lingered, a Cheshire apparition hovering over me. The harder I tried to steady my breath, the sharper the smile grew, the higher it floated into the air like a rising blade.

I shrank into the shadows, tucked behind the fanning palms guarding the alley. I waited until the sounds of the demonstrators faded. The sky would burn into the ashes of dusk before I could bring myself to leave.

*

A peculiar Mediterranean storm had reached the coast, the sirocco winds lifting from the desert and tearing across the sea. Rain fell in long, silver pins and shattered the dark water filling the streets. The humidity suffocated my small room until it shrank around me, and my breaths gained a cottony thickness. I sat in bed, listening to the whir of an electric fan and muffled ribbons of conversation trailing upstairs from the grungy, velour-laden lounge below.

The hostel was a terrace house in the heart of the old urban core. It was part of a winding ream of colourful facades, each one parched pink or scrubby apricot, with long-louvred shutters flung open onto dusky interiors. The piazza was a short walk away, and across the street stretched the harbour, where the surf now broke in a wild, galloping spray.

I had been uneasy since the piazza that afternoon. I tried to read, but the words sifted from my brain, defying retention. I paced between the walls of dirty eggshell blue, under a bald grey bulb dangling from the ceiling and washing the room in an overcast dimness. The room's dimensions did not allow for truly productive pacing, but the space was sparse enough: wall mirror, brittle brass bed frame, wicker chair chained with cobweb, haunting me from the corner. The wall mirror watched me as I moved, its glass mottled as though time had spat on it and let the saliva rust.

It was the American distracting me. His freckle hovered in the periphery of my mind like a voracious fly.

I could not explain it. The encounter had been so transient that my memory had already smudged even the barest features of the other demonstrators. But still it churned in my stomach. There was a potency to the moment, warm and pained like a ruptured blood vessel. As I studied my books on Corsican territory — Ajaccio being Napoleon's birthplace was rather celebrated, it seemed — my hand wandered from my notes to scribble a tangly portrait in the margin. Once I noticed the American's face, ink saturated and smiling, I ripped the page into pieces. The sensation was visceral, like my own nerves tearing under my skin. I swept the shreds under the bed with my foot, then pinched my forearm until it was warped with bruises and my mind was again calm.

Across the room, a ghostly film over the mirror obscured my reflection. I rose from the bed and walked to it, clearing the film with a shirt grabbed off the floor. What had the American seen when he looked at me? Lanky limbed, not particularly tall. Ruddy hair worn almost effeminately long. A paprika puff of freckles and a sullen mouth that had never suited me, set with all the plump severity of some ghastly child-baron. I stared into the mirror and tried to order my features, locate the face I knew was mine, but the reflection was too impersonal. An entirely separate person peering at me through the passage of a secret world.

I had once known that world, had I not? There was an Alfred Bloom who roamed the foggy green fens with other Fulbourn boys, racing through ancient peat and swaths of rustling grains. Where was he now? Even fresher iterations of myself, like the spirited one who had first arrived at Cambridge, were lost to me, severed and insubstantial as fading echoes.

I was staring too long into the mirror, the eyes growing strange. Watching and unwavering. I felt a leap of panic and turned away, kneading my palm into my chest. I thought of the classmate standing behind me, positioning me before the mirror in his room. *Your bones are sharpest here.* Touching my slice of collarbone. *And here. Down here too.* My jawline, my ribs. *It's like I can see inside you.* His

6

eyes, grey as dead teeth, running a cold glaze over me. *Like I've cut you open.*

It was his parent, not my own, who caught us. A small mercy, in a way — for me, at least. Maybe that was why I did not refute the classmate's claim that the affair had been my idea, my seduction — or maybe it was some notion of heroic sentiment. An effort to be honourable, to lend dignity to our shared intimacy, base and perilous as it was.

Though I was not so sure it could be called intimacy. I had come to see it as lower than common love, as mind-draining as two addicts passing a needle back and forth. Each time I left his room, re-emerging onto the brilliant green plain of the courtyard, I felt as though I had left a piece of my body behind, a vital organ or limb. Often what we did in bed was so painful that I would ask him to stop. When he did not, I would bite into the pillow, channelling the pain into my teeth until I slipped from my body, leaving it to stiffen and curl like calcified remains.

Sometimes, instead, I would look through the window and leaf through the stars. Watch them until they watched back. Though I could never quite see them clearly — only in small patches — through the fog and fingerprints that blinded the glass.

After the first time together, the classmate dabbed the red threads from my thigh with a wet towel. *See how I love you?* he said. *Who else would do this for you?*

Need for someone, that kind of desperation, was an addictive anaesthetic. It dulled the senses to the damage being done — the drilling of a hole in one's mouth, the gutting of one's body. And how could I blame the classmate instead of myself? I clung to him as though he had drunk the heartbeat from me, and to hold him was to be close to my own pulse, stolen and stowed in the hidden rivers of his veins.

Wind whispered through the poorly sealed window. A tatter of paper scraped out, like an injured moth, from the underbelly of the bed. Picking it up, I thumbed the inky corner of a smile and felt a curious frequency in my hand, as if I had placed my palm on a piano and the notes were still ringing in my blood. I squeezed the paper in my fist and sat on the windowsill.

As the wind swelled, the tree outside my window scratched the glass. The storm shook the droplets of red berries suspended between the leaves, as though the tree were quivering with blood. I leaned close to the glass and listened until the sounds of the storm became a lonely plea. The branches clawed, weak and whipped about, and I felt a pained palpitation deep in my core. Touching my fingertips to the glass, I nearly opened the window despite the cutting rain to let the tree crawl in, to let the stirring in my fingers seep out and cling like sap to its branches.

✳

All night, rain sparked off the road, and a dusty wind engulfed the commune. Even as the storm calmed, a feverish fog remained, rippling hot under my skin.

I tossed in bed, linens stripped, thoughts spinning and delirious. Each footfall from the stairwell was a police officer, chasing me from across the English Channel for gross indecency, or the classmate's father walking in with the winter air on his coat — and a bottle of dark scotch, soon to be smashed, the scent sticking to the floor for days — thinking to surprise his son before exams.

When sleep did come, my mind plunged into the slanted banality of the most terrible dreams. They came in fragments, fading in and out, like drowsy blinking. I dreamed of a figure lying in bed beside me. His fingers sank into the soft flesh between my collarbones, scooping out my blood to bring to his mouth like honey. Before us, too high on the wall, where no one could reach it, a mirror flickered like a choked light bulb.

And each time the dream faded, a pair of eyes broke through, startling and clear.

I woke with a jolt, my hand to my throat. My undershirt was damp and stuck to my skin. There was a pounding numbness in my chest. I pressed hard against it, imagined cracking my breastbone. The classmate had liked to push his weight onto it, and the terrifying breathlessness of the action swept through me now.

I pushed off the mattress as if it were a trap door. Opening the window, I let the air rush in and widen the closing space around me. Memories pinched at the centre of my brain — the classmate's father, the bottle of scotch cast to the floor, cracking open, unfamiliar hands on me, throwing me like a shadow against the wall.

The sound of the nearby harbour waves became the torpid lull of the River Cam, cutting through campus, and I saw the classmate gliding in a wooden punt, standing on the deck with long spruce pole in hand, waiting like a ferryman in the mist.

I might have lost the night to this descent, but a cough startled me. I looked down from my second-storey room and saw a man standing in the middle of the empty road.

I blinked, still bleary. Was he lost? Injured? Common sense would have kept me in my room, but my muscles pulled forward, everything soft in me magnetized toward the shadowed figure below. I grabbed my umbrella and hurried down the hostel steps, out into the dwindling rain.

"Hey, mate, you all right?" I called.

The man turned, paused. My heart hitched higher. Our aloneness in the silent dark carried a sudden chill of vulnerability, like two wild and solitary creatures catching sight of one another in the woods.

It was the American. He was barefoot, and his clothes — pyjamas beneath a green jumper with heavily frayed cuffs — were soaked. Ducking his head a little, he squinted. His eyes tugged at mine as I looked away.

"We've met …" he said.

I stammered, feigning ignorance.

"I'm not stalking you." He ticked his head toward the street behind him. "I'm visiting my dad, just over there."

"Has something happened?" I glanced at his feet.

They moved swiftly toward me, seamlessly sidestepping puddles and stones, a blinking slice of glass I did not see until his heel landed softly beside it.

"Oh, no, nothing like that. I just have this busted shutter over my bedroom window. So I was trying to work, and the wind kept knocking it, just completely hammering it against the glass, and I kept hearing *come out, come out, I came so far.*" The ashen-yellow sky and gleaming rain-lustre of the road gave a bronze-cast beauty to the night. He inhaled deeply as he looked around, then laughed. "I actually don't know how long I've been out here."

A cigarette, streaming messy clouds, vibrated in his hand. He held it out to me. At first, I stared at it hovering mid-air, disoriented by such casual intimacy. I knew in taking it, we would be ushered into ongoing conversation, but the stirring crept into my fingers again, and they reached out, as if carried by a resurgence in the wind.

Our fingers brushed, light as soap bubbles. My voice rose to the roof of my mouth. "You haven't been out here all night, have you?" I asked. "During the storm?"

"Not the worst of it, no. I'm not as out of it as I look."

"No, yeah." I nodded, a little dazed. I was overwhelmed by his sudden appearance and the sweeping echolocation of the rain. In its countless fine points lightly striking every surface, I heard the vastness of the space around me. "I thought maybe you were someone who needed help, when I saw you. You're shivering. You can get hypothermia from the rain, you know."

A Song for Wildcats

He waved off the concern before letting out another gristly cough. "That was good of you. A lot of people wouldn't bother with that sort of thing."

"I'm sure they would." I surprised myself by gesturing with my umbrella, an offer of shelter. I watched my own actions with boggled detachment. My reluctant mind and persistent body were misaligned, stretched far apart and connected only by a tenuous elasticity. "You're going to catch pneumonia or bloody typhus," I said.

"Typhus." He laughed. "It's not the eighteenth century."

"Well, people *do* still die from typhus."

"You're right. I sound completely bourgeois." He rubbed his arms and let his teeth chatter. Rain, gathered on a curving frond, fell from the palm tree by the hostel steps and landed with a smack on his scalp. "Okay, cool. Thanks, man."

As he dipped under the umbrella, the sudden shift in proximity shook my equilibrium; it took a slow-reeling second for me to understand how closely we were huddled together. I tightened my grip around the umbrella's handle. My mouth felt heavy and warm as I spoke. "I'll walk you home," I said, taking a step in the direction of his flat.

"Were you watching me from the window?" he asked, without moving. "Did you know it was me?"

I froze, then stepped back in front of him. "Of course not. I don't even know who you are."

A current of electricity seemed to run through his lips, twitching at the corner. "I wouldn't have minded. I must look pretty bizarre."

We were so close that I felt the hypnotic pull of his pupils. I could not see his pale lashes so much as the harbour lamps glinting along each strand, like glowing flares of dust.

"Well, I wasn't." I looked down the street with searching fixation. "Which flat is yours, then?"

He did not answer. His eyes burned the side of my face. I worried he was studying me. Tilting me back and forth in his mind, in search of some impurity.

"Here." He tapped my knuckles.

My hand jerked away like it had touched a boiling kettle.

"I just mean ..." He indicated the cigarette. It had gone out, snuffed by a raindrop.

I looked down. "Oh. Sorry."

As he slipped it from my fingers, I filled with a high-floating nervousness, like gliding up and over a hill. To ground myself in some practical gesture, I reached to fix where the umbrella canopy had slipped loose from the tip. Then I shoved my hand into the pocket of my track-suit bottoms and squeezed the inner lining.

A silence fell between us. He took a lighter from his pocket, flicked it, cupped the flame. Over the edge of his hand, his eyes narrowed, flitting between me and the road. "What's your name?" he asked.

"My name?" I was clutching the handle with both hands now, close to my chest. "Right. Alfie."

"You seem unsure." Another twitch at the corner of his mouth. "What brings you to Ajaccio, Alfie? You here with family?"

A fine, pale sweat laced my forehead. The conversation could so easily spiral away from me if I answered — a seed of truth never stays a seed, and a lie sprouts in wily, uncontrollable directions.

My tongue went dry. I opened my mouth but said nothing.

He gave me a curious look. I recognized it from the piazza. "Now I'm intrigued."

"You haven't said your name," I managed.

"Felix Lispenard," he offered, quickly as a single word. "Here with friends? *Une petite chérie?*"

"No, I'm just ... here," I said. I could not think clearly. *Felix. Lispenard. Felix.* "Why do you care?"

He laughed. "Because you won't say."

My cheeks were flaming. *Fe*, soft as fabric. *Lix*, a sumptuous cut. Something inside me, shoved into shadow, was struggling to reassert itself. It made my marrow tremble, threatened to break the placidity for which I had fought these past months, for which I was still fighting.

I started down the street again, glancing at him to follow. "*Viens-tu?*"

"Are you here long?" he asked, catching up with me. "I could show you around. I grew up here as a kid before we moved. Watch yourself —"

Gently, he brought his arm in front of me, and stopped me before I tripped over a branch blown into the road.

I stared at the space between his arm and my body, the barrier of empty air. He stopped and stared too. I was overcome with the dizzying sensation of falling forward while standing still. As he moved his arm aside, there was a strange weakening in my chest. The excuses I intended to give him were suddenly thin and ugly deceptions, wafting like pond scum over some essential truth, and from the pure depths of that truth, before I could stop it, darted a flashing, irrepressible *sure, yeah, show me around*, flinging from my mouth into the open air.

After walking him home, I returned to my room and sat in the centre of the bed. My trainers still on and soaking the mattress. The umbrella puddling the floor, rain-beaded and glittering with light. I held my forehead in my hands and stared into the splotchy grey of the tracksuit cotton.

Dawnlight soon misted through the window. The brush of his fingers still clung to my skin. Clean and cool and eviscerating, like drops of bleach. What about him was affecting me so much? It was not his beauty. There were beautiful people everywhere. A beautiful appearance entrances, but it does not fascinate, it does not menace.

I curled onto my side to sleep. Stretched out on my back. Rolled onto my stomach, face in the pillow. My muscles retained his presence, invigorated all over, like I had run a great distance. All I could do was give in and stalk miserably down the hall to the shared facilities, where I undressed and stood in the scalding shower, one hand flat against the soap-scummed wall. I meant to expunge him from my system in the most physical and immediate way, but I could not do it. I felt sick, foolish, the act humiliating though hidden from view.

Pressing my face against the cold tile, a welt of disappointment deepened in my forehead. What had I done, agreeing to see him again? Had I learned nothing of the destructive nature of desire? Had its bruises camouflaged so easily that I would already risk them again?

I remained in the shower until my skin felt satisfyingly flayed, and the water in the adjacent stalls sprang on.

*

"You're sure your father won't mind?" I asked.

"Never you worry," Felix called, looking over his shoulder from the wheel. His voice threaded through the grating hum of the motor fitted to the back of the small boat. "He knows me well enough. He'd have hidden the key if he didn't want me taking it."

The sky was a clear, drinkable blue. We were heading to an archipelago, a low-rolling range of hilly islets on which sat a lone parapeted tower, giving it the look of a sinking kingdom.

Standing at Felix's front door the previous night, I had tried to deter him from wanting to see me by being sincere and suggesting that we go birdwatching. He had not laughed at me, instead pointing to a chain of islets and asking me to meet him the following afternoon at the pier. For hours I debated, in a spinning stupor,

A Song for Wildcats

whether or not to actually meet him. Had I not come here to experience the territory's natural, material beauty? Would the distraction
of a pleasant new friendship not help draw me out, pick me up?

There was more to it, of course, and I knew it. My impulses
conspiring, my blood effervescing. So I found my feet lowering un-
steadily into the boat, Felix offering his hand for balance, flashes of
sun in his dark-gold hair. And it was not until, with a heaving pitch,
we pushed outward into the bright blue gleam that I understood my
decision had been made the moment we met.

"You're not seasick, are you?" Felix asked, laughing. "You're
looking kind of woozy."

"I'm fine," I called back, signalling to watch for the boat ahead.
"Just — eyes on the road." My queasiness was merely guilt at
watching him so intently, turning the eye of my infatuation on an
unwitting participant. I forced myself to look away and leaned over
the side of the boat. Icy-pale pools of shallower water lay stark amid
the blue. White and featureless, like the souls of long-obliviated
species, coursing through seagrass meadows, adrift in a parallel and
unseen place.

Once on the islet, we dragged the boat into a sandy cove. I
followed his feet as they climbed nimbly ahead of me up a craggy
hillside, where we reached a sprawl of chalky paths. We spent the
afternoon roaming through waves of pink sea heather, hardy green
fennel, densely flowering maquis. We ate trail mix he had packed in
a canvas satchel and talked of childhood, school studies, the state of
the world. At one point, he indicated a silk-feathered heron wading
through still water, and without meaning to, I caught his sleeve,
drew his eye to a soaring osprey.

When I handed him the field binoculars I had brought, he
turned them over in his hands. I told him how my father had used
them to birdwatch, in moments of prolonged stillness, from the
muddy ditches of warfare.

15

A Song for Wildcats

"So you don't resent him for disappearing?" he asked.

"He was pretty rough with me," I said. "I just like the binocular story."

"That's a trick answer." He traced the aged binoculars as though they were a rare artifact. "My dad asked me to stay with him for a bit this summer. We've never done that before, but his wife left him, so …"

I learned that Felix's mother had sent him away to escape the draft. *More as a matter of principle than any maternal protectiveness,* he emphasized. *If she thought it would piss off the president, she'd drive me to the induction station herself.* Born in Ajaccio, he had been raised by his American mother on a communal ranch in San Francisco, a place I had never given much thought but that seemed, now, rather charming. He was studying political science in Paris and had been part of recent altercations between protesters and authorities, including the student occupation of Nanterre.

"Just another dirty commie." He gave me a second glance then, and smiled. "You've got …" he said, brushing his thumb against the corner of his lip.

I ran the back of my hand across my mouth, clearing away a salty crumb.

As we came upon a curve of shoreline, tucked low into a minor cliffside, he stopped. "Drink?" he said, offering me a water bottle from his satchel. "You're flushed."

I drank, as he said. He did the same without cleaning the lip of the bottle. He looked more polished than he had before. His shirt was pine-green, with the sleeves rolled to his elbows. Large, black sunglasses vaulted his eyes, giving his face an unreadable nullity, and sunlight ignited the fine gold hair along the nape of his neck.

I tried not to look at him. I tugged at the collar of my T-shirt, fanned some fresh air onto my chest. The intermingling scents of the maquis, a minty sweetness overlying cool citrus and crackling spice, were overwhelming.

Glancing around, Felix pulled a spliff from his pocket and lit it. He inhaled several short puffs with it pinched between his fingers, then held it out to me.

"I haven't, actually," I said.

"Oh yeah?" His brow rose. "Do you want to?"

I had always been too nervous among my friends at school, none of whom knew my more intimate leanings; I feared that I would drop my guard and let the truth spill out. I did not know why I felt so at ease with Felix.

"All right," I said. "Let's see what you American hippies are always on about."

"You sure, though?" he asked, so seriously that it surprised me.

When I nodded, he shifted in front of me. Falling still for the briefest moment, his chest seemed to rise two beats as he took a breath. He swallowed. "Here, lean closer, we'll shotgun. I don't want you going overboard."

"Shotgun?" I asked. "Aren't you a pacifist?"

He laughed and gestured me toward him. "Not a full shotgun, don't worry. If you don't like it, say so, okay?"

"Okay," I said.

"I mean it. An ex-girlfriend of mine used to get kind of sick, so just tell me if you don't feel well. It'll be totally fine, I swear, and I'll take you home if you want."

"Okay," I said again. As I leaned forward, sounds crystallized — gulls piercing the quiet, the ubiquitous breath of waves.

"Just breathe in when I breathe out," Felix said. Taking a tight drag, he planted his palm against the grassy slope behind me.

The reverberations of my heartbeat fluttered in my stomach, and the warmth in my face deepened, overbrimming and spilling across my neck. Felix's face was inches from mine as he blew a slow, light stream of fog into my mouth. It was damp and tasted of spoiled grass, burnt rubber. It astonished me to be tasting smoke that had rolled around his lungs. I held it until he told me to exhale, then swallowed the last of its soft cinders.

"How do you feel?" he asked, his hand still on the slope.

"Not sick yet," I said.

Everything beyond our small, secluded radius felt sealed off. As we looked at one another through the fading smoke, a weight pressed inside my chest, an agitated prod, as of someone wrestling with a door.

Then he coughed, apologized. He stepped back, eyes pulling away and searching the ground like he had lost something. "Do you want more water?"

I shook my head. Looseness unravelled through my limbs, and I lowered myself onto the ground. My thoughts thickened, turned sluggish. Sunlight glowed through the wildflowers beside us, blazing-blue petals like bioluminescence, the light of creatures guided by their own internal ignition. I thumbed a satiny petal and felt the thrill of its frail solidity. The rocks along the shoreline and the brush over the hills felt momentarily real — breakable and flittering, as though I were sitting in a paper diorama being teased and torn apart by the wind.

As if from a distance, beneath the drone of cicadas, I heard myself speak. "How do you know if you can trust yourself?"

Felix looked at me with the narrowed curiosity of peering through a keyhole. "How out of it are you?"

I rubbed my eyes, smearing away the heaviness. "Never mind."

"I'm kidding," he said. "What do you mean?"

"I mean ..." I started. "How can you trust your own choices?"

He settled onto the ground beside me, running a hand against the dirt and breathing in the sea spray as it sprung over the rocks fortifying the shore. He dropped the stubby spliff into the water bottle, now filthy with ash. "The ranch family is a bunch of *make love, not war* idealists. They'd say to root your

A Song for Wildcats

choices in love, or something like that, but I doubt even they know what they mean."

"Aren't you?" I asked. "An idealist, I mean."

He shrugged. "I like to think I'm a little more pragmatic. Honestly, all they talk about is love as this stagnant abstraction, like if you feel it, then it will just surge out of you and harmonize society — but who's actually helped by someone *loving* the idea of love? Day to day, who does it feed? What unjust policies are overturned by them not voting?"

"I don't know if something as irrational and destructive as love can be the core of a good life."

Felix drew his legs up and propped his elbows on his knees. "I don't know, I think ..." he said, then paused. I could see him holding his thought, letting it flicker into full form. "I think love is like kindness, like how you can carry out an act that embodies kindness without it genuinely coming from a place of empathy and altruism. Maybe it's, you know, ego using an act of kindness as a vehicle to satisfy itself. So people *say* love, they say they *feel* love, but what's the substance of it?"

"I had love back at school," I said. "It just felt like someone knew where all the bruises were and how hard to press." I sat forward, hunched my shoulders, felt my joints readjusting inside. I was becoming somatically aware of my skeleton, the clean precision of bone. I felt its bare exposure against the erosive air. "But that's the thing, love isn't conscious, it's not a choice."

"I think there's choice," he said. "Love is just perception. It's like what Galileo said about colour and taste, it exists only within consciousness and is otherwise completely extinguished. And we have to be able to rationalize and make sense of our perceptions. Everything is composite."

"Not love, though, right?" I said. "It's like *soul*, it's the beginning and end of itself."

A Song for Wildcats

"Listen to you!" He had collected some of the climbing tide into his palm, and he flicked his wet fingers at me. "It's hormones and neurons, you occultist."

I made a clicking sound with my tongue. "Well, that's not very transcendent."

Felix's eyes widened. "Here I was thinking you were a malcontent, but you're a *romantic*?"

"*No*," I said, turning to face him directly, eager to be understood. "I just mean, love could be this vast sea, something varied and evolving, but we reduce it to a puddle that reflects only ourselves, our weaknesses, and — what?" I asked, as his smile grew.

"You've read too much Plato."

"It's hard to explain," I said.

"Okay, hold still." He mirrored my position, the toe of his shoe touching mine. The space between us fizzled. "I'm going to read your mind."

"Wait," I said, for some reason shielding my eyes.

What I wanted to say then was hopeful. That I believed there could be a kind of transcendence, deeper than want and greater than possession. That love, in its truest form, was a kind of seeking. The soul rushing against the chest, ecstatic at the prospect of creating something sublime, of its own eternal nature, yet pained to reach only as far as the boundary of its body. The thriving space between searching and finding, exaltation and grief.

But my breaths came quick, pumping the words out of me. I lowered my hand from my eyes. "I want an experience of the world that's iridescent and unfixed. A pure, beautiful life. And love diminishes that — at least when it attaches itself to me. It's depleting. It's poisonous."

I waited for him to argue, but he went quiet. He looked at me for a beating moment, as though he intended to speak. There was a nearly indiscernible way in which his body retreated, and then he was on his feet so quickly that he unsettled the soil into sudden dust.

"We should head back," he said, throwing his satchel over his shoulder. "It's going to get dark."

"Sure. Of course," I said, but he had already started up the path rounding the cliff.

The boat bobbed in place on the low, heaving waves. I sat on the rear seat and stared at my hands wrapped tightly around my binoculars. My thoughts were sharpening with sobriety, turning their ends on me. What was I doing here? What had compelled me to talk so openly with a relative stranger?

The sun spilled across the sky, electrifying the waves, transfusing its revitalizing warmth into the chilled patches of water. Felix's gaze was fixed on the floor of the boat. He looked occasionally in my direction, some private thought shifting in the gleaming chrysalis of his eye.

Eventually I asked, "What is it?"

"Nothing," he said, reaching to start the motor, then stopping again. He opened his mouth, and hesitated. "I like talking to you."

There was the mildest taper in his voice. All attention to his looks, all intoxication of his odd flavour of confidence, were replaced by an innocent desire to wrap myself around him and shield him like a shell. Words sprang off my tongue: *yeah ... same.* As I sat grounded in my seat, the heaviness of my heartbeat, the steady cadence of my lungs, filling and emptying, held me in my body so I could not float away.

✳

For a time, we ran smoothly. April melted into afternoons wandering the old quarter, lost in circuitous debates. And evenings loitering on the sea wall of the marina, watching the mountains blend with the sky like a fading afterimage. At night we read in my hostel room or listened to Felix's portable record player, worn at its brown vinyl edges and resembling a struggling salesman's weary suitcase.

We had become friends, quickly and absorbingly in the manner of small children. Often there was an exultant pain, being near him, intensifying when we playfully shoved each other or he tapped my hand for his cigarette, which I gave and received, in an unconscious pendulum of gestures. Or once, when he surprised me by grazing my back as we turned into a crowded street.

Yet I trod the platonic parameters of our friendship with caution. Whatever impelled me close to him found a reassuring safeguard in his casual, mildly grating anecdotes of former girlfriends at school in Paris, beachside flings in San Francisco. Nothing gratuitous or posturing; in fact, he spoke well and matter-of-factly of these girls, and I worried — somewhat indignantly — that his speaking of them at all was a way of preventing any sort of confusion between us.

I met one of the girls, among his student activist friends, when we all went out to a smoky, ultraviolet discothèque behind a hotel. The way they danced together, how she touched his shoulder, a mark of possession — I was convinced he was sleeping with her. On nights when he was unavailable, I imagined them together, a writhing heap of limbs in his bedroom, which he had never shown me. Still, it helped me hold onto the firm reality that he was unattainable, that there was no room for desire to squirm in and ruin us.

One evening, we were drinking red wine in my room — crassly, from an unwashed tea mug and a water glass with dried toothpaste on the rim — and rifling through each other's books. Felix was impressing on me the necessity of integrating Marxist thought into common political discourse, for the sake of social expansiveness — adorably heated, barely breathing between sentences — as I was impressing on him the necessity of beauty, and reverence for nature, to the expansion of the soul.

"Whether you see it as psyche or spirit, the soul extricates society from ego. It roots us in meaning," I said, slurring but adamant. "There's a soulfulness, or a presence, in the natural world, and it's trying to reach us, or we're trying to reach it."

"Honestly, Alfie, are you a scientist or a Druid?"

"I don't think they're mutually exclusive."

I lay on the mattress, sopping drunk and holding over my face his collection of Marx's articles on the tumult of mid-nineteenth-century France. The words had begun to thread together.

"So he's a man of multiplicity," Felix said to an invisible third party. "You have to come with me when I go back to Paris. They've shut down the university. It's absurd. France is finally pushing forward into the modern world and they just want to hold it back."

I rested the collection on my stomach and rose onto my elbows. "When do you leave?"

"Soon. I should already be there, but — you'll come, right? I rent a little place in Pigalle. It's above a grimy sex shop and the hot water never works, if that entices you at all." His voice went dry. "Let me lure you into a life of embattled radicalism."

I laughed. "Tempting."

Felix looked down at the book in his hand, my collected Keats, and traced the smudged annotations beside a poem. "You like this one," he said. *"Bright star, would I were stedfast as thou art ..."*

He was smoking out of the open window, wearing my crimson cardigan over his T-shirt, the buttons all misaligned, and a boxy pair of black-framed glasses that he wore on occasion, and that made me feel heady and lopsided. He rested his elbows on the sill, his spine long and elegant, with the marble-cut suppleness of a sculpture.

He seemed utterly innocent, as ever, to his own incidental poise.

23

"What's your favourite constellation?" he asked, looking through the tree's restful leaves into the night.

"The Lynx. You wouldn't be able to find it." I breathed deeply, the air low and languid on my skin. "It's famously hidden. It takes the preternatural, truth-seeing eyes of a lynx to spot it. Scientifically speaking."

Felix grabbed a crumpled ball of paper from the floor and threw it at me.

I shielded myself, batted the paper away. "I saw it once when I was little. Without a telescope, just out in the snow one night." Wandering through the field by my house, away from the yelling and clatter of thrown cutlery. My boots breaking through the fresh snow and the long, blue shadows of the trees. "I stared into one of the stars until it stung and blurred. But I've never been able to see it again."

My head rolled to the side, and I found Felix watching me. It shook me into a startling reminder that we were sharing physical space — that I was compact flesh in a mutual reality, and he could see me as clearly as I could see him.

"What?" I asked, pretending ambivalence — but I liked him watching me. It was soothing and warm, so different from the class-mate's wintergreen glare, his dull blinks like secret cameras clicking behind his eyes.

Felix released a stream of smoke into the tender-blue evening. "Nothing. I just find it interesting."

"What, watching me?"

"Yes. It's fascinating to me that you exist."

A whistle rose from the sidewalk. Felix laughed as he looked down at the street below, then meowed like a wildcat. "*Pas ce soir, mon ami,*" he said. Turning away, he settled clumsily onto the buckled hardwood, among the empty wine bottles, and let his head fall against the side of the mattress.

Something in the quickness, the lightness of his actions, sent a low tremble through my stomach. "You still haven't answered my question," I said.

"About childhood?" he asked. "It's embarrassing."

"Good," I said. "I hope so."

Before he had redirected the conversation to politics, I had asked him to tell me of a childhood treasure. Something he had once loved, achingly, that had lost its place in his life so gradually he could not remember when or how it disappeared.

He eyed the ceiling. "My first merit badge."

"You were a *Boy Scout*?"

"See, this is why I didn't want to say."

"My, my, what would the Bolsheviks think?" I flicked the hair by his ear. I loved moments like this, when my hand passed through my aversion, as if through rain, to touch him. Quick little teasing things. The sort of lapse I could blame on dramatic inebriation.

"Up yours," he said. "I was a fantastic Boy Scout."

"Oh, I bet you were." I patted my hand around the bed in search of my mug. "Just a proper little American."

"Fuck off." Felix took my mug from the side table and handed it to me. Face warm with wine, he raised his chin in sarcastic triumph. "It was for Citizenship in the Community. I loved it. I was so proud of it. I slept with it under my pillow, *holding* it, like someone was going to steal it away from me."

I rolled onto my stomach and folded my arms, so that we were both facing the opposite wall. The room whirled around me as I moved, swaddling me in loose swaths of colour. I was enjoying such buoyant liberty, and I accepted Felix's cigarette as he reached up and placed it in my mouth.

"Now I'm sad for your poor little merit badge," I said. "Who knows what's happened to it. What if it got all torn up and thrown away?"

25

After a moment, Felix took a breath as if to speak, then waited. "Alfie," he said, carefully. "Can I ask you something?"

I swatted at the air until I caught the wine bottle by the neck, then poured the last splash into my mug. "About ..."

"The person you were going with at school." He turned around, resting his forearms on the bed so that they lay over mine. My breath caught. I was rapidly blinking, his closeness fogging my vision. "What exactly happened with that?"

"What do you mean?" I asked.

He took the cigarette from me, the paper burned short enough to bite my fingers. He dropped it into his glass, where it hissed against the dregs. "You know what I mean."

"No, I don't." I pulled away, sitting too quickly. I smoothed my hand over my forehead and tried to solidify my runny thoughts. "We were both a bit mad, that's all."

"You called it poisonous," he said.

"Did I? That was rubbish, it was nothing." I swayed pathetically, catching my balance against the headboard. "I just never really understood what was happening."

"As in, whether it was a relationship?" he asked.

"No, I mean ..." I was conscious of myself lowering the mug onto the side table with an unsteady clatter, but I was not inside the body performing the action. My hands stretched far in front of me, as though I were looking through the wrong end of a telescope. "Why does it matter?"

"Just makes me worry, I guess," he said.

I had lost track of my body's orientation, the room aslant, the ceiling unstable. "So you feel sorry for me. That's brilliant, thank you."

"Alfie, you know that's not what I'm saying."

"Look, it was complicated." Involuntarily, my hand drew to my neck, half expecting to touch air. "In private, some things were ... I don't really remember."

Felix was looking up at me from the floor. He struck me as somehow innocent, his gaze sweetly open and receptive. "What things?"

A cold ghost of a tongue behind my ear. A damp whisper. *Say you're nothing without me.* I shuddered, rubbed my face. "There are things ..." I said. "You should have to ask first, that's all."

"But what things?" he asked.

"I don't *know*, Felix, I've never talked about it." I dug my palm back and forth against a tension in my chest, my body unravelling like gauze. Memories slashed behind my eyes — the feeling of breath squeezed from my throat, smooth leather noosing me from behind, the clink of a belt buckle. I pressed my temple and flinched. "You should have to ask first, and you should stop if ..."

Felix had straightened. He remained still but for the pronounced rhythm of his breath. "It's okay," he said, when I did not continue. "It's okay, I'm sorry. You don't have to tell me if you don't want to."

... if you don't want to

In between the flashing memories, those glowing eyes appeared, tearing two holes in the darkness like knife cuts through cloth.

... you don't have to ... if you don't want to

The words circled, nonsensically, like an ink-blot zoetrope. I had to squint to see through them. "Did you say something?" I asked, though what I meant was, *What does that mean?*

I felt myself spilling, like water, through my own fingers.

... you don't have to

... if you don't want to

I could see myself in the classmate's room, lying limp with my arm slung over the mattress. Waiting for him to finish. Watching the polar-blue light of a lava lamp on the desk in the adjoining study. Wax spheres like eyeballs scrubbed vacant, breaking apart and floating to the surface, only to sink back down and be subsumed.

"I don't feel right." My hands were shaking. There was a protracted blur of movement, and soon a glass of water, smelling faintly of rinsed wine residue, hovered in front of me. I winced and leaned away like a child.

"Come on," Felix said, his tone comfortingly patronizing. "Will you drink the water?"

"You don't have to do this," I said. "I don't need it."

"I like doing it," he said. "And yes, you do."

Fingers tangled loosely in my hair, a steadying thumb against my jaw. I took a small, feeble sip. Then he was sitting beside me, guiding the glass back and forth until my breath evened.

My cheek eased onto his shoulder. I felt the gentle roll of him readjusting, and his sturdy arm around my waist.

"Alfie," he said, his breath in my hair. I watched the strained motion of his hand running up and down his jeans. "Don't talk to this person anymore. Okay? Please."

I nodded, but I would have agreed to whatever he said. A sedating drowse closed over my head, all thought bubbling out.

✳

A moment later, it was morning.

Sunlight cut into the dark haven of sleep, and when I opened my eyes, the ceiling throbbed above me, overbearingly bright. My body felt syrupy with sleep, thick and fluid and slow. I shifted to grab the glass of water on the side table, but there was an inexplicable weight over my hand.

Turning onto my side, I found Felix lying beside me. I fell stone still. He was asleep, serene in my dishevelled cardigan, squeezing my hand to his chest. How had this happened? I scanned the room, vaguely sequencing the previous night. A quivery nervousness set in. What had I told him? Had he meant to fall asleep here, or would he be mortified to find himself in my bed? My chest lay thin and damp over my heartbeat, my breaths so shallow I thought I might faint.

A Song for Wildcats

And then he murmured, still asleep. I looked at him curled so soundly, clutching my hand. The freckle by his mouth burned my retina, like the fine-point fire of sunlight through a magnifying glass. An aching tenderness cracked open inside me. His beauty appeared almost separate from him, a pure essence existing in the interplay between us, between his goodness and my cherishing of his goodness. I had never before desired to watch someone sleep; the path connecting me to other people had been shrouded, winding. Yet I watched him sleep as one watches a river, or a rare bird.

I reached out to stroke the hair from his face — and started at myself. He could not possibly have intended to sleep next to me. We had passed out in wine-headed exhaustion, and he had searched for my hand in the night as he dreamed of someone else. Perhaps it was pity, too, for the onset of my strobing memories. Or guilt, after prying into the affair, its unspoken strangeness always lurking on the leeward side of my mind.

I slipped my hand free. Moving to the creaky wicker chair in the corner, I sank into myself and waited for the distance to accumulate, for the floor to stretch into separate hemispheres.

It did not. The easy tide of Felix's breathing carried across the few feet between us.

I leaned forward in the chair, sitting at the edge. My hand, so recently nestled in solace, tingled with absence. I traced my palm as though he had left etchings of his prints. What if I was wrong, and it had been my anchorage he sought in the drift of sleep? What if desire could flourish bloodlessly, without suffering or defacement?

The sky floated high in the window, cloud swept and milky blue. I stood and lifted the sash higher, then dipped my head into the clean morning air. I looked back at Felix resting peacefully in my sheets. The breeze woke my skin, tasting of sea mist and salt. The waves hushed along the harbour, and in them I could hear a hidden language, calling to me in tumbling whispers I could almost understand.

A Song for Wildcats

*

That night, Felix and I met at the cinema. We did not sneak in a flask or spit popcorn at each other in the lobby, as we occasionally did. And we refrained from our usual whispers as we sat in the aged velvet seats and unventilated dark of the theatre. We watched Kubrick's new *2001: A Space Odyssey*, with our backs stiffened straight.

When I had woken again that morning, having fallen asleep in the wicker chair, the bed was empty. The cardigan was folded and placed formally, even coldly, on my pillow. Immediately, the bed took on an aura of the vestigial, a piece in a museum exhibit pulled from ancient palatial ruins, and I lay beside it, on my back, in paralyzing melodrama. In the debate of what next to do, the unreasonable side — teetering on delusion, egging on pursuit over retreat — somehow won, and finally I sprang off the floor and called Felix's flat from the front-desk phone.

At first, he did not pick up. On my second try, he let the phone ring for so long that the shrill monotone hammered my ear. By the time he answered, I was so nervous, I felt ill. His voice made my heart lift and my stomach sink simultaneously, and without the faintest idea of what to say, I invited him to the cinema.

I wore the cardigan, unwashed and carrying his scent, with the sleeves rolled to the elbows, in his fashion. A peace offering or a petulant taunt, I could not decide. I saw his folding of the garment, and his choice to leave it rather than take it home as he usually did, as either a retaliation for abandoning him in my bed or an erasure of intimacy.

As we watched the film, I could not concentrate. I hardly heard the dialogue, and the story's threads tangled into an austere, oddly tranquil incoherence. Being together in such enveloping darkness, even in a crowd, felt breathlessly private.

A blue sheen of sweat shimmered on my palm as I tilted it, on my lap, in the screen's light. I was filled with a heightened anxiety to grab hold of the moment, and not be swept outside of it — and without registering any pain, I had dug purple thumbnail-crescents into my skin.

Felix folded his hand over my forearm. "You okay?"

"Yeah," I said, though sound began to blur. "Yeah, I'm fine."

He touched my palm, and I let it lie open. "What did you do?"

My eyes were lost and hazy as I looked at him. I said nothing, merely stared as his question fell away. As if to extend a bridge across the silence, my leg shifted until our knees touched.

He did not move away.

A rustle in my chest. Nerves fluttering up my spine. I leaned my leg closer and took a slow, thin breath. I could not get enough air in my lungs. We looked back to the immensity of screen, where bleary bands of neon streamed from a nexus of ineffable light.

Afterward, we walked from the cinema in silence.

The air hung close, too balmy to breathe, and the streets vibrated with the quiet but kinetic energy of warm evenings in small towns. People lounged against open car doors parked on crooked, undulating roads. The yellow burn of old iron lanterns was bittersweet — fiercely radiant at the core, yet dimming at the glass's edges, the inevitability of light's fading made stark by its confinement. Electricity scaled my arm as we walked close together.

The sound of our shoes on the pavement clipped my ears. My footsteps responded to him; I had noticed this soon after we met. They slowed when I caught fresh sight of him approaching, and quickened to keep pace, like an erratic metronome. They did not follow his rhythm or get lost in it, but they knew it like a tempo. I heard his footsteps as singularly as the echo of my own in vast, empty halls.

Nearing our little region of street, my mind groped about for an excuse to stretch the night. I was about to suggest a nightcap, despite having nothing in my room to drink, when Felix halted.

"What's the matter?" I asked.

Expressions flickered across his face like crystal catching light. The palm trees lining the sidewalk, leaves caught in a gust high overhead, shook their shadows onto the street.

"I just ..." he started.

I waited, watching him. "What is it?"

He swallowed and continued staring, his mouth parted. To my astonishment, he looked impossibly shy.

It had not for a second occurred to me that his confidence might be as susceptible to crumbling as that of anyone else. That having let me press my leg against his, and having pressed back, he might now feel rather lost and helpless. For this was uncharted territory for him, whereas I had navigated it extensively, and he knew it, despite us having never broached the matter.

"Alfie," he said. "I've been trying to wrap my head around things ..."

He trailed off, though I could tell that a quiet reconfiguring was taking place. I realized, then, that he was waiting for me, trusting me to take care of us both in this decisive moment.

I looked around; the night stragglers had drained away, and the street was empty. I took his hand. Holding his eye, I gave the slightest nod to say *it's okay, it's okay*, and led him into the alleyway ahead of us. I had not decided what to do, and was propelled only by an amorphous determination.

The alley was windowless and cut short at the back door of a café whose neon sign glowed, spilling pink light from the roof. We stood by an empty bookstall and a gurgling drainpipe, hidden between the alley's cracked stone walls. Dry black dribbles of graffiti declared *soyez realistes, demandez l'impossible.*

"This is good?" I asked, quietly. He nodded. I touched beneath his chin. "Felix, look at me. Is this good?"

"Yes." He looked at me, unblinking, and squeezed my hand. "*Yes.*"

I moved closer until our foreheads met, his features abstracting, and he was only the light washing his skin. Our mouths caught one another, as if by accident. Then again, and again, each time more firmly, lingering longer and more deeply.

Blood burned and beat in my ears. Under his solid hands, I was suddenly aware of my own contours, the materiality of my existence and the space it occupied. At the same time, my body expanded. It was not invisible; it was dark matter, powerful and mysterious and the only constant thing. It was not my hand roaming under Felix's clothes but currents of electricity, his chest lifting in soft resuscitation. And at the back of my mind, I marvelled at how something so palpable could conceive such impalpable beauty.

But it was an insidious desire. Lost in impulse, I pressed him against the wall, held his face in my hands, drank him like a thirsty wanderer. I could not think straight over the roar of breath, his primal shudders into my mouth. An inverted viciousness rose in me. The sharp corner of his loosened belt buckle dug into my waist, and I grabbed it, drove it into me, as if to break the skin and sap myself dry. I wanted to ask him to speak strangely to me, cruelly. To hurt and terrify me.

Felix's mouth touched my throat then, the daintiest bite, and a clammy shiver ran through me. I could feel the classmate all over me. His arm against my neck, his belt strap, the biting that drew blood, the hitting without asking, without stopping.

"Wait, I can't —" I said, pushing away.

"What's wrong?" Felix's shock was plain and pale, then twisted into worry. "Alfie, what's going on?"

A Song for Wildcats

"I can't do this." My voice came out fractured. I was not sure what I was saying. "I can't feel my hands. Felix, I can't feel my hands."

My vision reeled, hyper-blinking and hot. I was shaking so violently that I could not button my shirt. Felix had to help me. He kept apologizing and assuring me that he would get me home. I felt too sick to even be embarrassed that I was crying.

On the hostel steps, I would not let him come inside. It took me an hour to climb the lobby stairs to the second floor. I paused along the way to sink onto the dingy wood and peer into its stained-black whorls. I threw up in one of the shower stalls, rinsed it away. Locked myself in my room and crawled under the unmade bedding. The sheets smelled of Felix, his heady sweetness. I could not tell if I wanted to wrap myself in his scent, breathe in his body like a narcotic, or set the bed on fire.

*

It had to end. It had to be me who ended it.

For days, I ignored him. I wrote letter after letter, trying to explain the inexplicable, then proved incapable of carrying any one of them beyond the threshold of my doorway. None of this was out of anger; it was my fault, letting it happen all over again, offering my veins for exsanguination. But there was no pursuing what had happened, and there was no undoing it. We were suspended over the consuming chasm desire occupies. I could only return to my side, and push him back to his own.

Felix, more a creature of the moment than myself, continued to call the hostel. He went so far as to leave a note at the front desk, without the discretion of an envelope. Just a folded piece of his father's letterhead. It was addressed formally, a little cryptically, with an eye-roll baked into the tone.

Dear Alfred,
Something has come up. Quit being an ass.
Warm regards,
F.

Finally, he lost his good humour. It was early twilight, and a clipped moon bobbed out of the blue as if it were drowning. A firm knock dragged across my door. He was drunk.

"I'm not here to beg," he said. "Talk to me now, and that can be the end of it. But you can't just pretend I don't exist."

At his voice, my nerves turned jagged. The friction of glass scraping glass ran up my spine. I set my book on the bed, pressure beating behind my eyes, and opened the door.

He gave a fleeting smile that split my stomach.

"See?" he said. "How hard was that?"

The room was humid, and he blundered through the top buttons of his shirt as he nudged past me, tiny discs flashing between his fingertips. His eyes were misty and unfocused. He leaned against the wall and glowered at me through sweaty bolts of dirty-gold hair.

"So?" he said.

"So what?" I asked.

He made a short chuffing sound. "So, what the hell is going on? Are you okay? Are you not okay?"

Blood was draining from my body, trickling through my legs. I stared at my feet, waiting for red pools to start seeping out the soles. "I'm fine. Trust me."

"Well, we both know that's a lie. But I expected it." He remained uncannily still. "Paris is on fire, you know."

"What?" I asked. "What's happening?"

"The police invaded the Sorbonne. I have to go. I should have left already. I haven't been thinking clearly for weeks."

"You're leaving?" I asked. "When? Tonight?"

"Do you care?"

"Of course I care." I rubbed my eyes just to look away, but his form lingered, luminous against the dark behind my lids. "Felix, I know you hate me right now …"

"I don't hate you, Alfie."

"But you're angry."

He pursed his lips, shook his head faintly. "Not angry."

"You must be *something*," I said.

"I'll be furious, if you want. Is that what this is about? You want to provoke some reaction out of me? Am I being tested or something?"

"No, of course not, don't be ridiculous."

"I'm not being ridiculous. What else am I supposed to think?" he said. "And stop saying *of course* like everything is completely obvious. Nothing is ever obvious with you."

"Nothing's obvious with *me*?" My voice thinned, flattened by the weight of all it was failing to convey. I wanted to gawk, root up his own bewildering opacity, but it would only have dragged us farther down. I lifted my hands to stifle the argument. "I'm not fighting with you."

"No, that would require us to actually be straightforward with each other."

I paused. My skin bristled with cold pins. "This isn't straightforward."

A sharp inhale through his nose. "Alfie, what does that *mean*?"

"It means *this*," I said, encapsulating us in some inarticulate gesture, "this will only hurt us. Look at what it's already doing."

"But *you're* doing it."

"I know," I said. "I know it's me."

"So all your talk of — what was it, transcendence, beauty, love," he said. "This is how you treat it?" Coming closer, he searched my face as though it were disappearing. "What's this wall of yours? I can always feel it. I can almost *see* it."

36

A Song for Wildcats

"Felix — there's something wrong with me. I don't know what it is, but it'll bring out the worst in both of us. You don't understand how bad it will get."

"Right." He used the cuff of his sleeve to wipe his nose, sniffed once. Then he brought his hand over his eyes, and cringed as he spoke. "Listen, if you're not into it —"

"That's not it," I said. "I don't want you to think that." I started toward him, but pitched slightly, my legs deflating beneath me. I lowered onto the edge of the bed and steadied myself.

As I did, he followed, crouching in front of me, clasping my knees. "Is it because of what happened at school? If you'd just talk to me —"

"I told you, that was nothing," I said, but my mind hardened. Was it nothing, or was it that I felt nothing? The *nothing* had burrowed into me. I could see flickers of my fear, my pain, locate it burning in some inaccessible core, but I felt only a flat numbness, like touching a wildfire on a television screen.

"It was as much my fault as his," I said. As I took a breath, a smaller one squeezed up underneath it, and then there was no breath at all. "I'm the one who let it happen."

Felix gathered my fingers in his hands, held them delicately as loose petals. "There's nothing wrong with you, Alfie. I don't think it's possible to *let* something like that happen."

"I don't want to get into it again," I said.

"We don't have to." He inched closer and rested his chin on our collected hands. "We don't have to say anything. We don't have to do anything. It can be on your terms, all of it."

The warmth of his hands bled into mine, rousing my body's strange occupant, that unflagging force so restless to break out. My shoulders softened, and I curved toward him, freeing his hand. Drawing his palm to my mouth, I kissed the salty hollow, as if tending a wound.

"Just tell me what you want, and I'll do it," he said. "I'll do whatever you tell me."

I pulled back, as though he had gone slack and was bleeding out on top of me. "I don't want that," I said. The cold pins sank deeper into my skin, shivery and damp. "I would never want it to be like that."

His hair fell, limp and stringy, in his face. Weary blue shadows wrung his eyes. "Then tell me how you want it to be. Because I don't know what I'm doing."

"No, Felix, that's not — please don't say that."

As I looked at him, the malleability of his autonomy and the depth of some invisible injury were as exposed as fresh abrasions scraped raw across his face. Nobody could miss them. Nobody could mistake them or pretend they were not there. I could ask whatever I wanted of him. Make him do anything, agree to anything. Make him slip into complicity, a participant in his own degradation, until he did not know the difference between desire and defeat, intimacy and control.

There was a crackle of clarity in me, fragile yet feverish, like an atrophied eye regaining light. I was waking from a dream, only the dream and reality were identical.

"You need to leave," I said, shifting my legs onto the bed, so that he was no longer cradled between them. The *want*, the *need* for one another — how could he not see the danger, like balancing on a parapet, like licking fire?

"You're not serious," he said.

"*Please*, Felix."

My muscles clenched, and my lower spine prickled. From the other side of the wavering glass, where Felix could not see me, I watched his face run through a scale of confusion. He touched my jaw, tilted it toward him. His mouth hung open, and my own ached. But the new waking dream flooded my eyes, stark and striking, and

I hardly recognized him. He spoke several words I could not hear over the torrent in my ears, and waited for one imploring moment, before standing and leaving the room.

✳

The truth, a patient predator, dogged me through the night. Down the winding streetsides. Across the commune's insular ecosystem of medieval stone and modern glitz. The shadows were still, at first, but for the stirring palm leaves. As they deepened, they swept forward in slow rushes and falls. Light from the street lamps sparked off what must have been broken bottles on the road, so that a prowling pair of small, gold glints crept, at a distance, beside me.

Glass shattered, somewhere far off yet so impossibly close it made my heart jump. Panic sprang from nowhere. There was nothing to fear, and yet my breaths strained and I struggled to swallow. I held my hand around my throat, unable to pry it away. And as I walked, the two little glints crept along, as if the trail of broken glass were endless.

I soon wandered onto the pale sand of an empty beach, edged in myrtle trees leading into the forested mountains. The dark water lay calm and carried the stars, a thousand unblinking eyes, on an easy current. I could not divert the truth, famished as it was for reflection, except by exerting myself to exhaustion — and so I walked the beach, rounded the woods, the sea's breath the only discernible sound. But there was no clearing myself of Felix. I carried him in my bones, where he lived restless as stirred silt.

Closing my eyes to him that evening, as he walked away, had been like locking a tomb. I closed them again now, more tightly. I imagined them sinking, burrowing into themselves, gutting tunnels through my memory.

A Song for Wildcats

It was a whimper that called me back to myself. I opened my eyes and looked around, but I saw no one. At my feet, dark trickles stained the sand. The night sky leaking, or my body bleeding out. I pulled my hand from my throat, expecting to see it drenched, blood spilling from wounds of my own doing. But my hand was dry.

The small drops formed a trail, and I followed it toward a puddled shadow beneath the trees. I stopped, squinted. Glassy eyes peered out at me, catching the moonlight with a mercurial gleam. As I leaned forward, I saw a tail curling under the nursing lick of a tongue. From the size of the creature, I knew it was not a stray. It could not be cradled and carried home. I stepped closer, but the creature shrank, tightening into its body.

I froze at once, not wanting to frighten it or worsen the damage — and something in the immediacy of that instinct startled me, springing forth with all the certainty of a sudden recollection. What had made me pause but a desire not to harm? What was that desire but a force within me, channelling my purest impulse? To stop, to wait, to perceive the vulnerability of another. Such an instinct was a blood-song, a vibration plucked across the veins; it came from nowhere I could name, and it outlasted everything.

The truth of this washed over me. He had come upon me, the classmate, and recognized a wound as opportunity. He had chosen not to stop, not to wait, but instead to impart a mimicry of love. To corrode an outlying creature, one boundary at a time, moving inwardly in concentric circles until there was nothing left.

A new shame lowered over me, chastising my sophomoric self for being so foolish, despite all my book-smarts, but also a shame at my own chastising — for how could one blame a lonesome creature for running headlong into the first open hand?

And was it so easy for anyone to tell when it was the soul speaking, and when it was the wound?

A Song for Wildcats

The creature rose and arched its back. The breeze, blowing off the waves and over the bluffs, shook the myrtle flowers — their petals wrung and wiry, yet incandescently white, like the pith of unpeeled stars. Carrying the injured end of its tail in its mouth, the creature straightened, raised its chin. It blinked its lunar gaze through the trees' gathered shade, curious yet calm, as if transfixed by a tempered fire, and then darted away into the safety of the woods.

For the rest of the night, I sat by the water on a long, dark spine of rocks. I watched the glinting grey waves as clarity continued to strike like drops of rain. Now and then, the protective glaze over my mind rinsed away, and I was a small part of the trembling enormity around me.

Dawn began to warm the horizon, igniting the powdery-blue sea-line and combusting the clouds. I stripped my feet bare, rolled my cuffs to my knees, and slid my legs into the water. They turned an unearthly pale. I had sought a purified existence, consciousness dipped in ambrosia, all fear and suffering burned away. But did I want a dispassionate life, or had I merely stumbled into one while running indiscriminately from danger, and no longer knew which way to turn?

I kicked, slowly, wayward against the tide. Even in movement, my limbs looked death-marbled. But the water soon flushed a lively pink, and without thinking, I slipped into it. I let it lap against my neck and warm the cold glow of my skin. I felt the sun's unfettered heat soak my face, and the shriek of gulls crack open my ears. For an instant, as I breathed the boundless air, my heart raced with the stamping run of a lost child catching sight of home.

*

When I arrived back at the hostel, clothing sundried and stiff with salt, guests were gathered around a hulking wooden television in

A Song for Wildcats

the sitting room. A nervous cloud clung to the air. News from Paris, crowds marching the Left Bank through the night and into the morning. The screen streamed with dark, grainy footage of baton-battered faces, sparks showering from broken street lamps into the Seine. Desks and chairs and wooden crates were piled into barricades, the exacting veneer of the city crumbling into a surfeit of squalor. Fires had raged, left ashen heaps, blackened banners. Recordings of the noise — the chants, the screams, the gun-cracks of long-cloaked police firing tear gas — played over the blood-slicked arrondissement, scattered with paving stones torn from the road.

Every face belonged to Felix. He had left the island, I knew it. Flown back to the mainland. He had been there, among the riots; he had been the riots. Sound fell away under the blood-pummel in my head, the pounding of the impatient occupant inside me. I thought of how my heart rushed toward Felix, buoyed on a swelling tide, how his name flew moth-like from my mouth. And of the far-reaching search outward, the far-plunging search inward. Through the open hostel door came the soft thunder of the waves, and I looked out to where the sun had fully risen, casting a beckoning path of light across the sea.

Heatstroke

The wallpaper was an inferno of curling red acanthus. If Fiona looked at it for too long, she felt it moving inside her, slipping among her organs. Other oddities: she noticed that gravity was strongest in small, atmospheric pockets right around her temples and was weighing against her shoulders. In a water-warped corner of the ceiling, fruit flies barely moved in counter-clockwise rotation.

Fiona sat by the motel window, looking out at a corner of downtown Vegas. Electric outlines glowed above darkened storefronts, green light harnessed and bent into the shapes of women's bodies. A pair of pink neon lips twitched.

Fiona got off the bed, rings of cereal crunching beneath her bare feet.

None of this was right. She was not the way she was supposed to be. It was as if she had exploded and been too hastily reassembled, pieces misplaced or fitted upside down. All she knew was this: one week earlier, she had headed out of Reno in her uncle's car toward the Red Rock Canyon National Conservation Area. She had hiked at least as far as the limestone ridge of the Moenkopi Loop — and then, a time-jump. She had awoken on her side, in the sand, the sun exhaling its molten breath over her skin.

A map of Clark County and the Mojave Desert lay unfolded at all times on the motel floor. Fiona ran her finger along the lines, trying to channel her memory like a spirit through a Ouija board.

A route drawn in Sharpie led from Reno to Red Rock, among the easternmost parts of the Mojave, then to the salt flat called Groom Lake — *AREA 51* scrawled in big, daggered letters, more of a joke than a destination — before circling backward to an abandoned gold-rush town in the Bullfrog Hills occupied only by the ghosts of murdered prospectors and miners with phantom lungs like sacks of coal dust. It had been meant as Fiona's own bespoke road trip, marking the end of high school, the beginning of the newly unfurling world. As far as she could tell, she had reached only her first stop, Red Rock, when the journey ended.

Fiona understood that it was July 5, 1982. She remembered her mother and sister, their clapboard bungalow. Her friends Jody and Easton Maxwell, a pair of brothers who had left Reno the previous summer and now lived with their father on an old ranch in Moapa Valley. And the robot they had constructed in middle school, out of scrap metal and a toy astronaut helmet. The siren they had set into its chest — found in a ditch, cracked through the centre, like the once-wailing blue heart of a disintegrated spaceship.

She knew she should reach out to someone. Jody in particular would have understood, but each time she picked up the phone, an inexplicable hesitancy sacked her voice, and she hung up before the first ring.

Once she had found her uncle's car in the conservation parking lot, Fiona could have sworn she saw a second road float into view, like a soul ushered from a body. There were two roads now, over-lapping. The correct one, and the one that she was on. But it was an error, a mutation of fate. She was stuck in the aftershock of some sudden divergence, a reality that never should have been.

July 2 — The Dream of the Wrong Turn

> *Four hundred miles from the heart of Reno, the Creamsicle-orange Cutlass drives through the Sierra Nevada range. Soft white headlights pass us, their silence almost wild, like the eyeshine of a deer.*
>
> *The driver taps the wheel to a euphoria of synth-pop on the radio. In the passenger seat, a child reaches out and tangles the wind between her fingers. I watch her from the back seat, far away in the side-view mirror. A deep, steadfast light blinks from the black night of her pupil.*

So the dream played out. Wound back, played again, my mind swallowing itself until I woke, left to stare into the motel's comatose ceiling fan, the red wallpaper like a window into the bloody viscera of a whale. The dream had followed me from the desert and played continuously the past two nights. I sensed that its persistence was intentional. That it knew what had happened, wanted me to know.

Outside, people roamed Fremont Street under the winking observation of a carnival-lit cowgirl perched above the Glitter Gulch. I half watched them from the bed by the window, pulled back in time to a day I could not remember, the square cut clean from my memory's calendar. If I squinted, I could see the outer edges of the lost day, a shimmering dissolution. But the hours between had collapsed, sealed themselves off, left nothing but a black hole.

*

Fiona bolted up on the mattress, breath squeezed from her body. She felt the coarse tongue of desert heat, tasted the grainy air between her teeth. The dream again, every night for that first week of July. It was 3:00 a.m. The clock, knocked onto the floor, branded the darkness with an insensate red glare.

In the dream, the child was always gone when the car stopped. Fiona would get out and follow the driver — known only as M., and identical to Fiona but for muted eyes unsullied by any puncture of pupil. Ahead lay the Mojave's burning sandstone, its sweeping rings of red and white, and distant mountains with gentle peaks and slopes.

M. would stand ankle-deep in a prickly haze of desert needle, taking quick-flashing photographs that shook the darkness like dry lightning. She would turn to Fiona and speak of an orange spider weaving her web, until her egg hatched a hundred hungry spiders who devoured their mother.

Fiona curled up again in the motel's thin sheets. She clasped her head as if squeezing a splinter from her mind. Of all the films, why had M. chosen *Blade Runner*? The spider story, the last line from Rachael before android hunter Deckard reveals to her that she is not human, and her understanding of herself splits: *Real. Unreal. Before this moment. From now on.* Fiona had seen the film in theatres twice that summer, her eyes wide and shining like coagulated wonder.

She fell back asleep and the dream resumed its loop, only now the green highway sign had changed. Before, its taunts were simple: *Wrong Turn Up Ahead* — a perky little arrow tilting left. Now there were a thousand arrows. It had replicated itself, split radially into an inescapable warning.

*

Heatstroke

The owner of the motel never seemed to unplug herself from the network of hanging keys behind her, a broad wall of multidimensional connectivity, like an old telephone switchboard. Fiona scanned the keys, each one able to unlock a portal into someone's fitful world.

She had received an unexpected call from the lobby. Some business about a letter.

"Yeah, I'm pretty sure it's for you," the motel owner said, looking slightly confused as she handed over an envelope. "Fiona Moss?" When Fiona nodded, the motel owner clicked her nails on the counter. Her eyebrows pulled together. "Was it your sister or something?"

"What do you mean?" Fiona asked.

"Your sister, bringing the envelope."

"My sister? Not in Vegas, no, she's fourteen."

"She just looked ..." *Cleaner? Chattier? Less blood-flushed in the eyes?* "She just looked an awful lot like you."

Fiona felt an eerie omnipresence. Was the letter from M.? How could that be? She scanned the lobby's dimpled ceiling, the vacant cherry vinyl chairs, the magazine rack neatly stocked.

"It's kind of like ... what was that episode ...?" Fiona pressed the heels of her palms against her eyes. In the blotchy darkness, she saw herself huddled with her sister on the sofa, their faces a weird embryo-pale in the glow of *The Twilight Zone*. Watching as poor Millicent Barnes, once a sensible girl, is tormented by the sudden appearance of her doppelgänger in a bus depot.

"Honey, are you okay?" The motel owner touched Fiona's hand, startling her. "You seem a little young to be on your own out here. Are you meeting friends? Family?"

"No, I'm here for ..." Fiona's thoughts knotted. What could she say? A small white statuette of the Virgin Mary stood on the counter by the window. Its reflection in the glass, cast in the ceiling's fluorescence, appeared superimposed onto the scene outside, an attentive presence watching over the cars in the parking lot. "I'm here because ..."

Was it the light? Yes ... a moth-like longing for the light had drawn her here. A lifelong reliance on the stars, or whatever light was most at hand for comfort, navigation. But how can one say *I came here to curl up in the city's manic radiance*? How does one explain that if one could not burrow into the space between the stars, hold oneself in place with the pins of Orion, then Vegas would have to do. An electric star cluster within driving distance.

July 1 — The Day After the Wrong Turn

The morning cracked open, spilled onto me. I found myself staring at the prongs of cholla cacti, fuzzy and forked like freezer-burned coral reef. Strands of hair beat against my face. I swatted, saw browned blood on my knuckles. *What happened?* It took a long, sinking moment for me to ask: *What happened to me?*

Pain flooded my body as I tried to sit. I caught my breath, gazed into the clear, watery strata of blue sky streaming between the clouds. I was still in the Mojave, with the giant sandstone forma-tions, the occasional Joshua tree, branches contorted as if fossilized in a state of hysteria.

I could do this; I could make sense of things. Find the ridge. Follow it back to the visitor centre, the parking lot, my uncle's bright orange car. I tried to trace my movements backward, salvage some sequence of events, but the harder I concentrated, the faster my footprints burned up and blew away.

*

48

Heatstroke

Evening fell as Fiona sat outside by the edge of the motel pool, afraid to return to her room.

When she had left the lobby and opened the envelope, she found a Polaroid of herself standing by her school's flagpole. Wearing her burnished-blue graduation gown, tipping her mortarboard like a Stetson. She had intended to give the photo to the Maxwell brothers but held onto it instead, struck by a sudden self-consciousness. Written on the back was some ridiculous joke about a Vulcan *passion fight* for her affections. Had it in fact been a joke, or her egging them on, trying to make Jody jealous, or Easton jealous, or both for some reason, or no reason at all?

Fiona's breath tightened. Perhaps cross-contamination had occurred. She had failed to decipher the dream, and so the dream had come to find her. Fed up and determined, M. had attached herself like a burr to Fiona and travelled into the waking world. Fiona was not one to jump to impossible conclusions — but then, deserts and other untamed terrain had long been breeding grounds for unexplained phenomena. Geometrically pristine patterns in the wheat fields of Wiltshire. Claims of portals appearing, quietly timed for twilight in the Verde Valley of Arizona.

Fiona walked the length of the pool, intercepted by the shadows of zany-legged flamingo ornaments. Opening the envelope again, she eyed the photograph without touching it. As she searched it for meaning, studying the tie-dye sneakers and blooming cottonwoods, a clot of dark hair appeared in the pool. Fiona watched, alarmed, as it drifted toward her like the inky curlicues of a squid. She knelt and looked closer, a girl's figure taking shape in the pool's icy-green light.

Only now did it occur to Fiona, blood-rush filling her ears and body bracing to run, that she might have been wrong about the other girl. There was M., floating in the pool water, looking every bit as lost as Fiona. Staring up at her with a helpless look of embalmed serenity, like a specimen preserved in a jar. Eyes scrubbed of aspiration, of memory, no future or past. A self suspended in time.

Fiona crashed through the water, pearls of air spilling wildly. She swam to the other girl, took her hand, kicked to propel them both to the surface. But with contact, a sudden tessellation occurred. The two of them began to merge — a unifying feeling at first. Fiona could see M. as a little girl, crouched on her knees among the wispy wild rye, watching mustangs in the meadow below. There was a delicate, pinkish rain, each fast-falling drop catching the sunset. M. was trying to memorize every detail of the horses, the full breadth of their peacefulness. Incubate them in the warmth of her memory, so that they might be cherished, kept safe.

No. I know this memory. Did M. mean to consume her, like a fetus absorbing its twin?

Fiona pulled away, afraid of draining from her own body. *It's mine. It's mine.*

✳

Back in the motel room, the fruit flies had grown busy. Congregating in sticky takeout containers and pockmarking the walls. Fiona felt the doppelgänger fusing with her, inhabiting her. She tried to will her pores to filter out the other girl, let M. drip from her hair like the pool water. But her body only absorbed the invader more fully, locking her inside.

Fiona leaned over the sink and peered into the uneasy depths of her pupils, waiting for M. to Bloody Mary herself into the mirror. Fiona's mother used to call her own reflection her *better half.* Glimpsing it in the department store window, a puddle in the yard, the hallway mirror: "She never has to feel anything, does she," she would say. Fiona remembered the punched purple lids struggling to open, her mother's clear blue eye like the sky squinting.

Heatstroke

She hurried to the phone on the nightstand and dialed the number to the Maxwell brothers' ranch. Nausea burned her throat as she forced herself to listen to each taut, frenzied ring.

For Fiona and the Maxwell brothers, the otherworldly, with all its strange possibility, had always been a conduit for shared curiosity. Jody had joined her sixth-grade class mid-year, but Fiona did not particularly notice him until the day he presented a shoebox diorama of post-apocalyptic San Francisco. He spoke softly under the class's laughter, in his green-corduroy overalls, holding a creased copy of *Do Androids Dream of Electric Sheep?* Fiona admired the glittered cotton balls stretched into golden radioactive mist, the plastic farm animals broken apart, hollow insides stuffed with wires.

Jody, soon accompanied by Easton, began to ride over from the suburbs to camp in Fiona's backyard. Easton would roll up singing off-key before dropping his bike onto its side with a hard clatter. Jody would carefully wedge his bike's kickstand into the mud as Fiona waited inside the lopsided tent, wherein fervid debates arose over closed loops in space-time, the grandfather paradox, the diplomatic merits of Kirk versus Spock.

One morning in eleventh grade, Jody pulled Fiona aside by the foggy bleachers. He had been quiet throughout their usual walk to school. It was just the two of them by then, with Easton getting his licence and, along with it, a newfound embarrassment over public contact with his little brother. In the school hallways, he passed Jody without acknowledgement, and threw Fiona consolatory side-smiles that left her oddly thrilled.

"What's the matter with you?" she asked.

Jody was agitated, readjusting his glasses and looking over his shoulder. He reeked of wet grass and unbrushed teeth as they sat on the dew-chilled steel of the bench.

"Something fucked-up happened," he told her. His lower lip was swollen. His sweater had a ruddy, poorly soaped stain down the front. "I can't remember it all," he said. "It's like the whole night's been scooped out of my head."

By his account: Easton's recent spurt in size and confidence had shifted everything. Now, the absence of such a spurt in Jody formed a channel, hovering invisibly in the air, redirecting his stepfather's violence. Whatever had happened that night, Jody never said, but it had caused him to bolt out the front door and race through the neatly hedged cul-de-sac — only to wake up lying in the middle of the neighbourhood baseball diamond, the night instantly gone, dawn clicked into place like a picture in a stereoscope.

"But that's not the fucked-up part," he said. "I saw myself, Fi. I could see myself standing there, watching from the infield. It was my face, my clothes — then it fizzled out. It was like radio static or something." A duplicate, staring at him with an almost feral tranquility, the soft black eyes of a raccoon.

As Fiona placed her hand on Jody's shoulder, he shrank into himself. He rubbed his cheek and forehead compulsively, as if confirming the fixed existence of his face. "I look like me, right?" he asked, gripping her leg. "I'm still me?"

✳

The phone shrieked to life. Fiona clutched it to her ear with both hands, nearly knocking the base off the nightstand. "Jody?"

"... Fiona?" It was his voice. The shy, ever-sleepy mumble.

"Did you get my message?" Fiona listened to his breath, caught and trying to loosen itself, before a fumbling click. "Jody? *Jody.*"

She lowered the phone, stared at it in her hands like she had cracked it in half.

Her message on his answering machine had been clear enough for Jody and no one else: "The morning at the baseball diamond ... it's happened to me too. Can we talk?"

Heatstroke

Jody had never again spoken of what happened. That he had experienced some ripple in reality had never occurred to Fiona. And yet, reasonable people reported doppelgängers, catching sight of their own likeness on a bridge, a terrace, striding down the street in the opposite direction. Fragments of themselves roaming the world.

He had not seemed himself the last time she saw him, about six months ago, when he visited his mother in Reno over the Christmas holidays. He had called Fiona in the middle of the night, pleading with her to drive over. Fiona had peeked out the window at her uncle's car, occasionally parked in her driveway since her father died. *Come on, Fi. Easton wouldn't come up with me, and everyone's out at some tacky office party. Will you come? Please?*

Without waiting for her to take off her coat, Jody had led her, awkwardly by the hand, through his living room. Fiona knew the feel of the furniture's strawberry-mousse silk, the precise position of the coffee table, black-lacquered like a marbled oil spill. Yet, it struck her now that she had never invited the boys into her own home. Maybe it was something in the way Easton tugged the string of her shorts, causing her body to seize up, or Jody's sulky conviction that his brother always got his way.

Jody, the carpet ... Fiona pulled back and gestured toward her soaked boot prints on the floor, but Jody ignored them. His dark-syrup eyes peered into her, and though she could see him working through whatever he wanted to say, he never managed to say it.

Fiona clapped the motel phone onto its cradle. Why had Jody been so oddly tender that night? Watching *The Exorcist*, he had volunteered his shoulder for her to hide her face against, stroked her hair behind her ear when she thought she might throw up.

She grabbed the car keys from a heap of dirty clothes on the floor, shook off the flies.

Had it even been Jody sitting with her in the dim intimacy of his house? Whose eyes, when he drew so close his breath warmed her collarbone, had she been looking into?

✳

Light slipped over the hood of the car as Fiona drove down the Strip. Glancing in the rear-view mirror, she caught her eye, a bright gash of aquamarine — though the other eye was somehow bigger, somehow smaller, older, younger.

Fiona felt the city's wired, red-eyed restlessness running circuits through her, well after she had driven outside its borders, until somewhere along Route 95, when her heart began to sink. The roadside thickened with brittle saltbush and cacti. A tremor electrocuted the small bones in her hands. They vibrated against the steering wheel.

She shook her head. "I don't want to," she said. "I've changed my mind." But as if on its own, the car slowed and parked by the unpaved road leading into Red Rock.

Fiona went still. Here was where the world had split in two. Become *before* and *after*. She looked out the windshield at the vast, open flatland. Listened to the low-roving wind, the screech of a bird in the reeling blue overhead. What good was it to remember? After her father died, she was asked to recount her memories, brutal and loving alike. Would a counsellor have her squish another squeeze-toy and explain her every bruise, her mother's history of fractured bones? What purpose had it served to understand the violence? She wanted the violence gone. Dug out of her body like a bullet.

Dust skirted across the road. An inviting breeze rolled through the window and lapped against her cheek, but she could not get out of the car. The minute hand on the dashboard clock clicked with feeble determination as time lay slumped and rotting around her.

It would only continue mounting, this mass of wasted time, fortifying and isolating her. She hit the steering wheel. A hot, foul rush of memory began to rise, a magma chamber in her chest bursting.

June 30 — The Wrong Turn

"Moss, wait up!" Easton readjusted his backpack, watching his step on the slick rock. I had darted up a crumbly incline near the base of the Calico Hills. I was showing off my stamina to Easton and laughing at Jody, who was flushed and panting behind us.

After nineteen years of living in the soft-palmed suburbs, helping out at his father's ranch had given Easton a quiet earnestness. He paused to study the asters and mauve-veined lilies, and photograph the mottled cliffsides. He had drifted back to us, too, since leaving Reno: going to see *The Thing* in theatres with Jody, calling me late at night to discuss alien sabotage.

He and Jody would be attending the University of Nevada in the fall, Easton having deferred for a year, while I would be moving to California to start at Berkeley. We had planned this trip together, a proper send-off, the sort of foray our childhood selves would have wanted.

We hiked through hills of rusty stone, where trees rose aslant, branches low to the earth, as though their bulk had been swallowed by quicksand. By early sunset, we began to wander off the trail, settling near a ground-level cavity among the giant sandstone forms.

Easton sidled up next to me, startling me as he touched my wrist. "What happened? Did you nick yourself?" There was a scrape on my forearm from the whip of a branch. "I have stuff in the pack. You should have said something."

I shrugged, but he waited with his elbows out, hands tightening around the straps of his backpack.

"Fiona. It'll get infected."

I sighed, held out my palm.

Rather than give me the antibiotic, he took my hand. "Be more careful, okay?"

Easton had a way of falling still, fully occupying a moment with his presence. He would seem to me then, as he did now, somehow altered. Eyes cool with jarring clarity. As he dotted the scrape with ointment, gingerly thumbing grease into my skin, I smiled at Jody, unsure what else to do. I could read his irritation; his mouth had thinned, tongue running along the inside of his lower lip as he watched Easton's hands, the little wound near my wrist.

Maybe nothing would have happened had I reached out for Jody. Had I not simply stood there, bewildered, as he stalked off into the tall, tunnelled complex of stone. Had I not watched him disappear so quickly that, after searching in flustered circles, calling for him, yelling at him, Easton and I could do nothing but return to the cavity and wait.

The sun hung low and full-blooded, gradually disappearing behind mounds of scarred rock.

"Don't worry, he'll find his way back. He has a map, some water." Easton's cigarette dangled from his fingers, emptying itself like an exhaust pipe. "It's been rough for him without you. He doesn't know how to make new friends."

"That's not a reason to just take off like that," I said, pacing and itching at my shirt, the swampy feeling of sweat under my clothes. "He has no idea what he's doing out there — he could get hurt, or lost." I was beginning to feel faint. I sat down next to Easton, leaning back against the rock wall, now varnished in shadow. "I think I'm going to be sick."

Easton rose onto his knees and rested the back of his hand against my forehead. He took my jaw, gently tilted it back and forth. When I winced, he laughed. "Just checking your pupils, like Deckard."

Heatstroke

The empathy test — how bounty hunters decipher who is human and who amounts to nothing more than an assortment of parts, sentient shells planted with seeds of untrustworthy memory. "If I were an android," I said, "you'd never know."

I would never remember exactly how it started. Why he leaned forward and kissed me, what I did in response, if the twist in my face came before or after the stiffness in my spine. Nor the moment it all slid away from me, surprise at his eagerness swerving into swift, suffocating panic like a plastic bag over my head.

What would remain clear, palpable as the nightly chill of sweat on my scalp, was Easton's forehead hard against mine. His heated voice, *Don't be like that, don't make it weird.*

My eyes opening to find Jody watching motionless, shock bleaching the sunburn from his face. The surreal terror of my inanimate body manipulated by another's hands, another's intentions, like a necrophiliac with a corpse. My helplessness, stunning. The weight of it, crushing me into the dark, breathless, bottomless cracks of the earth. And I felt some small part of me eject from the rest, free itself, as if I could preserve a single unbound piece, cast it like a bottled message into the light.

✳

Fiona drove away from Red Rock without thinking, other than a nagging worry she had forgotten to return her Vegas motel key. The car now sat in the middle of Moapa, on the highway's muddy shoulder. Beyond it lay mangy flatland, a lone ranch, a laundry line bearing nothing but faded blue strips of sky.

There was a word Fiona would not use, the word for what had happened to her. And a name she could not say out loud, a name that would slowly become only *the boy who ... the man responsible for ...* She stared at the nearby ranch, but she did not entirely see

A Song for Wildcats

it. Only its curtains, framing the kitchen window. The thin, weary cotton, a print of large green roses. A wholesome quality like the prairie-girl patterns of her childhood bedroom. In the window, a boy washed dishes over the sink.

On the drive to Moapa, Fiona had first stopped at a hospital, where she was told an examination would be performed. Police would be called; yes, she would need to provide names. Photographs would be taken.

"Photographs?" she had asked the nurse. "Photographs of *what*?"

Before she changed her mind and hurried out, carrying all her weight in her knees, a doctor instructed her to lie back and concentrate on the poster stuck to the ceiling. Puppies wearing birthday hats.

Fiona touched the hospital wristband. *MOSS, FIONA. VALLEY HOSPITAL* — she stopped, looked away.

It was easier for M., untouchable in the darkening windshield. Fiona had nearly given the name Millicent to the hospital, but when her own name fell out, she was sorry for offering M. only an initial, an incomplete piece, like that was all either of them deserved.

The boy in the window dried the dishes, dabbed away the suds. Straightened the curtains. Such gentleness applied to cutlery and cloth. Fiona finally looked away from him and pulled back onto the road as quietly as she could. She drove into nightfall, past exits, down roads where salt grass and downy seep willow sprouted. She drove until she was bordered by valleys, where stars collected on still, black ponds. The dream had not stopped, and she understood, with a knowledge stored marrow-deep, that even once it did, it would continue to swim up from the time-drowned murk of the past while she prepared breakfast or stood on the crowded bus in a nerve-spun cocoon. She knew, indefinably, that something — a way of being in her body, a certain freedom with which she might have moved through the world — would never be quite what it was supposed to be.

Heatstroke

Fiona stopped the car and rolled down the window. She listened to her breath, how it mimicked the quiver of the grasshoppers in the valley. She conjured the scent of violets lifting from the resin-glazed evergreens as she and her father hiked along Lake Tahoe. His hand reaching back for hers, their hair flying in the winds of the foothills.

The moon drizzled its reflection across a pond. It hung full and so gauzed with light that one did not always see the heathered bruises, its surface cratered from the chaos of other bodies. The moon itself a piece broken from the earth, shoved into silent orbit.

Fiona looked through the windshield, into the sky, until the natural rhythm of her breath returned. Until there came a flickering recollection, an awareness of how she matched the moon, bright and pithy-eyed and solid. For a faint moment, she felt its enduring glow deep in her pupils, casting its beam down forgotten caverns and buried causeways, where she housed every ghost of herself — from that first small, balmy-faced progenitor, all the way to who she might become, and every self in between reaching out to one another — illuminating the ever-rippling collective memory of a life.

The Islanders

I.

TIGER SONGS

You could not compete with his mother's mouth. The ceaseless stoking of a fire fermenting inside. Hard candy cracking between her teeth, tongue twisting cherry stems or prodding the inside of her cheek. Restless tics that caught her son's eye like an exposed nerve as she sat by the front door in the paisley-papered hall, listening for the signal.

Then it would come: the sound of neighbours clanging tin lids against the footpaths outside.

Her whole body would be wound and ready to spring, to let in the men with the shiny black guns. The back door in the kitchen would already be ajar, waiting to spit the men out into the tiny courtyard, among the linens wrinkling on the laundry line. And the men would disperse into the alleys between the blowsy-brown houses so they might hide from the Brits, or the peelers, in the outhouse with the rippled tin roof. Or jump into a car packed with still more men and still more guns. Or disappear through another sympathetic door.

A scream had nestled inside Jamie's mother. He saw how it burned her throat if she held it in too long. Even in the midst of the densest riots, in the ripe, roiling heart of west Belfast, he heard her. In his sleep, he heard her. Yelling at the men in the blue berets until her voice blistered.

And where had it gotten her? Where had it gotten any of them? Jamie could tell you where it got him: the arse end of nowhere.

✳

The morning dripped blue. Rain sharpened the wind as it rushed off the dimpled silver of the North Atlantic. Jamie paused and looked over his shoulder. He surveyed the grassy acres flowing unencumbered but for craggy outcrops and the occasional bright, whitewashed house — some with neat, fern-green shutters and red-berried vines, others ill-kept, dark cracks in the brick like vein-rot.

He was sitting alone on the shore with his aunt's umbrella. He had kept to himself since she moved him out of Belfast. He had done the same back home, preferring the reliability of his own company. But roaming solitude had not often been possible in the city, or within the anemic avocado walls of St. Brigid's Home for Boys, where the relentless tumult of other people crowded in on him until he felt only a loose, downy sense of himself, like a dandelion clock coming apart.

Here on the peninsula, he could be alone. He opened the umbrella his aunt had badgered him into taking — what adult owned a million silk scarves but only one umbrella, and it was *broken*? — and tilted it against the sand, obscuring himself from view. From his pocket, he took the lighter his only friend, Grady, had given him. A dirty old brass Zippo they figured had once belonged to a cool-tempered cowboy all the way in the American West, who taught his sons to tame horses and chewed on cheap cigars.

An orange bud sprang from the lighter, and began to feed on the riddling patterns of purple embroidery along one of Aunt Lydia's scarves. He did not know why he had stolen the scarf, or why he wanted to burn it. But a pain churned in him when she asked — again and again — how he was feeling, and this was the only thing that eased it.

For the briefest moment, as the scarf burned, Jamie's heart stopped spinning. Seabirds circled overhead, and he felt their whirlpool rhythm deep in the stillness of his body. The electricity of oncoming rain prickled his lungs. In his hand was a contained chaos that he could ignite and extinguish at will. He let the cold ruffle of the tide roll under his toes, and tug at his feet. He dropped the scarf into the water and watched it be devoured as it drifted away.

It was then that the girls appeared. He saw them on the viridescent fields that swelled and sloped into tumbledown rocks leading to the beach. They were barefoot, with matted oat-blond hair and dirty wool jumpers hanging down to their knees. They made their way across the beach, lugging a tin wash bucket between them. Jamie thought they looked like lost, limbo-bound children from some terrible fire-and-brimstone tale.

The girls crouched and began dipping red, roundish items from the bucket into the water. They rinsed and scrubbed with their little thumbs, minding their own, until the younger one let out a throat-frayed cry.

Thinking she might be hurt, Jamie ran toward them. *Did a jellyfish get you? Let's see that foot, then. Where are your ma and da?* As he spoke, his voice grew distant, as if swept to the other end of a wind tunnel. All he fully registered was the blood smeared across the bucket, humming and frenzied with flies, and down the ropy knitwork of the girls' jumpers.

The smaller girl kept wailing. Her mouth widened, a pit of embery darkness. A fly crept up her tongue, flicked into the air, and disappeared into her eye.

Jamie was too frightened to move. His body felt reduced to a rootless pulse — until the older girl reached up and set the salve of her hand on his forehead. They stared into each other's eyes. Hers were silvery sage, like his mother's, and the arid cores of Jamie's own eyes filled with the nourishing rustle of trees, the flighty whistles and bleats of birds.

There was kinship here; he knew it instantly. He reached for her, wanting to hold her close. Through her small hand alone, he felt the strength of her command, the power to envelop and guide like a high wind. She spoke to him, a voice the green of sunlit grass: *You are a force, Jamie. A fighter. But a fighter needs a cause. Belong to us. Be one of ours. Just step into the water ... come along, a little farther, so we may be certain you are who we think you are.*

He was in the water only a moment before Aunt Lydia was standing in front of him, hysterical in a purple housecoat of tissue-paper satin. Trembling waist-deep in the water, soundlessly calling his name.

His aunt's voice slowly broke through as she hauled him back to the shore. "Jamie? Can you hear me?"

"Did you see them?" he asked.

Lydia clutched the collar of her housecoat and tried to hold the flimsy umbrella over both herself and her nephew, who would not stand still. "See who?"

"The little girls." Jamie looked around, but the girls were gone. It was only him, alone with his aunt, as she hounded him with her dainty tiptoe run. Not letting up an inch with that banjaxed umbrella, flapping its unhinged wing, half of its ribs snapped.

The Islanders

"Jamie, please, I need to get you inside," Lydia said. She worried he would give himself pneumonia. She had spotted him only by chance, glancing out the window to see him wading into the wind-roused ocean. "There's nobody here. Whoever it was that frightened you —"

"But they were *right here* a second ago." Jamie moved up and down the same patch of pebbly beach, one hand to his head, clutching a fistful of hair. His aunt kept trying to pin him to one spot, but his feet were agitated, as if sensing cracks in the ground, impending free fall. "I swear I saw them ... there was this bucket ..."

"What bucket?" Lydia asked.

"There was blood all over it."

"Goodness," she said. "A bucket of fish, probably." So much sudden movement had nauseated her, and she stared into the wobbly middle distance. "Places like this, you know ... maybe that's normal around here."

It was the blood that set him off, she was sure. What other reason could there be for two small girls upsetting him so much?

"Look, Jamie ... look," she said, gesturing to the water running clear along the shore, quivering over sand and smooth, black stones. "Right as rain. Any blood's been washed away by now."

She waited for some sign of relief to pass over him. Though if it did, how would she know? In their time together, Lydia had come to know the quietly stormy expression and sharp, glittery-green eyes that defined his face. The impossible bed-head of his badly trimmed hair, the same cool black as his mother's. The stomp in his step. Shoulders hunched and taut as he walked, though he was all of eleven, as if he were moving against his own private squall. Yet she continued failing, day in and day out, to reach him. To open him up.

"Catch yourself on," he said, growing frustrated. "You're not going to faint over a wee bit of blood, are you?"

A Song for Wildcats

"It's you I'm worried about." She touched his arm, inviting him closer, but he shrugged her off. "Jamie, what you say happened doesn't make any sense."

"What I *say* happened?" he asked.

Jamie wondered at the look on his aunt's face. Soft pity, a flinch of wariness. Like he was a helpless wild bird she meant to stifle in a tea towel and take home. He turned from her with a sense of both reeling and sinking, the disorienting blow of not being believed.

"I'll run you a hot bath and that's the end of it," Lydia said, at last managing a feeble grip of his shoulder. "A nice hot bath fixes everything, or it bloody well ought to."

Her nephew said nothing, just stared into some internal projection being cast over the water.

Turning him toward their house and nudging him along, Lydia took in the peninsula's mild mounds and squat, scruffy cliffs — the village as a whole closed off by the ocean's steely bastion — and she was comforted by the thought that their new home looked like either the beginning or the end of the world.

✳

Lydia dreamed in a blue world, where the pell-mell demands of her day subsided, and she fell through sheets of sky like fluttering laundry. There were no scalding lights in sleep. None of the looming, eggy eyeballs overseeing concert rehearsals or doctor's appointments, no sidewalks and roundabouts worming with people. She could sink away — or was it that the blue world floated up around her while she remained still? Was there a difference when relativity was unmoored?

Awake, Lydia carried in her mind the thick residue of her sleeping world. A blinding, almost granular fog. Some days it flowed through her whole body, until she felt it materializing into heaps of soaked fabric stuffed inside her rib cage. She would find it hard to breathe, to move, to lift her torso. She would droop over the dressing table and stare into her irises in the mirror, thinking maybe she could pluck one of the tiny blue fibres with a pair of tweezers, unspool her eye like thread.

A strip of static warbled across the portable television set.

"What now?" she muttered, rubbing her fist into her eye. She had moved the bulky little television to the kitchen countertop, where it was easier to monitor. The news kept reporting more bombings by the Ulster Volunteer Force. Four nearby, in Monaghan and Lydia's own Dublin. Thirty-three civilians dead.

She felt light-headed. Light-chested, too, like a heavy bolt of wind had rushed through her. Bombs dropped in milk vats, planted in cars and King's Cross and courthouses. And it was not just the paramilitaries; British soldiers were massacring people and running around instilling terror. And she found no matter where she went, she carried the dread that any street she might be walking down could come flying up around her.

The recent attacks were just over two weeks apart from the UVF bombing a pub in south Belfast. The broadcast had come on as Jamie was stuffing his foot into one of his tadpole-green wellies by the front door. He had stopped to watch, one socked foot on the brown shag of the sitting room. He gave a sudden spasm of a blink, before walking outside with the other muddy boot in his hand.

Lydia turned the dial and the news winked off.

Squinting at the fierce midday glare through the window, she sank back into the breakfast nook's dowdy beige cushions. For the past two hours, she had been falling in and out of sleep to BBC news and sitcoms. She knew a long rest was needed, that returning too soon to her grinding routine would break her, but boredom had become as exhausting as overexertion. To play the piano — Tchaikovsky's *June: Barcarolle* unfurling its supple petals, Chopin's nocturnes balancing on the cusp of dreamy despondence — required unified choreography of the entire self. The body as apparatus for the soul. Rolling shoulders, precise and determined fingertips, pounding feet.

For Lydia, there existed no calmer, fuller state of being. No safer state either. Music could be remedied. One could play a composition as many times as one pleased, until it sounded just right. Mistakes could be fixed or obscured, pieces perfected.

Her hand, slack at her side, played lazily on the air. Not a song, just soundless notes attached to nothing. At first, she was not aware she was doing it, but her fingers missed running over the keys of the London Symphony's glossy black concert grand. The elderly widower who owned this house had left most of his furniture, but he did not own a piano. All the better, according to Lydia's doctor.

Don't put so much pressure on yourself, he had said. As if it were so easy. No pressure! Sure, why not. Rest, rest, seaside air, like she was some ailing Georgian heiress. Everyone always gave the same well-meaning and insipid advice — and perhaps there was something to it, but it seemed to follow the impression that Lydia's pressure was a levelling weight on top of her, to be lifted and abated, rather than a sinkhole deep inside her, constantly shuddering.

Pulling her knees under her chin, Lydia squeezed as compactly as she could into the nook. She leaned her temple against the windowpane and watched Jamie idle along the rocks and slippery, gangrenous clumps of seaweed, no doubt repeating yesterday's desperate search for the two girls, who were either a figment or a fabrication; she was not sure which was worse.

Since their arrival at the Inishowen peninsula in late spring, Jamie had spent most of his time outside, while Lydia hardly left the kitchen. It was an immaculate hinterland of cold tile and soapy-pink pantries, tucked at the back of the house. The unfinished touch appealed to her; it had been partly lost to flooding the previous year,

and it was in the paint-and-polish phase of reconstruction when the
widower decided he could not stand the sight of the place and threw
it up for rent. White slabs of lime were visibly scraped over cracks
in the stripped walls, and the cellar door was sanded bare. Only
faded patches of mint paint were left in the wood's carved furrows.

The kitchen reminded her of the home she and Eabha had lived
in. The Sisters of Mercy was a barren space of spastic lights, and sag-
ging wallpaper like the plaster cast of someone's water-pruned flesh.
Growing up in a place like that, Lydia had become accustomed to a
permanent unease, as though bad dreams were being alchemized by
the teaspoon and mixed into her food. The place where she had found
Jamie had seemed no different: a roof and some clothes and three meals
a day, but utterly unable to conform to the loving contours of a home.

It was no wonder the boy was struggling.

Still a strange matter, though, his episode on the beach. And the
look on his face, as he marched into the water, had alarmed her as
much as everything else. She knew it — a look of delirious hope,
like a castaway spotting a ship on a horizon that had, until then,
offered nothing beyond a final view of the world. Where would she
have seen such a look before?

All of this was unnerving enough on its own without today's
fresh crisis.

"Eabha, what do I do?" she asked. "Do I punish him?"

The empty room glared squarely back at her.

"Not like at Mercy, of course not. Just a normal punishment."
Lydia chewed her thumbnail. She could see herself in the dark glass
of the wall oven. Her other hand had worried itself flat across her
collarbone, like it meant to strangle her. "What does normal punishment look like?"

Three years since her sister's death, and she could not quite
shake the desire, the phantom habit, to reach for the telephone and
dial Eabha's old flat by the docks in Dublin. Though Lydia had

A Song for Wildcats

been living at the music conservatory at the time, she had always thought of her elder sister's flat, with Eabha's thin cotton dresses hanging from every curtain rail, as their first real home.

Lydia waited now in anticipatory stillness, as if for a response from the bare chamber around her. Of course nothing happened. She picked up a slice of dry toast lying, barely eaten, on the plate in front of her. It had gone hard and cold. She dropped it and sighed. "Fine then," she said. "Let's get this over and done with."

Gripping the edge of the table, she pulled herself up. The tile was patterned in quaint barns and watermills, idyllic creeks and sturdy silos, so that as she stood, she felt a vertiginous lightness, as though looking down onto a village through a glass floor high in the air. The industriousness of these imaginary people made her want to crawl back into bed and bury herself under the blankets. But she could not go on avoiding her nephew all day.

The trouble was: where could she possibly begin? A flick knife, of all things! A knife, stuffed between the pages of Eabha's dog-eared copy of *The Marriage of Heaven and Hell*, had plunged toward her feet as she was tidying Jamie's desk that morning.

She smoothed her skirt, several times, and shook her mind clear. Instinctively, she opened the cupboard under the sink to check on the fire extinguisher. She had seen the boy with that filthy lighter, the one he swore he did not have.

"Everything is perfectly fine," she said, repeating it to herself as she stood at the back door, squeezing the glass knob.

Her nephew would not become another cautionary tale. Lydia would not allow it. She owed it to him as his only known relative, the only adult in the world on whom he could rely.

And she owed it to Eabha. It was Lydia, after all, who had effectively destroyed her sister's life.

The flick knife waited on the table, extending its steel fang. It was powdered with rust, and the smell of it made her want a tetanus

The Islanders

shot. She folded it and placed it in her skirt pocket, rubbing her fingers clean on a crumpled tissue. As if tiptoeing around his mercurial moods was not doing her in enough, now she felt like a prison warden collecting contraband.

Then again, what had she expected when she took him in? The boy's life had been porous, huge gaping holes for fear to flow through. Lydia knew that fear — true, long-lingering fear — was not atmosphere, not environs or predicament; one could not be extricated from such fear. It was swallowed, inhaled; it broke the skin and infected the blood.

And he had been made to survive it all on his own. The looks some people gave her, the bloody nerve, asking without asking: *Where were you? Where have you been all this time?*

Nobody quite understood how Lydia had not known about her nephew until the past winter. After Eabha's accident — faulty explosives she was driving, and Lydia chose to believe her sister had not known — a few years back, in '71, Lydia had visited her sister's plot with annual regularity. She did so, in the cemetery between the motorway and the muraled sinews of the Falls Road, on the first of every February. It was only this year that someone else was standing there when she arrived. A spiky fellow with bedraggled hair, glancing at her over the upturned collar of his leather coat. *The sister, is it? Aye, she mentioned you, she did. Kept a photo in her wallet. Me? An old colleague, an old friend. Visiting the wee nephew, are you?*

Lydia remembered the slow sensation of her heels sinking into the wet, mud-spongy grass. Cold drizzle spitting in her face.

She opened the back door and called Jamie's name. He was crouched in the sand at the bottom of the slope, which rolled from their yard into the beach. No coat, just a jumper over his freshly washed pyjamas, begging to catch a cold. He was observing something through a large magnifying glass, making a shifty orb of his eyeball.

A Song for Wildcats

Jamie pretended not to hear her. The way she called from a distance, unable some days to drag herself beyond the porch and come get him, filled him with dull resentment. At least she had finally emerged from the cold tomb of the kitchen. He looked up the slope toward her, and found her dressed for a boozy garden party. Billowy turquoise skirt, with big globs of pearl stuck to her earlobes. Hair, a tea-stained blond, falling in gentle waves. Yet tissue poked out from the sleeve of her blouse, bunched up beneath the embroidery, and her voice had a dozy grog, though it was past noon.

Jamie turned back to his magnifying glass. He continued examining a braided strand of wire lodged in the sand.

The previous night, the girls had returned to him. Or, rather, they had sent a signal. From his window he could see only the moon-etched outlines of the grassy banks, and the glinting curves of Aunt Lydia's roadster in the drive. Then, a glowing curl of smoke had risen from the shoal. He heard the same voice as before, somehow inside and outside his head. *We do not create the flame, Jamie. We recruit it.*

"What flame?" he had asked, the tip of his nose against the windowpane.

The one you feel inside you. It has drawn men to fight for millennia, since the Battle of Mag Itha. With us as their guidance, their mothers of war. You feed our flame, and we feed yours.

Jamie hesitated. "What if I don't want to fight?"

You will. And we will help you do it. The smoke broke apart, fell away, like feathers. *A cause will never abandon you, Jamie. And it cannot be taken away.*

By the time he had pulled his jumper over his pyjamas and slid out of bed, the smoke had melted into the night. He waited for hours for the signal to return, his arms folded over the windowsill. Nothing else appeared that night, but for a grey crow clapping her feet across the roof of Lydia's car.

The Islanders

Jamie had tried to force himself to sleep. But the smoke lingered in his thoughts, and sharpened into the great sword Excalibur as it pierced the water's surface, lifted toward brave young Arthur by the watchful Lady of the Lake. Or the long, barbed spear of Cú Chulainn, a warrior called mad for his battle-bred rage. Feared men, commanding and unyielding. In control of everything, afraid of no one.

He lay straight and stiff, body thrumming. If his mother were here, what would she say? A sudden sadness bubbled up in him, but he hardened against it, forcing it to dry out and crumble like ash. He tried instead to concentrate on his mother's bedtime game, a trick for easing his jumpy heart. *The moon is older ... the moon is older than ... King Arthur ... and older than the Book of Kells, and the invention of the magnetic compass by ... diviners ... in China ... and older than gunpowder, and older than the Dead Sea Scrolls, and ... what else, what went even farther back? Dinosaurs, all the way back to the Jurassic times, it was the same moon all the Brontosauruses looked at ... and the first tree grew from soil that fed off the light of that moon.*

Perhaps the girls were older than the moon. They were not girls but enchantresses, or Druids — that was obvious enough. And while he was no Cú Chulainn or Arthur, still they had chosen him. *A force*, the green-eyed girl had said. *A fighter.* He rolled onto his side and wrapped himself in his blanket, as tightly as he could. *A cause will never abandon you ... and it cannot be taken away.*

Come morning, Jamie had thrown on his boots, stuffing in the hems of his pyjama bottoms, and trudged down to the spot on the beach where the smoke had appeared. There he found a peculiar scrap of barbed wire, sprouting from the sand like a seedling. Around it, the water pulsed in rapid, incongruous ripples.

He leaned in close, peering through the magnifying glass he had found in a drawer filled with the widower's colourful stamps — pictured with yellow palms and ancient ruins, all backdrops to the huge imperial head of the British queen. Looking at the wire, Jamie realized it was the same sort that prickled across the roads in Belfast and spiralled in bright rings along the brick-walled alleys. As he reached down and touched it, he felt a wince in his skull, as though his brain were being wrung out.

Jamie clamped his hands over his ears. Sounds poured onto him, pelting him. His and Grady's cackles as they whipped rocks against the Peace Wall, a stubborn sham of steel and concrete. Armoured cars wrestling their angular bulks onto the sidewalks, and rumbling, mud-green military trucks idling in noon traffic. The dirty purr of helicopters, and bombs in the night, and the held breath between gunfire, so brief but like a slow drop in time, and even now, all the way on the farthest tip of the south, Jamie could not pull his heart up from that drop, soothe it, make it run steady.

"Jamie!" his aunt yelled.

His chin shot over his shoulder. "*What?*"

Vitriol filled his mouth. Why could she not just leave him alone? He bit down on the urge to snap, to tell her to knock off her blethering, the endless surveillance and fussing, to stop throwing more noise into the maelstrom.

The wire stabbed his finger, and he snatched his hand away. "Shite!"

"Language, Jamie!" Lydia called.

"I didn't say anything." He brought his finger to his mouth, eyeing the blood smeared over the thorny knot in the water. It was oddly distressing, a part of himself scraped away.

Then the voice again, whistling through him. *Now you may come to us ... Be ours, and we will never leave you ...*

The sand caved in around the curlicue of wire, and a small hole widened like a trap door in the ocean floor. A perfect circle, through which the wire dropped and disappeared.

Slowly, he pulled his hand away from his mouth. The blood was gone. Even the taste of it.

The Islanders

As he made his way toward the house, Jamie was not sure what he had seen. The past couple of days had not felt entirely real. He looked at the cut on his finger, clean but raw, and pinched the cuff of his sleeve against it. Better to hide it from Aunt Lydia, keep her from losing the absolute run of herself. Not that she would believe the cause of it, anyhow, if he cared to tell her.

"Well, if it isn't yourself." Lydia rested a hand against one of the porch's pillars and tapped an impatient rhythm. "Come along. I'll put the kettle on."

Jamie looked up to find his aunt struggling in the confines of the porch like a kite in a tree. With a pang of guilt, he noticed the unsteadiness of her gestures as she inched forward, waiting for him. Cú Chulainn and Arthur probably never hurt their aunts' feelings, if they had aunts.

The back porch was the size of a wardrobe, built of milky-yellow pine that now split along the floorboards. It had been invaded all over by blithe tufts of grass, with a low-slung roof tipped to one side beneath the weight of muck and scrabbling dog roses. Hand to her temple, Aunt Lydia looked the uneven pillars up and down, doubting their sturdiness.

She watched her nephew sigh and take his time up the hill. A slow lumber, dragging his shadow behind him like an iron ball.

"Honestly, any more of this and there'll be less of it," she said, chasing a fluff of lint down her sleeve. "I must have called half-a-dozen times."

"Got you out of the house, didn't it?" Jamie held the magnifying glass to his face, moved it back and forth. "I spy with my little eye ... someone who is ... going to go swimming today."

"The child's gone mad," Lydia said to the empty space beside her. "It's too chilly, the water. And there are little bitsy crabs hiding all over the place. You're going to get pinched."

Jamie had to laugh. "You're going to miss the whole ocean."

75

"Another day," she said. "Come inside a moment. We need to have a chat."

He began to protest, then froze. Pale mortification trickled down his face, and the magnifying glass slipped from his hand. "It isn't mine."

Lydia glanced at the knife handle peeking out of her pocket. She tucked it away and forced a smile. "You're all right, love, you're fine. Just a chat, that's all."

He was twisting the end of his sleeve like he meant to bleed out the dye in dribbling saffron. He had wanted to be honest about the knife from the start — truly, he regretted ever letting Grady talk him into taking it — but it was a serious matter, he understood that, and one could never trust how another person might react.

His eyes remained low, lifting only briefly like a tenderfoot bird, before falling back to the ground. "It's Grady's."

"Is it now," she said.

Jamie glanced again at his aunt, carefully measuring her degree of anger. "He said I had to hold onto it because we couldn't afford to lose more of our ranks."

An indignant laugh shivered through her, but she pressed it down. "Oh, good grief. Ranks."

"It's *true*," Jamie argued. "What would you know about it?"

Lydia inhaled with purpose, ready to make a point, then recognized she had none. She sighed, frowned. "That's a fair cop, I suppose. I don't really know what it's been like for you."

She fell into a patio chair scabbed in peeling red paint. It never ended, did it? She had deliberately lost track of her anguish over the conflict in the North, refusing to hold onto her allegiances or rage. Instead she had cast a sodden exhaustion over those plummeting feelings, like a tarp thrown over a bottomless well.

"What I mean is … you're a child, you don't need to be thinking about ranks. Is this Grady one of the older lads? Was he trying to get you involved in something?"

76

"No, but you still don't cross him," Jamie said. He heard his own voice racing ahead of his thoughts. Too quick, too high and breakable. "Once he walked right up to one of them soldiers patrolling the market on McQuillan and aimed his cap gun at him, and he could've been shot dead. He's completely mad." He paused to catch a hiccup of breath. "And it's not just the Brits, you've got to worry about the Prods in the Shankill jumping you too."

"Jamie, don't say *Prods*." His aunt smiled at him then, with all her quivery warmth. "Let's calm down. I just want to make it clear that you don't need something like a knife here. Everything is perfectly safe."

Jamie looked at her like she was speaking another language. He took a shallow breath and held it at the top of his throat.

"Jamie?" Lydia asked. The boy could go so terribly quiet, she almost wanted to shake the voice out of him. Some afternoons he holed away for hours in silence, curled onto his side, listening to records. Songs of lonesome journeys to outer space, or of driving by fields and turnpikes with a lost, empty wanderlust. And she could do nothing, shut out as she was, but hover in the hallway or press her ear to the door.

He said nothing, only stared with his mouth closed tight.

"Your eye, the first day I visited ..." Lydia's voice came out blunt and clumsy. "The home told me you got into a lot of fights." She recalled the sight of Jamie shuffling into the hall, fidgeting with the grease-stained tie of his ill-fitting uniform. Shrinking away from her hand. He had been sporting a shiner behind the shaggy bangs, a nasty dark purple, and a split in his lip the shape of a claw. "You know, there's no one anywhere near here who'd want to hurt you. Is that what you're afraid of?"

He had no answer. It had never occurred to Jamie to centralize his fear on a single possibility; he had always staggered under the fathomless immensity of the fact that anything, everything, could happen at any time.

"They were talking about Mam," he said, remembering the taunts, the hailstorm of knuckles. "They're always talking shite."

His heart was beating in his fingertip, where the cut now dilated with a fresh sting.

Lydia squinted at a spot of blood on his sleeve. "Did you hurt yourself?"

"No," he said, shifting his hand out of view.

She drew closer and he stepped back. "Jamie, let me help," she pressed, at the same time worrying that she was making matters worse, like trying to scrub away a stain. "Do you need me to bandage it? Have you washed it clean? It could be infected."

His foot poised to back farther away. She was only trying to help, and he was spoiling everything. He could see it, and he hated it — but it was always going to be spoiled, eventually. His aunt beamed with open kindness, but she was so delicate, a moth flitting aimlessly, trapped behind the blinds. Less than a month together under the same roof and she was already banging herself against the glass.

"I don't need you babying me," he said. He lifted his chin to prove it, his shoulders stiffening. But his knee would not stop bouncing, and his breath kept piling up in his throat.

They looked away from each other, at nothing in particular. The clear, dizzying sky widened overhead as the last traces of cloud pulled away.

✳

Inside his bedroom wardrobe, Jamie sat squished between a box of ornaments that jingled whenever he nudged it and a wicker bowl of dusty knitting tools and yarn, where he felt as though he were hiding in a forgotten corner of someone's memory.

The Islanders

With great care, as if the cardboard might crumble, he lifted the lid off a shoebox. He kept it buried in the wardrobe, behind a blockade of fusty peach-tweed coats and purl-knit jumpers. Stored within it were his comic books — his serious books were stacked on proud display beside his bed — and a crinkly picture torn from a dirty magazine, showing a topless woman posing on a motorcycle. Grady had given it to him on his birthday. He had presented it while wearing his wide and ever-spontaneous grin still clinging to several baby teeth. The picture and the Zippo were treasures of enormous sentiment to Grady, so Jamie treated them as such.

Jamie took the lighter from his pocket and flicked the rusty spark wheel. A soothing warmth bloomed in his chest. He knew he was a freak for loving fire, but what else was there to singe the edge off his nerves? There was just enough light to see, huddled within the wardrobe, and pore over the shoebox keepsakes. Age-sallow sheet music bound in a frail yellow ribbon. A sparsely tasselled plaid shawl. Forgotten sundries his aunt had left lying about the house, like clicky batteries and purple sticky notes she had scribbled on, half-conscious in the kitchen nook. His mother's tatty collection of William Blake.

Pulling his mother's crucifix necklace out from under his collar, he clung to it as he thumbed the pages of Blake as gingerly as he could. Here lived the source of her lullabies, mild and ruminative poems set to playful tunes.

Tyger Tyger, burning bright
In the forests of the night

He had always loved the lines about the Lamb, though they made him feel far away from the poem, shirked by it somehow.

Did he smile his work to see?
Did he who made the Lamb make thee?

A Song for Wildcats

Emptiness swelled in his stomach. It felt bigger than him, some-how, and he wanted to curl inside it, alone and unseen. He closed his eyes and imagined this cavernous space, and just as it began to feel real, so did the weight pressing against its stony walls. Waves bat-tering to be let in, trickling through cracks and weeping onto him.

His eyes flew open. He hurried the necklace back under his shirt. Shook his head and swallowed the last pinch of bad feeling.

He looked down at all he had stolen from Aunt Lydia.

There were postcards. One from Zurich depicting the dusty gold light of a concert hall. Another from Paris, with a sunny haze of chalky facades and faded black rooftops, which Lydia had explained to him was "very Belle Époque, very decadent," but which seemed to Jamie like a rich child's old dirty dollhouse — too wearied to be truly restored but too lavish and fiercely loved to be thrown away or replaced. Lydia had postcards from across the continent. Jamie had found them sitting in a bowl by the telephone, with the mail, as if she still intended to send them — the back of each left blank but for the adjourned greeting of *Dear ...* in the top left-hand corner.

It was not that he disliked Lydia. Really, he did not know her. They had nothing much to do with each other, no bond but the blood between them. She had arrived at St. Brigid's Home for Boys like a whirlybird seed on the wind, all fluttery spontaneity. Jamie had never seen anyone so glamorous. Not like his mother at all. He watched his aunt from the window in the room of twelve beds — each one with the white uniformity of pill capsules — as she tot-tered up the pitted stone steps in a lilac dress, black boots up to her knees with heels like golf tees. Occasionally she was hilarious because she swore in different languages. *Scheisse! Merde!* To bury the vulgarity, he figured, though she failed to realize that he and Grady had devoted an entire afternoon to scouring translation dic-tionaries in the library on Lisburn, compiling a dead funny list of cosmopolitan profanity.

The Islanders

But she talked too much like a Brit, after living so long in London. His mother must have hated that, both the talk and the leaving. Maybe that was why they grew so far apart, why it took his aunt eleven years to find him.

Jamie brought the lighter closer to the shoebox. He savoured the bruisy ache of his mother's memory as the eyes in Blake's illustrated hellscape were enlivened by the roving flame. *Rintrah roars and shakes his fires in the burden'd air.*

His mother would have known he was telling the truth about the girls on the beach. He might have told her of the tremor he could not shake from his hand, and trusted that he had nothing to fear. But Aunt Lydia did not believe him — and were she to come around, what good would it do, given the state she was in? The other day he had sat in the hallway, back against the wall, listening to her scrape her way through a bowl of porridge for nearly an hour.

As it stood, there was no one to rely on but himself.

Aunt Lydia's house was just above the strand of beach. The girls would surely appear again, seeking him, and he would be ready on the shore to meet them. The problem, of course, was the risk of his aunt interrupting. It would take only a minute for him to sneak away, once she was asleep — but her sleep was irregular, and he often found her curled up in unexpected places, like a forgotten orange peel. She would be monitoring him more keenly now too. The knife was bad enough, but then he had gone and made matters a hundred times worse.

Returning to the kitchen that afternoon, Aunt Lydia had put the flick knife in the press, among the black-and-gold teacups "from Munich" that he was not allowed to touch.

"That Grady seems like a budding thorn in the penal system's side, if you ask me," she said, fastening the press doors with a plastic child lock.

"Just had that lying around," Jamie said.

A Song for Wildcats

"Less of the cheek, you." She gave his arm a light swat. "Though if you must know, one of the Brothers did mention some stolen cigarettes."

He rolled his eyes. "I found those."

Jamie was no thief, not of anything important. That pack was acquired fairly enough by anyone's standards. In fact, about all Jamie knew of his da was that he did a stint in jail, as his da had done before him, and Jamie was so terrified of this generational passing-down of iron bars that even when he had found the pack stashed in a drainpipe, he waited two days before taking it to sell to the other boys, for fear of a sting. Some smug, tweed-clad peeler like Dirty Harry spying from a rooftop.

"You don't even smoke," he said.

Lydia tugged the press door, testing the lock. "Well, if ever I had cause to start." Matching mugs of peppermint tea — patterned with purple foxgloves, one with the letter L, the other J — steamed aromatically on the table, set with teaspoons and a bowl of sugar cubes. Jamie threw an uneasy look at the breakfast nook, where his aunt set their plates each day, their snacks and tea, as if trying to lull him like a lonely siren, draw him down with her to the bottom of the sea.

"Will you have your tea?" Lydia sat at the edge of the nook, on the cushioned bench. A single chair was placed at the end of the small table, and she pulled it out. She waited a beat, tapping her foot, then nudged the chair toward him with a woody squeak. "Let me have a look at that cut on your finger. What happened? Does it hurt at all?"

"It's nothing," he said.

She leaned toward him. "Let me see."

His shoulders tightened. He kept his eyes low, concentrating on the miniature farm machinery illustrated on the tile. Some by-gone mower with long, sharp bullet teeth. He inched his foot over

The Islanders

it, wishing the teeth would bite and sink between his tendons, get him out of this conversation. "Why do you always want to talk about everything?"

"To communicate," she said. "How can I help you if I don't know what's wrong?"

"Who asked you to help me?"

"Jamie, I'm your *aunt*."

"For the past five minutes. You don't even know me." A real mower would tear his leg off. He could picture it shredding his trainer, then his muscle, spitting out rubber and bone.

Lydia took a deep breath and rubbed the side of her face. "It would be really grand if we could have one day —"

"Forget it," he said, turning away. He let his hair fall in front of his eyes. He was not crying. It was only that his face was so hot it was making his eyes water, like sitting too close to a campfire. But his aunt would assume the worst. An uncomfortable energy began fuming inside him, demanding to be expelled.

"What are you doing?" Lydia asked.

He had thrown open the refrigerator and began mindlessly emptying it, slamming an illogical assortment of jarred fruit and bland condiments onto the counter.

"What's wrong? I don't understand —" Lydia rose but hesitated behind the chair, bewildered by her nephew's stream of consciousness materializing. Untouched apricot preserves and crusting honey mustard and expired piccalilli she had completely forgotten she had bought, all confronting her from the countertop with their muted judgment. A coded message she was failing to understand. "Jamie, if you're hungry, there are better ways of asking."

"You don't know how to cook," he said.

"Neither do you," she snapped, then caught her words. She took a breath. "I can cook some things, Jamie. You haven't been starving."

A Song for Wildcats

"Yeah, you're a right cracker chef."

"Just tell me what's upsetting you." She spoke slowly, used her hand to temper her tone. "Maybe I can make it better."

"Stop *saying* stuff like that," he said.

Her bottomless blue gaze pressed down on him. She was always keeping an eye on him — waiting, he was sure, to catch him committing some act worthy of sending him away. Back to the home, back to Belfast. Sometimes she watched him so intently that he wondered if she was trying to read his thoughts, or bend his will like a psychic with a spoon. It was overwhelming, such scrutiny. No one was noticed at the home unless they had misbehaved or fallen ill, and then attention was purely punitive or functional, and delivered with the expectation that you would be assimilated back into invisibility as swiftly as possible.

"For crying out loud, what's the matter with you?" Lydia was shoving the food back into the fridge, only for him to pull it out again. "*Tell* me. I can't read your mind, can I?"

What *was* the matter? Part of him wanted to stop. The biggest part of him. He was ashamed of the swell he was bringing to his aunt's brittle voice, but the blood was up now, his momentum reeling outside his body, beyond his control. She wanted to know what was wrong? Everything was wrong, everything that had happened. His heartbeat drilled, the reverberations swallowing his eardrums like his head had plunged underwater.

The cold spark of Lydia's hand touched his temple. "Jamie, you're sweating."

He jerked away so sharply that the soda bread in his hand swung and smacked a jar of seashells on the kitchen counter. Jamie's heart sprang from his chest and hung mid-air.

For a strange, yielding moment, time slowed. He stared out the window, latching onto the leafy shag of the yew tree in the yard. The only tree in sight, his mother's favourite tree. Small and dark

The Islanders

and evergreen. The breeze loosened the branches until the rigid bulk seemed as weightless as a blade of grass. In that moment of pause, he remembered how it had felt to lose her. A rush of grief swept through him. There was so much of it, too much. Impossible to carry. Its enormity threatened to crash through his ribs like the sea through a sinking ship.

The jar hit the tile with a glassy shriek.

He and his aunt were both struck entirely still. Between them lay a wreckage of broken scallop shells and glittering bits of amber glass like scattered fish eggs. Dark, wiry cracks appeared in the tile, fracturing a sheep pasture in the little blue village.

His aunt looked at the mess. It had spilled just out of reach of her bare toes.

"Mind out," she said, so quietly he barely heard her, as she grabbed the dustpan and shooed meekly at his feet. "There are more broken bits than we can see. Don't cut yourself."

As she swept, Jamie searched the past few minutes to pin the precise moment he had lost grip of himself. If he could find it, he could grab hold of it, press it like a bruise.

Maybe saying the right thing would lessen his aunt's disappointment. *Apologize. Say you're sorry.* He could offer to walk down to the beach and get her new seashells. *We could make a game of it together.* His aunt would love for him to be the sort of boy who reciprocated her friendliness, who understood how to give back to her.

Instead, he stood there blinking uselessly. Staring at an iridescent shell with a dark fissure down the centre, still perilously in one piece.

He wanted to take the shell and cradle it, take it somewhere soft and safe, but his fingertips felt fuzzy and the hum in his ears sharpened. "I didn't mean —"

"Jamie, will you give me a minute, *please*." His aunt closed her eyes, lifted one hand. "Please. Just go to your room."

85

Here in the wardrobe, there was no one in the world other than him. After leaving the kitchen and running upstairs, he had been unable to sit still. He had kicked the door. Hit his face to knock out the incessant hum. Bullied himself to stop crying. The right thing would be to go back downstairs and take hold of Lydia's hand when she reached out to him. And he almost did. Almost told himself *enough*, opened the door, and walked back to her. But hands let go, hands disappear, and he was tired of longing for what could not be relied upon, the weakness of the need itself.

A new voice crackled in his ear. *We are here with you, Jamie. We are always with you. Do you feel us stirring in your blood?*

"I think so," he said, squeezing the lighter. "Yes, I do. I always have."

Then you are ready. Come to us, when the sun begins to fall. We are waiting.

The flame drew his eye toward it as he lifted the scroll of sheet music. The loyal fire was an elixir, and he could not tell you the revelation of relief it brought to light the pages of Aunt Lydia's music, let the corners curl and taper into smoke.

*

Blinking out of a cloudy daze, Lydia peeled her sprawled hand off the kitchen tile. A prickling sensation gradually became apparent. Yet, even as she stood and walked to the sink, she remained only peripherally aware of the pain caused by the sticky flecks of dark glass dusting her palm.

Look at all these treasures, Lyddy. Eabha had seemed quite grown up to her then, two decades ago, but she could not have been older than ten when she lifted the lid of their jewellery box and revealed broken amber glass from a medicine bottle, see-through as syrup

The Islanders

and smelling of garden mint. *It's from the grey crow, the one at the beach. She's been bringing me gifts.*

It was shortly after the beach picnic at Portmarnock, the only field trip that Lydia could recall taking while living at Mercy. It was all a little hazy now. Hands brushing tall, breeze-tousled beach-grass. Stockings torn off, bare legs free and clambering up sand dunes. Her stomach warm with tea, the breathless luxury of raspberry jam on scones. And the grey crow that nobody but Eabha could hear.

The hot tap water began to sting and Lydia swore under her breath — at what, the water?

Who was she angry with: Jamie for being destructive or Eabha for cornering him into it?

What had her sister been thinking, keeping the boy in Belfast? The sheer, astounding recklessness of it. Had it been a matter of means, Lydia could have understood — though she would have helped them if Eabha had allowed it, or done her the great courtesy of letting her know Jamie existed. It was that dogmatic fury of Eabha's, compressed for too long, until it ripped the whole radiant patchwork of her personality. She stopped answering Lydia's calls and letters, moved about Belfast so often that Lydia could hardly keep track of an address, until finally Eabha did not leave one.

A photograph appeared in a small newspaper the year they lost touch, a woman with slender defiance in her shoulders and dark hair feathering out from beneath a balaclava. Lydia cut it out and hid it, pressed like a flower between the pages of a book.

Standing at the sink, she grabbed a tea towel and dabbed at the wet heat rash on her hand. She tossed the towel over the faucet and squeezed her arm over her torso, sickened by a bad mixture of resentment and guilt.

Eabha's dismissal of everyone in her life beyond the IRA, her cultish devotion to what she called the *fight for Ireland's soul*, could be forgiven. Had to be forgiven, in fact. It was Lydia's birth that had derailed her sister's life, torn her future and her family away from her. Eabha would lie in bed, longingly recounting memories of their mother sprinkling sugar onto apple cake; the flat above the bakery, its white wallpaper with rows of blue rosebuds; the kitchen window overlooking the quiet River Liffey and the emerald glow under the stone arch bridge at night.

Lydia had no memory prior to being hurtled into the Sisters of Mercy in the Northside of Dublin. Eabha was five, Lydia just beginning to bead her words into sentences. Their mother, all of twenty-one, had managed one daughter just well enough on her own, but could not manage two. As for their father, Eabha often told the story of him dying in a standoff against the Germans, alone in a wintry forest with dark spruce and prowling wolves, so deep within the French Alps that his body was left to be buried by the wind and snow. Such a noble vision fell apart once Lydia reached Second Class and began puzzling together a map of the war, but this fabrication of a father remained vivid, cherished; she preferred it to any living man unwilling to die for the safety of his girls.

How could Lydia not forgive her sister when her sister had never blamed her? Eabha would have been justified in hating Lydia for forcing them both into the bleak, frigid warehouse of Mercy. For being squished into one stiff, sterile bed until they grew too big to fit and took to kicking each other over the edge. For the pasty-blue walls that had not been freshened since the founding of the home in 1912. The beatings and upbraiding and mouth-soaping. Among Eabha's few acts of childhood rebellion was hiding a gold tube of lipstick under her mattress, and the Sisters had practically torn her hair off, cut it blunt up to her cheeks with poultry shears.

A shroud was cast over her life by the toll of Lydia's birth. And what had Lydia done to make it right? Certainly she had tried, with a sort of possessed vigour, to insulate them both with money.

Protect them with prestige. But to what end? While Lydia grew glamorous, basked in applause, bought a big flat in Kensington, Eabha shrank farther beneath the shroud, vanishing into shadow.

It was only upon learning of Jamie that Lydia's guilt met a wall: what about once a child became involved? The boy had been a defenceless little thing bobbing in Eabha's womb like a berry in a jelly dome. Eabha had made a choice not to put his care first. Did the blame for that choice wash back to Lydia too?

Even squinting, Lydia could not see the bitter woman her sister had become cradling an infant, fiddling with his toes, reconsidering the role that squibs and gun-ferrying could continue to play in her life. Had she wanted to leave? Had she tried to break off those radical pieces of herself like rib bones she could bury out of sight? Had the bloodhounds, with their noses for vulnerability, dug up those bones and brought them back to her?

Lydia clapped her hand over her mouth as cries began throbbing through her. She could make up for it all now, do right by her family, if only she could pull herself together. Their lineage seemed to be one pulsing, pouring hemorrhage, and it was time to cauterize the wound.

The telephone rang, sharp as an electric shock.

Lydia unclipped her earring and answered the phone.

"Hello? Yes, this is she." It was her manager in London. "Of course, my apologies. This phone is turn-of-the-century."

An autumn concert cycle was being suggested. Something about session recordings. Lydia heard herself say *well, my sabbatical ...* and *you understand, with my current family situation ...* in between her manager's insistence. The phone gradually slipped down her cheek.

"Lydia? Are you still there? Lydia?"

She listened to her name with detached fascination, as if someone had dialed the wrong number, was asking for the wrong woman. Eventually, her manager hung up.

89

A Song for Wildcats

What people wanted was Lydia Flynn the performer. A musician regarded as uncompromising and bold, known to infuse her performances with dramatic energy.

Unapologetically daring, she had been called. Dazzlingly dynamic.

Nobody had noticed the change in her after Eabha died. How even standing became laborious, carrying the iron bulk of her bones. She had made sure of it. Until her last performance, earlier in January, when she rose from the piano bench with the feeling that her body was hollow porcelain, her brain crystal glass. Her joints made a chalky grating sound as she walked across the stage, through the back halls, and out the nearest exit, wearing only a thin silk dress, with the frosty air biting her throat. She walked the city until her body cracked and crumbled away, and she was only the floating essence of herself. Nothing more than a handful of music notes, collected in her glass-blown brain like candy in a bowl.

An odd scent tickled her nose and brought her back to herself. She was suddenly unsure how long she had been holding the telephone, listening to the dial tone. The cord had somehow wound itself around her wrist. She examined her fingertips. They were swollen and red, like little wild plums, from loss of circulation. Beads of blood percolated like sweat where the glass had pricked her palm.

Lydia unravelled herself and rubbed the sore pink spiral on her arm. "Jamie?" she called. "What are you doing up there?"

She followed the scent toward the stairs in the hall, where the air was sharp with the unmistakable smoked tinge of wood burning.

＊

He had a handle on it, at first.

Sitting in the wardrobe, Jamie leaned against a long, white dress printed with sunflowers. Let the cotton brush his cheek. His eyes

The Islanders

closed for only an instant, lulled by the burning paper, and the flame took the chance to latch onto the cotton, devious little fire burrs leaping and flickering, and they spread too swiftly to catch, surrounding him in a hungry smog.

He stumbled out of the wardrobe and threw what he could onto the bed. He ripped off the blanket, meaning to tame the rest of the fire before any real damage was done. No one hurt. Just the loss of some abandoned threadbare clothing, a little charred wood already warped by wet rot.

Only a bilious fog had formed, and it seeped into him, clouded his head. He stared into the fire as it roared and surged, until heat ran along his veins like a lit fuse.

Then a hand thudded against his chest and shoved him away. Aunt Lydia moved in front of him, directing the white drift of a fire extinguisher over the luminous streams flooding the hollow in the wall.

Jamie watched, numb yet mesmerized, as the crackling gusts died down. A dirty, acrid taste stuck to his tongue. Stung his nose, made it warm and runny. He was coughing; they both were. Aunt Lydia got onto her knees and smothered the last scraps of fire, in the far corners of the wardrobe, with the now-ravaged blanket.

Slowly, it dawned on him what he had done. He hurried to the window, threw it open, started ushering out the smoke. "It's clearing out. See? It's not serious."

His fingers prickled. He spread them out and looked at them. They floated in front, as if separate from the rest of him, bobbing on water. His eyes itched and watered from the smoke, and he tried to rub them clear before his aunt saw and misunderstood.

Lydia's legs shook as she pulled herself up. Sounds swelled and echoed. Her nephew was mouthing words at her, buried beneath a blurry ring. "What?" she asked. "What did you say?"

Coughs grated her throat. She coughed until she half expected chunks of charcoaled lung to come flying out of her. Once she

A Song for Wildcats

stopped, gained composure, it fell so quiet she could hear the grass-hoppers in the field outside. For a moment, Lydia let her mind blink away. She wondered how grasshoppers distinguished between their various songs, all an identical crinkled chirrup to her ear. How they conversed and understood.

"I'll make up the sofa bed for you downstairs," she said. "You'll sleep there."

Jamie nodded but could not meet her eye. Soot raked his old orange jumper. "What should I —"

"Nothing," Lydia said. "Do nothing. Just wait for me downstairs."

The jounce in his leg quickened. "I can put the blanket in the laundry," he said, kneeling to collect it.

Lydia stopped him as he reached toward the tattered heap. "The blanket is ruined, Jamie. Look at it. I'll have to clear out the entire room."

"It was an accident."

"Was it?" she asked.

Her gaze was caught then, curving around him to the items thrown onto the bed. Jamie shifted, but she saw past him. He had tried to salvage his mother's book. The blackened pages of sheet music. A pink-and-white shawl, contorted with blind heat.

Lydia was near speechless. "Why do you have these?"

Jamie's mouth hung open. Time thickened and tightened around him. He had only meant to burn corners, edges, precise spots in precise ways.

"Why do you have these, Jamie?" she repeated. A lesion opened in her chest, and her warmth pour through it, draining away. Her eyes were glassy, her voice shaking. "Do you have any idea ..."

"I can buy new ones." He turned to the piggy bank beside his bed. "I'll replace them, I promise."

The Islanders

"These were given to me, Jamie. They can't be replaced." She leaned her forehead against her palm like she might faint. Then her hand lowered, fingers hovering above the burnt shawl. "If you'd just let us be friends ..."

It was almost a whisper. He could no longer tell if she was speaking to him. He kept waiting for her to yell. Slam the door, pound the wall, anything his mother might have done. But she only grew quieter.

Was she angry, Lydia wondered? No — *diluted*. Defeated. The wardrobe would need to be hacked and stripped. The frame was burned to a scaly crust, gaping at her like a secret passage to the underworld. It occurred to her, distantly, that raising a child who loathed you would be a fitting, if subtler, torment of the Nine Circles. She could see herself in a scorched blouse of galvanic violet, buttons dangling from the thinnest thread. Poised at the head of a sludge-soaked tea table, clinking her glass and straining a diaphanous smile: *"Here, too, I saw a nation of lost souls."*

"I just wanted to ..." Jamie started, but he could not find the rest of the words. In the grey light, his aunt had gone an oddly bright pale. She laughed faintly into the back of her wrist.

"I don't know why I'm laughing." She felt estranged from her voice as it fell from her mouth, flat and involuntary. "Not even one funny thing about anger. It just pours from one person to another and spills everywhere. Your mother —"

"Mam wasn't angry," Jamie said.

Lydia sighed, quietly, and her chest sank. "Of course she was angry. She was the angriest person I've ever met."

Jamie could not recall his mother beating him, or throwing bottles at him the way Grady's mother had done. Now and then she had a habit of grabbing his hair and yanking his head back, sending his heart flying. But were those not the dark moods of all parents? Given all that weighed on her, was it not his share of the burden to shrink behind her like an adoring shadow and absorb her incandescent flares of pain?

"She wasn't angry," he said. "She was a soldier. The rules are different in a war. She wouldn't have done any of that, she wouldn't have left me if she'd had a choice."

"Enough of that." Lydia ran her hand through her hair, held onto it, knuckles close against her skull. "Brainwashed, the bloody lot of you …"

"I'm not brainwashed." A searing itch crawled up his arms, flushed across his neck. "Nobody did anything to me. People aren't brainwashed just because they don't agree with you."

"I'm not having this conversation," Lydia said. "I had it a hundred times with your mother. I'm not doing it again."

"How can you talk about her like that?" His voice came out strange, slipping away and floating high out of reach. "No wonder she didn't want to talk to you, if you just called her brainwashed, like you know everything."

At school, when Jamie learned of Joan of Arc riding out to claim the *bastille de Saint-Loup*, it was his mother he saw, black hair ablaze with battlefield firelight. Though at night, the proud image transmuted. In his dreams, she stood roped to a burning stake, only the stake was her own unbreakable spine, extending high outside her body, and she could not peel herself free.

He pawed at his arms, but the itch ran deep, like fibreglass muscle. Something he could dig into and tear out.

"Don't do that." Lydia started toward him and in one step felt like she had run a mile. She swallowed, her breath pinching. "Stop it, Jamie. I'm serious, you're hurting yourself."

"There's nowhere …"

"What do you mean?" she asked.

"There's *nowhere* …"

94

The Islanders

Nowhere he could run to, nowhere he would not have to defend his mother or untangle her from other people's stories, nowhere she could just be his mother.

He turned to leave and nearly tripped over the long foot of a rocking chair. His heart skittered, and he shoved the chair without thinking, let it snap against the floor.

"Everyone thinks they understand, but they don't know anything." He kicked a broken spindle across the room. It whipped against the wall and went spinning. "You don't even care about me, you just feel guilty or something." He was yelling, all pink and blubbery, wiping at his eyes. "Why would I need you now? Mam needed you and you just forgot about her."

"*I* forgot about *her?*" Lydia's voice rose and cracked. "Nobody *made* your mother get involved with those people. Nobody *made* her put you in danger, or stop answering my calls. Those were *her* choices, not mine. You want to be angry with someone, be angry with her. I sure as hell am."

The boy's face was flushed and emphatic. Lydia meeting his outburst with her own had surprised them both, and she stood there winded, hardly registering his footsteps storming out of the room and down the stairs.

It was quiet again. The grasshoppers chittered outside. What she wanted to do was call out to him. *Come back. I can hold us together, our family. I know you're hurting. I'm hurting too.*

She tried to gather her voice, hold onto it as she had a moment ago, but it was like trawling with a sliced net.

What good would it do to chase after the boy, like she had chased after Eabha? Haul him back inside when he wanted nothing to do with her, force him to be near her, within reach, within view, when all he wanted was to be left alone? It was just like her, always clinging to the naive belief that people could be saved against their will. She had been digging her nails into that same

95

old muddy bank, but the current flowing toward defeat continued to grow stronger.

As the front door swung open downstairs, then slammed shut, a renewed rush swept over her. It pulled her under, rolled over her head. And in imagining herself letting go, she did — for only a moment, which of course is all it takes.

*

Too far. It had all gone too far. Remorse began to set in once Jamie was down the front steps and the wind, brisk and salt rich, cooled his forehead. How long would it take for Aunt Lydia to arrange a return to the home? A month, a week? She would probably have his suitcase packed by morning.

Well, fine. So be it. Why continue holding onto what could never last? Besides, he had more or less arrived here prepared to leave, and he had done well enough on his own. Aunt Lydia could not step in now, after eleven years, and act like she was needed. Who was that for — him or her?

"You're a force," Jamie said. "A fighter." Maybe Arthur had his round table, but Cú Chulainn, the Hound of Ulster, fought best alone.

A new path stretched before him now. He ran down the slope until he reached the shore.

"I'm ready!" he called. "I'm here!"

The girls would be like Scáthach the Warrior Maid, the Hound's teacher and protector. Jamie knelt on the sand, sank his hands into the water where the coil had disappeared. Any minute now, any minute.

Though the sun was still falling, the twin beaks of a crescent moon pierced the sky. The breeze tugged at the back of his collar, and he looked over his shoulder at the old stone house, with its tall chimney and grand windows that his aunt never opened. He could almost see her shrinking into herself, a wizened heap of hair and housecoat. Sometimes she looked so slight, she took on a strange transparency, like the film that peels off an egg.

His chest tightened. Would she be all right, left on her own?

Jamie considered how easy it could be to trust someone like Aunt Lydia. The freshly washed, matching linens she stretched over his bed, bought brand new for him from a store somewhere in London. The lavender toothpaste she had them both use, with the soapy aftertaste. The placid blue eyes, with glimpses of misty violet, like the sky above the water at dawn. Her clear-rimmed reading glasses, so unreasonably big that it looked like a giant glass moth was camouflaging itself on the bridge of her nose. And whenever she managed to leave the house, to drive into Malin Town for errands, he tracked the minutes. He checked through the front blinds for her car, anxious and unable to concentrate until he heard her tires crunch back up the gravel.

He had not so much as thanked her, or told her how much he loved the waterside. How excited he was when she told him that she had found a house right along the peninsula. There were no beaches he could remember in Belfast. His mother used to drive him out to the coasts of nearby counties — and if he held his breath now, he could be six again, on one of those beaches bordered by sylvan headlands, dipping his hands in the clear green shoal. He could be trudging along the sea floor, clouding the water with a flurry of unsettled sand. And she could be there too. Mam. Crouched with her arms around him by a low-tide rock pool as they studied the wispy seaweed, the fish darting like slivers of light.

Once home, she would rinse his beach pails and watering cans in the sink, and carefully scrape the sand out of the movable joints and impossible crannies of his action figures.

That was one of the worst parts: the erasure of her as his mother. Nobody talked about how her laugh was so loud he could always track her during water-gun fights, racing through the house and not worrying about the furniture. Or how she knew how to take a tumble if the water struck her, really drag it out, make it ridiculous. Not one news article noted their long walks through the hills overlooking their end of the city, spotting newts and damselflies in the ponds of the deserted quarries, or hares in the heathland — once, a fox drinking from a mountain stream. At his amazement that foxes lived beyond the woods, she knelt beside him and rested her chin on his shoulder. "They live all over," she said. "They're hardy things. Quick-witted, quiet. The fox survives."

As the sun sank away, it burst and bled over the water, as if torn by the beaks of the gliding gulls. *Red sky at night, sailors' delight. Red sky at morning, sailors take warning.* He could only recall his mother saying this once, and yet all his life, he had determined the weather according to the tint and timing of a flushed sky.

When the sun begins to fall.

Where were they? Why had the girls not come? Jamie's fingers dug into the sand, scraping his skin. "You told me to be here ..."

From out in the mist came the slap of oars, water trickling as they rolled in and out of the waves.

He stood, stepped back. "Hello?"

There was no one, yet somehow he felt watched, as though each particle of the thickening fog were an invisible, appraising eye. He began to follow the sounds, and soon he could not see beyond the reach of his hand.

The fog dampened and chilled his skin, though its scent was green and earthy, like a breath escaping from underground. A memory bubbled up: smoking skunk with Grady in the home's graffitied boiler room. Coiled on the cement floor, pressed against the sticky stains and rusty pipes, trying not to boke their rings up. How Grady laid his palm on Jamie's sweaty forehead, as if checking for a fever. How his wriggly curls looked babyish then, uncouth and

The Islanders

uncombed. His eyes rosy and tender with concern. How Jamie had shirked the gentle hand away.

But it was not right. The memory felt dredged to the surface. Pulled close to an intrusive peephole to be observed. Jamie rubbed his temple, struck by the sensation that his mind was being turned over in someone else's hands. Only who would want to look inside his memories, when even he did not? He shook away the feeling, fanning at the fog as it gathered on all sides. He kept expecting his foot to hit water; he must have gotten spun around and was walking in a new direction along the shore.

When the sounds stopped, he paused. Listened. Not far ahead, the shapes of three figures appeared — vaguely visible, more like faded grey imprints of long hair and hanging cloaks. The air, his own breath, fell limp around him.

Voices washed over him in rippling echoes.

Do you trust us, come with us, do you belong to us ...

Fresh, cold fear stirred in his stomach, but the urge to follow rumbled with warmth, like stoking a fire. From the folds of the darkest cloak came a low, elastic moan. It stretched over him, flying into a high shriek that batted his ears like tiny, crazed wings. The figure cast a finger toward him, then outward, as if to send him away — but soon shrank beneath its two mirrored shadows, all three submerging into a single grey cloud, coursing over him and scraping his throat like wood ash.

As the cloud blew away, an Old World deer swept by — giant and white, with antlers sprawling canopies of nerve and bone — and instantly vanished like a frozen breath.

Another sign, another guiding signal. Jamie chased after it. *Wait for me ... I'm right behind you.* He spoke silence into silence, the sound smothered by the blanketing fog. He shouted. *Can't you see me?* But the silence only deepened, a pressure ringing in his mouth. He swallowed, and his throat clogged.

Startled, he halted and grabbed at his chest. Dribbling coughs spurted out of him. Mouthfuls of briny water. For half a breath, he found himself underwater. Air rushed from him in a bubbly stream. Waves churned overhead, and around him drifted countless white flecks of sea debris like travelling stars.

Jamie looked down to where his feet flailed over bottomless darkness. Then sleep, deep and easy, as he had never known.

II.

VANITAS

Lydia thumbed the golden *J* on the mug before putting it on the shelf and closing the press door. She cleared the table setting, counting in her head the number of times they had eaten together. A stack of Sears catalogues sat on the hallway table, left open with a pen for Jamie to pick out new clothes or toys, supplementing the ones she had bought in advance of his arrival. Running her hand over the top of the stack, she cleared the dust from the slick, glossy cover. He wanted to be left alone, and she was not listening.

Upstairs in Jamie's bedroom, where the air still tingled with ash, she examined the ruined shawl. When Eabha used to wear it, the shawl was just another piece of clothing. It was never meant to be important. Using a pair of tweezers, Lydia found an untouched corner that could be snipped from the rest, like slicing the rot off an apple. Some small piece of the keepsake could be saved. Some small piece of anything could be saved, she had always believed.

The sheet music had been a gift from Eabha, celebrating Lydia's acceptance into the academy. Eabha had been proud of her little sister. *You're out, Lyddy. You're free.* Eabha would say the burnt music should be ground into a fine ash, sprinkled over the garden as nourishment. She had always known how to take care of wild

The Islanders

things, sinking her fingers into the dirt, listening to whispers of knowledge in the wind. This was why it had taken Lydia so long, too long, to realize that her older sister — protective and bossy and fierce — had needed taking care of too.

Once the grey crow — the one from the beach, Eabha was certain — began bringing treasures of broken glass, Eabha buried them in a box under the hedges along the courtyard's flaking-iron gate. The morning she first showed Lydia, she gave her a perfunctory shake before hauling her from bed, through the ill-guarded corridor, down the back stairwell, and out into the inviting chill of early spring. They ducked under Eabha's shawl and crept toward the gate. In hindsight, this could only have made them more conspicuous, but Lydia felt entirely hidden from the city in that known and trusted huddle, yet closer to her sister, and more clearly defined by her own inwardly turning eye.

Every morning there's something shiny on the windowsill. Just above the bed.

How can you tell it's from the beach crow?

Because she's always perched on the gate, waiting for me. She's grey and black, and her wing's clipped like she's been injured.

The crow had looked dead when they found it on the Portmarnock beach. The other Mercy children were kicking at the frothy water or waving dark ribbons of kelp, while the young Sisters strolled in billowy black habits and veils, looking from a distance like selkies still shedding their skin. Lydia and Eabha had drifted down the long, sandy stretch of the Velvet Strand when Eabha winced, cupping her ear. She began following a sound that Lydia could not hear, until they came upon a dark, soaked clump in the sand, being nudged by the tide.

Lydia came scrambling up behind her and instantly broke into tears. *It's dead!*

Stop crying, Lyddy, we're going to help it.

Eabha wreathed her cardigan into a soft nest and placed the bird inside. Drawing her hair back, she dipped her ear to its chest and listened for a heartbeat.

Lydia pawed helplessly at her sister's shoulder. *Do you hear anything?*

Not if you don't shut up. The bird blinked with a black, liquid shine as Eabha brushed aside a splash of grey feathers along the top of its wing. *Oh no … Lyddy, she's been snagged by a wire.*

They lifted the bundle to sneak it onto the minibus, but the crow's wings snapped up and it darted away over the swelling waves. Eabha sped into the water as if she could follow a parallel path below the bird. She looked transfixed with longing, arms reaching out like she meant to grab hold of someone.

Lydia remembered screaming at her sister to come back. And Eabha stopping, the sea lapping her ribs, blinking like a startled sleepwalker. Lydia was all spun up in her wailing by then, her little fists bunched in resolute terror. Even as her sister came to shore, she screamed. *Eabha! You're hurt! You're bleeding!* There was a long sliver of blood on Eabha's hand, where she must have been cut by the wire. *You're going to get tetanus and die!*

Eabha laughed and rinsed off the blood in the bubbly tide. It must have been her young mind, but Lydia thought the water came alive where her sister touched it, squelching around her hand. To Lydia, it was a thirsty, milkshake-sucking sound, and when Eabha lifted her hand, the bleeding had stopped.

Was that wailing little girl who Jamie saw when he looked at her? Someone who could not help an injured bird, or her sister, or him. Who seemed incapable of helping even herself.

Lydia returned to the kitchen, unsure what exactly she needed to tidy after a fire. Was there someone she should call? Of course not; that was silly. The fire brigade was more for putting the fires out; it seemed unlikely they would drive out here to help her clean the aftermath.

The Islanders

She stood in the centre of the room, rubbing her cheek. The boy would be stewing on the beach, or out in the fields, stomping out his anger. She started toward the back door, then stopped herself. No, a wide berth was best. Her hand flexed over the knob, and she breathed through her teeth.

There was no forcing some understanding between them. The day she drove him down from the North, pinballing between road closures, they were searched at the checkpoint by the border. Soldiers poked about the car with their rifles out, and while Lydia stiffened, Jamie sat on the side of the road, twining castaway dandelions, with all the casual boredom of a boy waiting for the bus.

And yet, some part of her did understand him. That same night, after the drive, she found him lingering at the edge of the darkened sitting room. He was staring at the widower's dead flowers framed on the wall. Greyed roses, shrunken blue irises, stringy yellow mums behind glass. "It's like those old death photos people used to take," he said, squeezing the collar of his pyjama shirt.

Lydia found the picture disquieting, but was too unnerved to disturb it. Preserving the semblance of life when life was gone was too horrible — worse than morbid, it was futile; it only affirmed death, made absence plain and stark and inescapable. The first time she saw it, she loosely crossed herself as she turned away. Something she had not done since girlhood. And the room became a sort of quaint mausoleum that they both took pains to avoid.

She picked at her cuticles, considering cleaning supplies, when she heard a tap on the window. She spun around, breathless. "Jamie?"

A crow was pecking at the glass. Lydia recognized the colouring, how its cloudy grey plumage looked spattered with ink. Her heart hovered, high in her chest. "It can't be …"

The bird's head ticked to the side, feet padding along the sill in a restless, staccato march. Of course it was not Eabha's crow, that would be absurd — but still Lydia climbed into the nook and leaned close enough to fog the glass.

"If it's Eabha you want, she isn't here," she said, speaking to the bird as though all birds, of any breed or time, communicated along the same liminal wire. "She isn't really anywhere. Or maybe she is. You'd know better."

The bird tapped its beak.

Lydia tapped back.

The bird struck so hard that the glass splintered.

She sprang back as the crow whipped up and flew toward the empty beach. Stunned blank, Lydia watched at first without any discernible thought or feeling, until the utter vacancy outside slowly settled over her, sharpening into rekindled panic. She ran to the back door and onto the porch, searching for a clash of orange jumper against the beach below or the green hillocks beyond, and saw no one.

✳

Curl up in stasis. Float, shielded and sheltered, unattached to the world. You are your own world, sole planet in a lightless universe.

But then, a shriek of brightness, and where did the universe go?

Jamie woke in a cramped sitting room of smoke-soured wallpaper and thick green carpet matted into weedy tufts. It held a distant familiarity, evoking scattershot memories of his own plump toddler fists grabbing clumps of carpet, the peppery scent of his mother's cooking wafting high overhead.

The curtains, the colour of hardened mustard, were tightly closed.

Across from where he sat in a sunken armchair, two men argued. Could they see him? Did they know he was there? Jamie felt both inside and outside of his surroundings, like lucid dreaming, though he was farther from consciousness than in dreams. A grasp of himself, his own sharp sense and feeling, seemed elusive and bleary, as a voice above water sounds to a drowning ear.

"He's got his mother in him, not only in his blood. You smell it ripe as I do," one man said. His leather jacket and feathery black hair were stark against the faded tweed of another armchair. And though his body held the bony edges of a man when Jamie looked at him, whenever he looked away, the shape was unsettled on the rim of his vision, growing wings like serrated shadows.

Jamie listened, puzzling over their conversation.

"Has to be a line drawn, do you see. The lad can't make the choice of a grown man." A younger man paced about the room, radiating doubt. His lips thinned and he shook his head. "You go too far and people turn on ye. Too young a soldier, and all they see is some wee lad kidnapped by the cause. War doesn't carry clout and glory anymore." He jabbed his finger into the air as the older man opened his mouth. "Don't you act like you haven't seen the tide change more each era, each century, like you haven't read the headlines."

Behind the curtains, branches rattled and clipped the window. Jamie's clothes were crisp with chill and smelled of salt. He felt the cold leaking into the room, and with it an unseen presence watching him, somehow daunting yet reposeful, in the manner of a mountain.

Whispering between the men's voices, a swell of leafy wind shaped into words.

You are drifting, all alone, in a boundless blue world. We have watched you.

The voice was cool, silvery smooth.

We can be mother, father, protector. If you let us.

"But I can't see you," Jamie said.

The two men stopped speaking. They turned and looked at him.

105

A Song for Wildcats

The younger one's eyes flicked toward the window. He parted the curtains, fingers furled around the edges, and leaned close to a pane of glass blinded with fog. "You hear her, then, do you?"·

Jamie's chest felt weak and clammy. He tried to straighten his shoulders, lift his head. "Where is she?"

The younger man glanced over his shoulder, rolled his eyes over the room. "If you can hear her, she's around. Our sister, set in' the Old Ways." His voice lowered as he turned back to the window. "Can't just have a bloody conversation."

"I came to find the girls from the beach," Jamie said. "Who are you?"

The older man sipped from a tall can of lager. He swept a streak of grey hair from his face. "Some call us phantoms of war."

"People make their own phantoms well enough," the younger man said, closing the curtains again.

"I see you're frightened." The older man smiled. He reached out and shook Jamie's knee, his grey nails piercing through denim. "Oh, but you've seen us before, lad. We take the forms that suit our needs. But you've no reason to be wary. We claim only those who wish to be claimed."

"For the war," Jamie said, his leg tensing under the man's grip. The wound from the barbed wire pinched, like a bird chewing on his finger. "You mean a Ra man."

He shrugged. "If that's your side. It was your mam's side. But it's all our war, any war of country, as long as we keep the flame going."

The younger man's distress rose from his body as he paced the room, a visible heat warping the air. "Aye, but this has never been my war, has it. And save that look on your face, none of that *war is war* load of shite." In his unseeing agitation, he knocked into an ugly cork lamp on the coffee table. "To fuck."

"All right, keep the head now."

The Islanders

"Piss off." He stabbed his cigarette into a small hill of ash, spilling the tray onto the velvet sheen of the sofa. "You never think of the cost, do ye? Just look at the lad, he's not but eleven."

The older man had hardly moved. A silver chain threaded from underneath his jacket collar and gleamed with lamplight. "They were all wee things once."

"Aye, but if it isn't always me cleaning the blood." The cigarette was gone, yet smoke seeped from his mouth, and his throat was lit with a frenetic glow like a jar of fireflies. "Never once seen you by the shore washing the dead, rinsing out all the bloody pieces."

The older man's eyes grazed Jamie's as they shifted to peer down the hall. They were acid-washed eyes, cold and raw, and the years piled up behind them. Jamie followed them to a closed door with a smudge of blood on the knob.

The room tilted. Jamie swallowed. "You want me to do what my mam did."

"We want to be your family, lad, that's all." The older man extended the can of lager. "Burn inside of you, where we can guide you, and fuel you, and keep watch over you."

Jamie clasped the can with both hands, taking a biting, lukewarm sip. He wiped his mouth with his arm. "What would I have to do?"

"Don't ask that." The younger man stopped behind the armchair and squeezed Jamie's shoulders. A shock of vibrations travelled from his fingers into Jamie's body, like flies let loose under his skin. "War is a gorgon, wee lad," he said. "You must never look it directly in the eye."

Turning in the chair, Jamie raised his eyes to him. The younger man's pale moustache looked tough as wire wool, and his eyes smoked and crackled, each iris burning through the milky whites.

"Let the lad decide for himself. You're outvoted on this, so that's the end of it." The older man hunched, with a decisive sigh, and set

A Song for Wildcats

his elbows on his knees. "Your mam knew what it meant to devote herself completely. And did you ever know her to be afraid?"

Jamie shook his head.

"Did you know her to rely on anyone? Need anyone?"

"No," he said. "Never."

"Because she had us, always with her." Fingers folded together, chin on his knuckles, he eyed Jamie squarely. "Your mam proved that she was worthy, son. Never turned on her own. Never put a thing above the fight." He ticked his head toward the closed door. "Head on down the hall and fetch us something. You'll know it when you see it. Prove to us that you're worthy too."

What choice did he have? Aunt Lydia had never wanted him, and what addled loyalty had driven her before was surely gone, after what he had done. Jamie slid off the chair, resolved to move forward on the only path he had left. His legs wobbled beneath him, but every muscle strained to hide it. As he started down the hall, the men's voices faded into fluted echoes lapping over one another.

You cannot leave him like this, even if he refuses us. But that is not the Old Way. I am tired of the Old Way. Are you not tired? I have given him a chance. Offered a warning. The rest is up to the sister. That is all I am willing, all I am able to do.

✳

Early stars clung like sparks of static to the soft, grey clouds. All was quiet but for the murmurous waves and the sporadic bells of birds.

Each time Lydia flung her nephew's name into the air, she had the urge to claw it back, clutch it close to her. She circled the house. Stalked across the fields without direction. Followed the single, sodden road to wave over the few passing cars and question the drivers, with wild eyes and a strained ringing in her ears.

The Islanders

As she stood in the middle of the road, blinking at the grimy glow of tail lights as they swept away, a horrifying possibility occurred to her. Perhaps Jamie, in his desperation to be rid of her, had driven off with a stranger. She ran back toward the house to call the police, tripping in the wet grass, her ankles like softened wax. The crow continued cawing. She looked down to the cusp of the shore, where it stood flanked by its own silvered reflection in the water and its shadow, dense as soot, on the sand.

Farther off, an orange jumper lay bloated between waves like a forgotten buoy. Terror seized her, yet somehow she was tearing down the grassy slope and into the water, where the engulfing cold cut into her calves, sank its chill into her ribs, and closed around her neck. Jamie's name ripped from her lungs as she swam, until she grabbed hold of him.

"I have you …" She gathered him in one arm, his head limp against her shoulder, dark hair slick as seaweed across his face.

Big, baleful clouds crowded the sky. Rain began to pinch the water, and soon a shivery curtain swept across the seafront. The waves heaved. Flurries of icy spray drove into Lydia's eyes. The shoreline bobbed in and out of view as the water broke over her and her nephew, and all the while the crow stood still, stark as a hole burned through the veil of rain.

Lydia grasped at empty air as if trying to climb into it. The ocean rose and shattered into froth, over and over, until a curling wave crashed down and dragged them both into suffocating darkness. There they floated in the shock of it. Panic surged through Lydia, and just beyond the breath bursting from her mouth, she saw herself sinking, as if looking in a mirror. And yet, she had the uncanny feeling that she was the reflection, the phantom self, watching helpless from within her glassy vault as the more solid, vibrant original was pulled downward — toward the sea floor with its ever-preserved, forgotten bones — the breath glittering out of her.

But that could not have been so, for the sinking woman before her was alone.

Jamie's weight started to slip. Just out of reach, the last of daylight bled through the clouding seafoam. Lydia clawed at the current as it rushed between their bodies, her muscles burning.

Cutting through a dark blue swell, she broke the surface. Her head tipped back and she inhaled, oxygen spearing clean through her body. She filled her lungs, began to float. Her arm was wrapped around her nephew's chest, his frozen cheek pressed to hers. The rolling tide carried them, and she held the boy close, her lungs ballooning, until her feet touched the merciful sanctuary of sand.

Out of the water, Lydia straightened Jamie onto his back and clapped his cheek.

"Jamie ... *Jamie*, can you hear me?"

She cleared the hair from his face, pulled the soaked jumper away from his neck. Her hands fumbled, numb and remote, as if receiving only partial signals from her brain. Jamie's lips were slack and blue. She leaned over to check his breathing, readying her hands to pump his heart — but a warm breath brushed her ear. Then another, and another, all steady and strong.

Taking his wrist, she pressed along his veins. Somehow, his pulse was racing.

Lydia buckled under the force of her relief. Though it did not last, for she saw now that, underneath her nephew's closed lids, his eyes were moving. Lifting the lids with her thumbs, she found his gaze alert and roving all around.

She rubbed the salt-sting from her eyes and tried to gather her thoughts. She waved her hand in front of her nephew's face, but he did not appear to see. He remained motionless but for his right hand, which bounced against the sand, as though absorbing an electrical shock.

The Islanders

"Jamie, it's me, it's Aunt Lydia … I'm here, I'm right here with you … tell me you can hear me."

She turned him onto his side to let out any swallowed water, but nothing came. She tapped his cheeks, shook his face, as if consciousness simply needed to be joggled to the surface.

It struck her then, with stunning clarity, the uncompromising fact of her helplessness.

Rain dripped from her nose onto her nephew's forehead. His face was warming, a little colour returning. But Lydia could not remember the signs of hypothermia, only that they could be confusing and contradictory. She had forgotten the crow, and did not consider the trail of claw prints surrounding her. It would occur to her only many days later how strange the prints were, unfixed in shape and size, breaking off into three trails at once, before melting into the wet mud.

*

High on the bathroom wall was a large porthole window. Beyond the glass, the clouds were lilac, filling the sky but for two wispy blue clearings. On overcast days like this, Jamie imagined the earth was a speck of grit caught in the wide-open eye of the universe. Though he was not sure if this meant someone was always watching, or that he was impossible to see.

What would be made of the sight before him now? He clapped his hand to the wall, unsteadied by a rush of sickness, as he stared at the boy balled up on the bathroom floor.

"Grady?" he asked. His friend was cuffed to the towel rack with cable ties. Blood caked his nose and soaked the length of his shirt. Jamie crouched next to him, reached for him, and the boy's entire body flinched. "The hell are you doing here?"

Grady was crying. He would not lift his face, though Jamie tried to tilt his chin upward.

A Song for Wildcats

"Why do they have you?" Jamie searched frantically for the mechanism to unlock the ties, then kicked them across the floor. The stench of freshly aired blood choked the small, closed space. "What did you do?"

"*Nothing*," Grady said, his face wet and twisted against Jamie's arm. "I didn't mean to hear anything, I swear."

"What do you mean?" Jamie asked. "Hear what?"

Grady's teeth chattered, cutting his voice into fragments. "I was just hiding to steal some chips, back of the pub. I wasn't spying, I *told* them."

"Spying on who?" Jamie asked.

"The *Ra*. Then these two men took me, brought me here. They said you'd know what to do with a traitor and a coward. What did they mean, Jamie? Why would they say that?"

The weight of his words sank through Jamie, settling cold and corrosive in his stomach. Everyone knew what the militias did with touts. "All right … you're all right," Jamie said, struggling to orient himself. "We'll go out and explain. Just look them in the eye and swear you'll be loyal. These types, they can tell when someone's lying."

Though Grady's head stayed low, his mouth firmed. "You didn't hear what I heard. They were talking about *bombs*, Jamie."

Jamie opened his mouth, but his tongue had dried and thickened, trapping his words.

"They know," Grady said. "They know I'll tout."

It was strange then, how the room inched closer on all sides. Jamie saw it clearly now. The thin yellow sundress hanging from the shower rail. The floor's tiny pink tiles. A brush bursting with dark, frizzy hair like burnt candy floss, and a cluster of bobby pins like a child's scribble of a spider.

The bathroom was just how his mother had left it, the last morning he saw her.

The Islanders

She had died for her cause, the cause Grady meant to under-mine. It had meant everything to her. More than her life, her sister, her son. A loyalty greater to her than any bond.

Jamie squeezed the dress hem and looked around at the incom-plete memory. Disembodied bits of porcelain and wood, a steely smudge of sink. He understood now, in the pin-prick centre of his core, that he was in the shadow of the waking world. Following alongside it, both connected and detached.

Blood ran from Grady's nose, plinking against the tile. The sound smacked Jamie's ears, loud as bullets ricocheting in a drum. "Stop bleeding," Jamie said, covering his ears. "Grady, *stop bleeding.*"

Grady clung to him, and Jamie buried his face in his friend's shoulder. How could his nails dig so deeply into his own skin, tear-ing at his ears, and he not feel it? The tremor had returned, mad thrumming all through his body.

Finally, Grady raised his face and looked at him. He cupped Jamie's hands, still clutching his ears. "You're so close to being part of something bigger than yourself."

It was something about the sound of his voice. Some note of warmth, an affectionate wryness that Jamie could not quite replay in his mind or recount accurately out loud, but that he knew was essential to his friend's voice, because it was missing in the voice he heard now.

On the wall above them, the porthole window squeaked. It spun, slowly, expanding into a view of the ocean.

"Quick, get up," Jamie said, shaking Grady's arm. "Get up, I can get you out of here."

"But you know I'll tout," he said. "A traitor. A coward. Good soldiers could be locked up for it."

"It doesn't matter," Jamie said. He felt a burn in his gut at the words *traitor, coward*, but he was on his feet now, hauling his

A Song for Wildcats

friend off the floor. "You need to listen to me, you have to let me help you."

The golden brown of Grady's eyes drained to the pale shrivel of dead leaves. His ribs slackened in the crook of Jamie's arm, dissolving like salt.

"No … no, come back." Jamie grabbed at the hollowness in front of him. "Come back, don't leave …"

The room fell away. Jamie found himself in darkness and a silence so complete that his ears could not spin a single vibration into a hum. There was silence even as he walked through the splashing black mirror beneath him. He called out for his mother, for Aunt Lydia, Grady, anyone. Paralyzed by a paradox of fear: *Am I alone? Am I not alone?*

Two shapes then appeared at once. A violet planet floated high above, twitching with bright threads of light. It was far away, yet still Jamie felt the overbearing tenderness of its gaze.

At his feet, a grey crow dipped its beak into the puddled black. "I saw you," Jamie said. "On Aunt Lydia's car."

The crow blinked up at him, eyes deep as dark matter. From the water it had pulled a beating, leaf-veined heart.

Jamie grabbed his chest, where he felt the slicing curve of the beak pinching frail flesh. The crow's bite tightened, and soon the heart began to beat with the even vigilance of a well-trained march.

Hone your suffering, Jamie. Sharpen it, like a weapon, and it will bring you peace.

Was this peace? He had thought it would feel fuller. That it might soften his memories, so that he could curl into them, seek refuge in them. But all he saw was the vacant doorway, the day his mother did not come home. An unoccupied space fitted to the dimensions of what was missing.

Channel that pain outward, onto others, so that it might never fester.

The Islanders

Bleed, and make bleed, and you will never be without us.
Each heartbeat knocked against the other, flint cracking flint, spitting sparks. Jamie squeezed his fists over his chest, twisting the fabric of his jumper, heat raving through his veins. Such heat could burn him hollow, scorch him clean. Everyone in his periphery peeling away.

Darkness crowded around him in a snapping deluge of feathers. His eyes closed tight, and somewhere in his mind appeared himself, much younger, holding his mother's hand as a bus erupted into a blazing barricade in the street. And again, younger still, squeezing her hand as a clipped flurry of birds flew up the bank in the park. And then clinging to her fingers outside the school, his first day, unsure if she meant to leave him in the squat brown building for good. And it struck him now, for the first time: why, in all those years, had she never squeezed back?

Jamie opened his eyes as the violet planet drew closer. He parted the clamorous wall of feathers, as if pushing through a storm-blown hedge. He watched the electric bands of light snap around the planet, growing louder, like plucked chords. *Jamie ... can you hear me? I'm here ... I'm right here with you ...*

An ache, wrenched from some unknown depth, shuddered through him. In one swift moment, it flooded his body and sprang from his mouth. His hands loosened, flew to contain it, but water streamed from his eyes and ears, stinging with salt. Jagged shards of shell cut his tongue and lodged between his teeth, and however he tried to will it to stop, the flood — full and total and agonizing — demanded to be unleashed. Jamie wrapped around himself. Let it tear through him. Even the heart poured, spilling from the crow's beak, leaving the bird to peck furiously at the current rushing away beneath it.

We see you for your weakness. Meek and helpless and soft. We offer you no solace. We will not come to you again.

A Song for Wildcats

The darkness fell still, and he was alone. For a long time, he lay in the ceaseless flood, pulled from a hidden well within him. He thought it would never end, that soon it would ferry his organs out of him — and when it did begin to slow, the ache was no less raw. But he could taste air again, one breath rolling into another, and each breath caught the tips of the waves inside him and rocked them back and forth into an easeful lull.

Jamie felt himself unfurling, even as he curled like a leaf against the brisk sea breeze. Somehow, he was lying on the beach. Warm breath flushed across his skin. Someone else's breath, falling over him, drawing into his lungs and tasting of lavender. A voice, gentle as vapour, was calling his name. Soon, familiar hands guided him upright, and he leaned into them. He wrapped his arms around the thin pillar of a person in front of him and rested his head against the steady raft of their shoulder.

✳

Lydia tugged the belt of her housecoat and grabbed her mug of tea, then walked to the back door and slipped on her boots. As she stepped outside, a welcoming breeze caressed her collar. It freshened her face, played with her hair. She cupped the mug of tea, biting hot against her palms and steaming with the vigorous scent of cinnamon. Eabha's favourite flavour. Lydia had not tasted it in years, but Jamie had insisted on it in hospital, then again on the drive home, his brow pinched and eyes fixed on the fields blurring past the window, as if even he could not understand the acuteness of his need.

It was nearly dusk. All along the peninsula, just above the water's horizon, stretched a sooty garland of cloud. Within the hour the day would fade, the sun draining away, replaced by the muted death mask of the moon. People of the island would sleep. But not

The Islanders

Lydia, not Jamie. They would read or watch television by the sitting room fireplace, Jamie in his blankets on the sofa and Lydia in the armchair beside him.

Shortly after she had pulled him from the water, Jamie woke on the beach with a jolt. Two days in the nearest county hospital, test after test, a vial of blood work, but no signs of injury or distress. The doctor could not quite explain it, and Jamie himself could not recall what had happened after he fumed out of the house, other than seeing what the doctor called a common scald-crow. Grey-feathered birds but for black poured over their heads, dripping down their chests, and with a gristly caw.

Jamie had spent several days more enveloped in blankets, under Lydia's unblinking surveillance. For reasons she could not define, this developed in her a sudden aversion to the far recess of the kitchen.

Though it had once been her corner of comfort, she found herself hurrying out of it with the pressure of another presence close at her back, a chill trickling through her arms. She saw it now, she supposed, as Jamie must have seen it. A crevice in which she had crawled and sepulchred herself. All this time, she had been extending her hand to him — but who would not retreat, in terror, from a hand reaching out of a tomb?

Lydia dragged the garden chair down the porch steps and planted it on the grass. Jamie was reading, a little way off in the yard, the yew tree's shady boughs curving protectively over him. He sat hunched, legs stretched out. His book rested on the ground in front of him. It was just as Eabha used to sit, down to the chain of his necklace — once belonging to Eabha, and their mother, and their grandfather before — pulled up around his jaw, with the slender golden cross dangling against his chin.

Like his mother, he looked at peace only when outdoors, alone and undisturbed. Solitude had not brought Lydia peace, however

117

deeply she encased herself within it, but perhaps being alone was not the point. It occurred to her that one is not truly alone outdoors, among the wild elements, and to be in private communion with the universe is perhaps the least alone someone can be.

And here she saw something of herself in the boy. An effortless attentiveness to sound, ear tilted to the wind and the ocean's pulse, the natural strains of song. How his eyes closed when the leaves above him lifted, and his shoulders slowly rose, slowly fell.

Their likeness emerged like smoke. He had her nose, her jawline, blended with Eabha's eyes and hair. Both her sister's shattered youth and her own, pieced back together and remoulded into a new face, a child's face. Lydia could see herself and Eabha as children again, as clearly as if these small selves were sitting in the grass. Helpless and blameless. Wondering and innocent. Clinging to one another like driftwood as they waited for rescue that would never come. And Lydia's heart, long strung up tight in a bleeding knot, loosened itself a little. Eased itself down as if into a warm bath.

Jamie glanced up from his book. He lifted himself off the grass, and Lydia waved faintly, fingers wilting in the air. He started toward the porch and she assumed he meant to join her, but instead he breezed past her and through the back door.

The nervous feeling returned. Lydia began debating whether to run after him to see what she had done wrong, but then the door squeaked open again behind her. Jamie stepped out, holding an elaborate contraption: a fusion of the plastic kitchen sieve, through which he had threaded long strings of yarn and dangling ornaments. Fragments of gleaming blue seashells from the rubbish bin, spotty teaspoons, and tiny sleigh bells. Jamie raised himself onto his toes, stretching the homemade wind chimes to the low porch rafter.

Lydia watched in utter confoundment. "Did you make that?"

The Islanders

Jamie dropped back onto his heels. "I can't reach that high," he said, staring at the rafter. From the centre of the upended bowl, in a pool of hardened glue, a strip of yarn drooped like a spent wick.

"Here …" Settling her mug in the grass, Lydia gestured toward the peculiar instrument.

The boy's gaze withdrew into itself, distant with doubt.

Lydia smiled, let her arm relax. "Keep trying, if you like." She lifted her tea and took a sip. "I'm here if you need me."

After a moment's consideration, Jamie reached across the swath of muddy grass between them. He gathered the chimes into his hands, and she tied the instrument to the rafter. Soon came the giddy stopping and starting of a tuneless, windblown song.

A memory struck Lydia then: the first time she had touched a piano. All of four years old, scrambling onto the bench in the Sunday school room, at the back of the weathered stone church by the river. Her fingers running freely, aimlessly, over the keys. A tumbling cascade of gleefully discordant notes. Had she laughed then, with the instructor glowering over her? Or was it the desire to laugh, lodged full and urgent inside her, that she remembered?

The wind swept the chimes into a tinkling clatter. A stitch tightened at the corner of Jamie's mouth as the yarn tangled, untangled, swaying the scavenged treasures. When the instrument remained intact, he crossed his arms with resigned astonishment.

"It works," he said.

The air, clear and reverberating, washed over Lydia. She placed her hand, tentatively, on Jamie's shoulder, and when he did not shift away, she let it rest.

"Did Mam ever play an instrument?" he asked.

"No," she said, "but she used to sing."

The surprise with which he looked at her was as delighted as it was sad. "I never heard her sing."

A Song for Wildcats

Eabha's crystal-cool voice bloomed across Lydia's memory like fern frost. "I wish you had," she said. "Your mother had a beautiful voice."

Boots in the untamed grass, encircled by a far-reaching nest of field and the sparkle and spray of the sea, here in this northernmost patch of country, they stood together and listened to the clink of shells, and the broken song of spoons and bells. And Lydia knew. Of course the little girl at the piano had laughed, her fingers wild, her blood enlivened and shimmering, as Lydia was laughing now.

The Wisp

The horses watched as the cab passed, their black-smoke manes blowing over the bright swells of their eyes, their legs like brittle stems of clay. It was late October 1933, and the drought had swept its indiscriminate scythe across the once sun-honeyed fields.

"You sure you've got the right place?" the cabbie asked, pulling into the gas station. "Lots of hamlets and villages in Mount Pleasant. Easy to get mixed up."

"I'm sure," Tessa said. She had asked the driver to hurry, hoping to avoid anyone she might know, but once one entered the slumbery port village on the east bank of the Hudson River, time had a way of slowing.

The cabbie got out of the car and looked her over from the gas pump. Her huge yellow coat, her hair long and veiling one eye. The jazzy white frames of her sunglasses, their dark green lenses, like an Emerald City starlet on her way to rehab.

"You're from the city?" he asked, watching the clock meter. Brown dust and burnt air filtered into the car through the open door. "Don't let the locals scare you with stories of the Headless Horseman. They love to spook visitors the most this close to Halloween."

A Song for Wildcats

As with all childhood homes, pieces of north Tarrytown — more colloquially known as Sleepy Hollow — still resided in Tessa, like embedded chips of glass that pinched when agitated. She looked at the cabbie from the back seat of the car. "My mother used to say that skeptics enter the hollow loud as woodpeckers," she said, "and leave quiet as ghosts."

Tessa had never meant to come back. She had left six years ago, at eighteen — the topic of which, her brother James had informed her, practically spun the gossamer of community scandal. After moving to the city to attend college, she had begun working as the assistant to a newspaper journalist. It took over a year for her employer to recognize her as a proper protégée. To him, she was the dour-eyed girl who failed, each morning, to recreate for him some quaint cup of coffee enjoyed two decades ago along the lavender banks of Provence. The memory of which, she was certain, was no more than a diluted phantom of itself, perverted by imagination and the passage of time.

But recently, matters had begun to change. He was instructing her with seriousness, eagerness, and Tessa felt herself jumping into a future broken free from her past.

And then came the call.

James's voice had crinkled through the telephone, a sound of locusts among the almond blossoms papered brightly on the walls of Tessa's Brooklyn boarding house.

Sabrina Jacobs. Found along the rocky bank of the deep ravine behind her house. Her skull fractured from the fall. A rusty hair comb lying beside her stony fist.

That was all. No conclusive explanation, no community uproar. Sabrina was an Irish girl planted in the deeply Dutch settlement, with no family left nor any claim to the old roots of New Amsterdam. For this, and her friendship with Tessa, she was deemed a peculiar bird. This seemed to suggest that a peculiar end could be expected, as though the natural laws by which the peculiar were governed existed separately from those of more orderly society. Sabrina had died mysteriously, and wild animals hunted one another among the mountain cliffs of the Catskills, and moss maidens of old country lore could either spur a plague or end it. This was just the way of things, and what was anyone, really, to do about it?

✳

The farmhouse sat caged behind the porch columns, its blue paint so faded it looked like little more than the ephemeral tint of the evening reflected off whitewashed wood. All the lights were off. Tessa figured her brother had gone to bed, and probably a good thing too. She had been half in the bag all day, sipping discreetly from a flask and soaking her brain into a pulp, unable to bear such proximity to Sabrina's unseeing face, her unmoving hands, once so light and agile.

Tessa fell onto the porch's wicker bench to catch her breath. Looking out, it was not all so different, so diminished. The trees were crisp golds and reds, like syrup-glazed apples. The family mailbox was the same as it had always been, standing in camaraderie with the lone tulip poplar. Dented on the side from the time she, Sabrina, and James had played The Three Musketeers, sword-fighting with steel rakes they found in the barn.

But the farmhands were gone. Meagre mounds of straw were stacked and bound upright in the yard like a dwindling army of corn dollies. A basket lay tipped in the grass, apples nibbled and browning and sticky with flies.

Lightheaded, Tessa bent over and stuck her head between her knees. Her pulse was light, flickery, like rustling paper. She stared at the dusty planks of the porch floor. Watched a long, deep-red strand of hair fall loose from its pin. Thought blankly of the porch swing that was no longer in the corner, trying to remember what had happened to it.

Homesickness, not felt while she was away, hit her heart like a pebble cracking glass. Real estate developers were scouting the property again. "They know people are desperate," James had told her.

The developers had been scouting all over Westchester since the Bronx River Parkway was built, the Tarrytowns' insulated tranquility threatened by open scenic highways.

She and James had seen each other over the matter only a month ago. They sat in two hard swivel chairs, in a New York bank lobby, looking like children playing Mom and Dad: Tessa in a pearl-buttoned dress, James in a freshly ironed herringbone suit. Everything too big and borrowed from a friend. More than anything she had heard from the loan officer that day, she remembered the earnestness of her brother's combed-back curls, the sweat on his collar, his dime-store cologne. How his fingers jumped on his knee, punching curt plumes of cigarette smoke into the lobby. And how their shadows, two sightless sentries, loomed from the grey-cracked marble beneath their feet.

∗

A voice startled her awake.

Tessa shot up from the bench. The voice beat through the wind, from far off in the Rockefeller forests. It had a cold, vaporous ring that pinched her forehead like brain freeze. And a remote weariness, like the frozen Hudson when she rested her ear against it and heard in its strange, high pitch all the places it had passed through, all the mouths and caves, the rib cages of whales. Tessa strained her ears, pulling every grain of sound from the air, but she could not make out the words.

The Wisp

Unexplained sights and sounds were accepted in the Hollow, attributed both offhandedly and reverently to storied spectres, so Tessa thought little of the voice when it stopped.

She straightened her clothes and picked up the bobby pins that had fallen from her hair. Tufts of late-blooming cottonwood seeds lifted from the porch and brushed her ankles. Startled, Tessa kicked them away, then opened the door and hurried into the shining oak hall. She closed the door with a thud before any of the seeds could blow in.

When they were ten, she told Sabrina that cottonwood seeds were will-o'-the-wisps. *They turn into ghost lights at night and lead people astray.*

"Back home, they're embers of hellfire," Sabrina had said, having come from an old Irish town of white bog cotton and castles. "They were once carried by a man who thought he could trick the devil. Or they're fairy lights that will guide you to buried treasure." She snatched some fluff misting the grass and examined it. "I think true will-o'-the-wisps are spirits from the Otherworld. They cross over on the night of Samhain and guide good people toward the right path."

"What about bad people?" Tessa asked.

Sabrina considered this. "Torment, I think," she said, and laughed. "They fly into your ear and buzz around until you're gone in the head, and then they lure you away to danger."

Since then, Tessa had grown frightened of cottonwood seeds, and wary even of fireflies and far-off lanterns pacing the pier.

✳

That same day, their legs knee deep in the pond where Tessa's yard slid into the road, she watched Sabrina's feet roll over one another like bony carp.

"Do you think I'm good?" Tessa asked.

"I knew you were good right away," Sabrina said, "when I came to your house that first time."

"Really?" Tessa could not recall any moral distinction about that day. "How come?"

"All those birds on your porch and pecking around in the grass. Birds are a good judge of character, you know, always watching."

But the birds could not know all of Tessa, nor the dark curiosities hidden on the far side of her heart.

Sabrina slid her leg behind Tessa's in the warm black pond and playfully rocked it back and forth. Though each kick was slow through the water, Tessa felt the woozy thrill of being swung high into the air. Her gaze followed the rhythm, wandered to where Sabrina's skirt lay tugged to her thighs, and where the fabric's shade formed a shadowy tunnel in between.

"I have a surprise for you." Sabrina lifted her legs out of the water and stretched them, bare and wet, over Tessa's lap. "Do you want to see?"

In a faint daze, Tessa asked, "See what?"

Sabrina pulled a jade hat pin from her pocket and held it in her palm. Their teacher had lost it the week before and asked them to search for it in the grass.

"A gift," Sabrina said.

"For what?" Tessa asked.

"Because you're mine." She lifted it toward Tessa's collar, her fingertips smelling faintly sour from stoning cherries with her father. "That's what my mam used to tell me whenever she brought me gifts. *Because you're mine, mo shíorghra.*"

Something in the invigoration of a treasure stolen for her benefit, the sickening guilt of it, the excitable spots of light in Sabrina's glassy blue eyes, made Tessa pull away from her and hurry half soaked and barefoot down the dirt path. She stepped on pebbles

The Wisp

and broken twigs, the tiniest fragment of a Coca-Cola bottle, and arrived home with a sweltering face and a bloodied big toe.

❋

Walking through the house for the first time in six years, Tessa touched the candlestick telephone on the table in the hall, the mildew-green wallpaper in the kitchen. Here was the queenly Glenwood stove, known to her and James as the Turquoise Fairy for magically burning their meals, and the black anvil of their grandmother's sewing machine, still sitting between the cotton lace curtains of the parlour windows.

Yet here was a change. The round-framed picture of their late mother and father hung above the fireplace, watching over the house like its own soft-glinting eye. For her sake, James had locked the picture away after they died. He was twelve when it happened, not much older than she was at seven, and she often wondered if the monsoon of paternal responsibility he inherited was the reason he did not catch the stormy sickness that overcame her.

She had not decided to come home so much as arrived, almost suddenly, with a stunned sense of purpose: to learn what had happened to Sabrina. This she understood, even if it mystified her — yet she felt an out-of-body loss of control. She had half a mind to think it was Sabrina's doing, that she had marched Tessa home, like the doll she once made of her. Dancing the figure across the floor and bending its legs when she was angry, sticking pins in its head.

Tessa walked in hiccupy steps to the liquor cabinet, sat on the floor, and took too large a sip of cheap gin. The cold burn eased down her throat and lit a glittering heat in her chest.

Why the hair comb, Sabrina? What were you doing?

She could not understand why it was there when they found her. She had bought it for Sabrina's fifteenth birthday from a peddler in a carriage painted gold, soured by sun, with toothy serpents spinning pearly green around the wheels.

And the ravine — I told you a thousand times not to go near it.

They had tried, once, to climb down the daunting fifty-foot drop into its narrow pit. The slope was soaked in moss, and they slipped their way down, digging their heels into mud, holding onto dangling branches. The rocks along the bank and rising from the water, some as foreboding and beak-sharp as the masks of plague doctors, eventually warned Tessa away. But they only tempted Sabrina deeper. Tessa had to beg her to stop, to climb back from the frothing open mouth of the forest.

Reckless. Completely, unbelievably reckless. Tessa squeezed the bottle to her chest. *What could I have done, how could I have helped, when you never listened?*

In her childhood bedroom, Tessa clicked open her suitcase and rummaged through clothes, books, fussy toiletries. A sea-blue ribbon of Sabrina's lay coiled in one of the pockets. Tessa had packed it when she moved and never taken it out. It seemed to vibrate with the memory of the day it fell from Sabrina's hair, when Tessa picked it from the grass and sneaked it into her shoe without knowing why.

As she traced the ribbon — remembering the queasy sweetness of lying in bed with it at night, twisting it around her fingers, pinching it between her front teeth — a pale blue light appeared in the corner of her eye. When she turned, it trailed toward the window. Tessa glanced around for whatever was reflecting it — a vase of blue glass, perhaps, set in her room by James — but the light flew outside and faded into the sky, above the stretch of forest and the peak of the Old Dutch Church.

She rubbed her face. Rest, that was what she needed. She pulled a small bottle from the suitcase. Veronal: pure crystals named for the star-crossed city. Bottled rain-shimmer of sleep. After a full dose, she changed out of her dress and threw it over the folding

The Wisp

screen in the corner. She curled on the end of the bed, above the quilt, her heart pressed against her ribs. The wrinkled white dress hung from the screen with all the ethereal doggedness of a ghost.

"Where are you, dark star?" she whispered.

She could not feel her friend's presence. Sabrina had made them take a blood oath, prick their left palms with the jade pin. *The left-handed path of darkness*, Sabrina had told her. They swore they would never lose sight of one another.

Well. You left first. She could almost hear Sabrina say it.

"You drove me to it. What else could I do?" she said, and waited.

The silence expanded, before thickening and closing in around her.

Tessa had read once that rage and loss could tie a spirit to the earth, reduce it to the very marrow of its suffering. So where was Sabrina? No one had ever had such an appetite for haunting, and yet now she was nowhere, and now she had nothing to say.

✳

The police offered little when Tessa called the station in the morning. A probable suicide, they said. Ruled as such by an overburdened coroner who knew nothing about Sabrina. And with her father dying years ago, and her mother disappearing one morning when Sabrina was small — *all dolled up in her perfect scarlet blouse with her perfect scarlet hat*, Sabrina had said, *too perfect to turn around when I ran down the steps after her* — there was nobody to bother calling at the Jacobs house.

Tessa did not know what she expected Reverend Hallamshire to tell her, but nobody knew the town's clockwork like he did, so she dragged her bike from the tool shed and rolled it to the dirt road. It was rusty from disuse and her adolescent habit of leaving it out in the rain, but it squeaked along, and in the perennial nature

A Song for Wildcats

of the past, she soon remembered how it felt to be a girl who rode every day through shivering tallgrass and gnat clouds, past wild hedgerows of fern.

Gold leaves lined the town's main road. Black cherry trees smelled of sugary decay, and smoke filled with clove and nutmeg escaped a corner bakery. Tessa breathed in this scent she had never realized she remembered. It was early and most of the storefront windows were still dark. Some boarded up or webbed in cracks. She glanced at her gliding reflection in the dim pharmacy window. Smart plaid skirt, hair curled and combed and pinned in place, every seam of her face stitched tight.

She looked away from herself, that double always nipping at her eye.

When Tessa fell ill after the loss of her parents, her grandmother sent her to a hospital in White Plains. The doctor told Tessa that she, like many patients, had seeds of hell planted at the centre of her mind. And she would nod along, hands folded, and try to hear him over the urgent red oak smacking its acorns against the window.

Tessa parked her bike by the Old Dutch Church, where Reverend Hallamshire had always been kind to her. His son Hector had claimed for years to love her and what he called her witchy habits, her contentious secrecy. But when she did not want to marry him at the enlightened age of fifteen, Hector grabbed the back of her head until her neck ached. *What better life do you see for yourself?* His eyes round and black as spider bulbs when she twisted away, following her into the manic light of the county fair. *We used to burn girls like you.*

Tessa climbed the church steps, beneath the broad white clapboard and the belfry sitting like a dollhouse gloriette. Her great-grandmother had witnessed the church burn in 1837, though she remembered only the smell of the fire's sooty breath. As a girl, Tessa

The Wisp

would stand in front of the church and imagine orange gusts crashing through the windows and blowing over her.

Inside, a man was leaning against the wall by the first pew to the left of the pulpit. He wore a long grey coat with a blood-purple scarf wrapped loosely around his neck. He brought a cigarette to his mouth, and the smoke hovered around him, as if he were burning, vampirishly, in the anemic light.

He was so deep in thought that he did not hear Tessa's footsteps until she was halfway down the aisle.

"Tessa?" he asked with a start. His gaze flitted around her, as though he did not trust the solidity of her presence.

"Hello, Hector," she said.

He was thin and gaunt. Hunger had remoulded him, pressed in the flesh under his cheeks. "You really aren't dead."

"Who said I was?"

The word *everyone* seemed to swell in his mouth, but he only shrugged.

"I need to speak with your father," she said.

"You're a little late. He passed a few weeks ago."

Tessa paused. "Oh. I see."

Hector gave a distracted nod, agreeing with his own private thought. "Fell down the stairs, if you can believe it."

"You must be heartsick," she said, heartsick herself, one wave spilling into another.

"Yes, well, you knew a very different version of my father."

"Will you take his place?" she asked.

"We're in dire need of it, so I keep hearing. But the seminary took as little to me as I did to it. Are you here about Sabrina?"

Her name was wrong in his mouth. Loaded to wound, like packed gunpowder. Yet, hearing it, Tessa realized that she had not spoken it in days, only *Miss Jacobs*; it had been lodged like a fishbone in her throat. "I was hoping to find out more about her life recently. Who she knew, what she was doing. You grew up with her too — what do you think happened?"

"We know what happened," Hector said, starting toward her with more life than she had expected. "So like you, Tessa, to think you're catching something nobody else can see."

"You don't honestly think she did this to herself," Tessa said. "That can't be what you all believe. For crying out loud, Hector, she wasn't *so* unhappy ..."

"If that eases your conscience," he said. "You know she was never the same after you left."

Tessa stared at him in the pressing silence, struck by the force of the suggestion. "You think this was *my* fault? Nobody could have stopped her from hurting herself, if she was set on it. Not even me. And I don't think she did, I think she fell in with a bad sort —"

"What *bad sort?*" Hector swept his hand toward the open door and the clear view of the village, as if the absence of any visible delinquents in that moment proved they did not exist.

"There had to have been *someone*," she said.

Tessa winced against a sudden sharp flicker in her head. A taunting mimic of her own voice whispered in circles, *nothing, you did nothing wrong, you did nothing.*

"And what would you know of it?" Anger flared, momentarily, across Hector's face. Its razored heat ran against Tessa's skin. He drew closer, tapped his knuckle against the rhinestone brooch at her collar. "I remember you in these loose farm-girl frocks, all patterned with tulips and ruined with mud. They dress more conservatively in the city, do they?"

His fingers, clean and smooth, a whiff of ink under the nails and a gold ring like a Roman coin. All these years later and his hands still snipped at her nerves.

"Some do," she said.

132

The Wisp

He eyed the collar's worn lace, veining across her throat. "It suits you. The visage of progress."

Tessa glanced at his ring, once offered to her, and a point of pride for Hector. He had always said it was imbued with a feeling of home, brought by his family, generations ago, from the green canals of Utrecht.

He lifted his hand to contemplate it. "Humiliation aside, I'm glad you rejected my proposal. I can't imagine parting with this ring now. It might be the one truly beautiful thing I own."

As a youth, Hector had held a voyeuristic conviction that Tessa and Sabrina had eyes like magic lanterns, projecting a secret beauty onto the world, and this made him all the more aware of his own shadowy passage. Once they caught him spying while they dipped into the creek that ran through the field and spilled, green and foamy, into the wooded ravine. They would often do this on late afternoons, wearing only their underclothes, and smoke cheap cigarettes in the grassy water. Savouring the scent of damp nicotine, and the freedom of wet skin pressing against thin fabric. Sabrina blundering her way through smoke rings, with their clothes draped over a branch of the white-flowering dogwood bowing over them.

When the sun began to dissolve into the clouds, in soft yellow drifts, they would sink to their chins like watchful mermaids and look out over the empty field. That was when they found Hector spying. Sabrina laughed and yelled fake incantations to scare him away, and Tessa climbed out and chased after him into the woods. By the time she knew she had lost him, she was so angry she could hardly breathe, and her bare feet burned from the prick of pine needles. She could not bring herself to let Sabrina see it, the red unfurling of feeling. So she hid in the woods until it stopped, listening to Sabrina's voice call out for her, and underneath it, her own stabbing heartbeat.

In the quiet of the church, a sound caught her ear.

A Song for Wildcats

"What's that?" she asked. It was coming from outside. "Is someone singing?"

Hector looked at her, amused. He gripped the back of a pew. "It's Scandinavian."

It was the same high-curdling echo Tessa had heard the day before.

"Her name is Alva," Hector said, approaching the window. "She's sort of the village ward."

"What on earth does that mean?"

Yet another dawdling tourist, falling for the rustic fantasies and sleepy romance of the place. They came to the Tarrytowns from all over to see Washington Irving's riverbank home or Ichabod Crane's long-disintegrated bridge. You knew them by the way they walked, out of step with the Hudson Valley's lulling pulse, and how they stared at the townspeople like pieces of some forgotten ethos.

"Father called her the ghost of Hulda the Witch," Hector said, flicking the raggedy tassels of his scarf against Tessa's arm.

She rolled her eyes at the thought of a tourist being as useful as the great doctor of Spook Rock.

"She showed up about a year ago. No money, no shoes. Incredibly odd if it were any time but this one."

"Where's she from?" Tessa asked.

"She won't say. Anyhow, it hasn't proven to be a problem, her being rather different. From what she tells me, the town is grateful to have her."

Tessa could not help an incredulous laugh. "This town?"

"I don't see why she'd have any reason to lie."

"What kind of singing is that? The inane yodelling."

Hector shook his head. "Some old mountain song, I think, for herding cows."

"I heard it last night, coming all the way from the eastern foothills."

134

The Wisp

He smiled. "You've never had a strong sense of direction, Tessa. She was here in the village yesterday. She helps at some of the local farms for practically nothing. Soup, fabric, board. The Van Wyck farm, especially, I hear — though usually she stays with me." He glanced around at nothing. "She stayed a fair bit with Sabrina too."

A knot tightened in Tessa's chest, coarse and twisting like a ball of twine. "Sabrina hates people in her house."

"Other than you, right?"

The words jumped out of her. "Yes, as a matter of fact."

"Always in your own private world, the two of you," he said. "Until you left, of course. Just took off like a change in the wind. You always were good for a shock, I'll give you that." An ashtray sat on the windowsill, and he brushed through the stubs for any salvageable remains. "*Little Tessa Hemlock, mad and locked away.*" He spoke in the singsong cadence of a nursery rhyme. "*Singing to the moon at night, but silent come the day.*"

The other children used to sing it while playing hopscotch, and shout it as Tessa walked by. She had gone a bit strange when she was young, leading to the stay in White Plains. She stopped speaking for two years after her parents' deaths, one in the war and the other in the grip epidemic. Her grandmother said she had the look of an ancient sibyl, with wide, portentous eyes. Each night, Tessa woke with the fear that her body had come apart, held only loosely together with string. She would dig through her blankets for her legs, her bones, her teeth, only to find that they were just where she had left them.

The rumours of her condition were made worse by her being routinely found, violet lipped and frozen in hypnagogic peace, up in the boughs of the tallest trees. It would take James and the reverend, and the occasional firefighter, to get her to climb down.

She could never explain it to anyone, or make much sense of it herself. That is what they never tell you of madness, how you remain unchanged. How it is the world around you that slips and shivers out of place. That soundness of the mind is a pulsing thicket of moths, and with or without provocation, it can flutter apart.

Hector surprised her by laughing. "I haven't thought about that song in years. What comes next? *If you listen by her window, you'll hear her solemn tune.* Duh-duh, duh-duh, I don't remember the rest."

"*She's quiet as the winter now,*" Tessa said, "*but once she was the Queen of June.*"

"Children are cruel."

"I wrote it, you know."

Hector blinked at her. "You didn't. Whatever for?"

She made a gesture, as if she could not be bothered with an answer, but really she had none.

"I know I wasn't always kind to you," he said.

"You're not being particularly pleasant now, either."

He knocked the windowsill, where his arm rested. "Old habits."

"Old habits. Right. Where is she, then?" Tessa asked. "The *ward*."

"Just down the way. You can probably see her by now."

Tessa leaned toward the window. The tip of her nose touched the glass as a pale girl trudged across the field by the adjacent cemetery. She was wearing a red raincoat and large rubber boots, climbing over fences, fey and invasive as a dandelion ghost. She looked around with a sort of fascinated skepticism, as if marooned on an island of luxuriant promise, where bromeliads shot up like small geysers of fire, instead of a town of greying birch and bread lines, of damp moss and mud.

The girl stopped and peered into the grass.

"So they were friends," Tessa said, "Sabrina and the ward. I'll need to speak with her."

"She doesn't say much." Hector moved behind her, and his fingers fell like pinpricks on her waist. "Look," he said, pointing toward the distant shapes of cows moving in a rippling drove across the field. "Quite the little spell-weaver, don't you think?"

The Wisp

✳

"Mushroom rings pop up wherever the devil puts his milk churn," Tessa said.

She lit a cigarette from the crumpled pack she had stolen from James's bedroom, where he could not be found that morning. She handed it to the girl, who took it without looking up from where she crouched, examining a ring of toadstools.

"Why would the devil need to churn milk?" the girl asked. "We call them fairy rings."

"I've heard of that," Tessa offered. Mushroom rings formed by giddily noxious creatures, all dancing together, their synchronicity webbing an illusory net. "Alva, is it?"

"These mushrooms are poisonous," the girl said, uninterested. Her hair, twisted in a long braid, was the white of raw silk. Beneath the unbuttoned raincoat, her dress was folksy, with a drawstring at the neckline, and baptismal white but for a hem of blue-stitch garlands. "Who are you?"

"Tessa Hemlock. A friend of Sabrina's."

Alva finally looked up, eyes bright and flashing. She straightened. "You're not usually here."

"I'm visiting." Tessa stretched out her hand in what James called their father's buckram manner. Alva gave it a slow, wary shake. "Hector says you don't speak much."

"Not in English. Does he speak much in Swedish?"

"Sweden, then." Tessa nodded, mind rolling over itself, searching for what to say. "*Nej, hej då. No, goodbye.* That's all I know. Does your family live here?"

"I came alone. I think I've been alone a long time." Alva continued to stare. "They're called the fly agaric. The mushrooms."

They were a peculiar breed, the sort illustrated in storybooks, with roundish red caps salted in white spots.

"We used them as a bug killer," she said. "A long time ago."

Tessa noticed a gap in the circle. "Poor thing. Looks like an animal has gotten to some of them."

"They're not deadly, most of the time," Alva said. "Just confusing. Things get bigger or smaller, seem closer or farther away."

"Ah, like in Wonderland," Tessa said, but the girl's brow only narrowed. "Well, I've never seen them grow here before."

Alva moved in front of them. "If you don't bother them, they'll go away on their own."

Tessa was struggling to get a proper read on her. She had eyes of effervescent grey and a look of innocent uncertainty, like a fawn or someone raised in a cult. Tessa did not for an instant believe the girl knew her way around a farm. Cow-calling aside, there was not so much as a thread of dirt beneath her nails.

"How exactly were you and Sabrina acquainted?" Tessa asked.

"Why does it matter?"

Tessa had seated herself on a tree stump and the dampness was seeping through her skirt. She shivered. "It just seems a little curious."

"She hired me to go to the market for her," Alva said, after a pause.

"Sabrina loves the market. Why would she need you to go for her?"

"I did other things. Cook for her. Tidy the house. Garden." Alva reached outward to avoid sprinkling ash on the toadstools. "She was sick."

"Nonsense. If she was sick, she'd have told me." A fetid breeze blew by, and Tessa held the back of her hand to her nose, turning from the nauseating stench of the nearby waterfront. Nets of oily green bodies were being flung from modest fishing boats and piling up on the slippery pier. "She wouldn't have kept that to herself."

"She didn't," Alva said. "She told me."

The Wisp

Tessa swallowed the urge to argue. The girl was like a rabbit quivering with readiness, about to dart away. Tessa searched the air for the right approach. "What did she have, then, if she was so sick?"

"Loneliness can be its own sickness," the girl said. "Are you lonely, like Sabrina was?"

Tessa gave a dry little breath of a laugh. Holding up the pack of cigarettes, she tried to pry out the last one stuck at the bottom. "Do you have a match? I'm all out."

Rather than a matchbox, Alva pulled a lighter from her raincoat pocket. A cloisonné piece, ornate as a jewellery box. It was glazed in patterns of tail-chasing fish, their scales turquoise and gold-rimmed and bright as stained-glass seawater. She looked pleased to see Tessa admiring it. "It's very valuable," she said. "A family heirloom to a berry farmer. Very precious to him. I picked strawberries for a week to get it."

"And the farmer agreed to that?" Tessa leaned toward the flame. "For only a week of strawberry picking?"

The girl shoved the piece back into her pocket. "It's what I was owed."

"Have you tried selling it?" Tessa asked. "With things as they are —"

"Objects dense with memory serve a greater purpose," she said sharply. "You don't sell the only key to your house." Tessa gave her a puzzled look, but before she could speak, Alva asked, "What do you want from me, Miss Hemlock?"

Tessa sucked in a sharp drag, let the sooty smoothness line her throat. "Sabrina had a hard time making friends. We both did. But I suppose you knew her. And you've made your way around town, so I've been told. Maybe you know something I don't."

"I know a great deal that you don't." Alva gave an unpleasant laugh, almost imperceptibly soft. "Are you playing detective?"

A Song for Wildcats

"I'm a journalist," Tessa said, stiffening. "Or nearly one. I work for a newspaper."

With an expression of sterling obstinance, Alva glanced over Tessa's shoulder at the cemetery. Tessa had been careful to keep her back to it, and now it inched up behind her in a phantom tide.

"There's a woman who comes here every day to visit her husband. His urn," Alva said, gesturing toward the back of the gate, "buried just over there. She never spoke to him when he was here, and now she talks to ashes."

"We all need to hold onto something," Tessa said. "How do you know the woman?"

"I told you. She visits her husband."

"But you said she never spoke to him when they were married. Did you know them?"

Alva eyed the burnt cigarette stub in her hand. Loose hairs blew in white drifts across her face as she bent toward the toadstools, flicked away a bit of fallen ash.

A lightly ringing hum rose from the girl, and Tessa felt herself fall under a hypnotic drowse. She was suddenly at ease, her distrust disappearing, as if sifting through her pores.

"Sabrina said you ran away." The girl's mouth balled up as she moved closer. "Left home like it didn't matter."

"I wanted a career. It's hardly mysterious," Tessa said, but she was struggling to concentrate, like pulling herself out of a barbital dream. She rose from the stump, her thighs freezing, and nearly tipped over. She grabbed hold of Alva's arm. "I'm sorry ... I'm feeling a little dizzy ..."

"Home doesn't wait for us the way we think it will," Alva said. "Turn your back on it, and it will forget you."

Tessa squinted, her eyes clouding. The hum grew louder, even as the girl spoke, a fragile resonance stinging Tessa's ears like singing glasses. "I didn't turn my back."

140

The Wisp

"I don't mean the village," Alva said. "Sabrina isn't yours anymore. This is no longer your home."

Tessa felt a prickling exposure, as if her chest had been pulled open, fitted with glass like a shadow box. She brought her arm across her chest to shield herself. She tried to speak, but her tongue felt sewn to the roof of her mouth. There was no explaining, openly to anyone, her reason for leaving home, for pushing Sabrina away so suddenly, and for turning into an insoluble vault. No explaining the black blur of the week before she left. The dare at the quarry. The fierce, fast clap of water against her body, and the slowness of sinking. Or Sabrina shouting from the porch roof — *Why won't you talk to me?* — tearing her skirt on a rusted shingle, the scrap of white fabric flickering for days like an injured bird. *Can't we just forget it? I'm sorry, I didn't mean anything by it.*

"Listen to me, Miss Hemlock," Alva said. She touched Tessa's wrist, her fingertips like ice drops. "What happened with Sabrina — there are things you couldn't possibly understand."

The church doors opened and Hector shuffled down the steps. The birds on the rails snapped up in a cutting, feathery gust, and with the doleful keen of a banshee. "Get inside, Alva," he called, looking at the sky. "Now, Alva. It's going to rain."

Tessa was still holding the girl's arm, steadying the quivering murmurs in her head.

"What do you hear?" Alva asked. A thought seemed to hook her, and for the first time, her face softened. "It's a terrible thing to not understand the world around you. To not be understood by it. To be lost." She took out the lighter and placed it in Tessa's hand. "Keep it," she said, as she pulled free and started to walk away. "And remember that I gave it to you."

✳

A Song for Wildcats

Lying back in the bathtub, Tessa sank into the comfort of her grandmother's good hand towels, still unused, and the white porcelain of the tiles, the pill-pink wallpaper. She turned her hand in the dozy sunlight falling through the open window. She looked, again, through the crack in the bathroom door, down the hall to James's empty bedroom.

She had always pretended not to remember the night at the stone quarry. Standing with Sabrina, both of them shaking and stripped nearly bare, their feet tempting the edge. *Are you scared, Tessa?* Sabrina's hand slipping into hers, squeezing it. *We'll do it together. I won't let go of you, I swear.* She had dared Tessa to jump with her, a bond of unbreakable trust. Much stronger than the blood oath of their youth. More permanently binding. *You'll be mine, and I'll be yours.* But as Tessa stared down into the mesmeric stillness of the water, she thought only of childhood nightmares, of darkness filled with vague faces, their waxy casts of anguish floating to the surface, like the murdered witches of the Iron Age released, all at once, from the airless prison of the bogs. Tessa stepped back, breathless. *You're going to get us killed — stop it, let me go.* As she jerked her hand free, Sabrina looked down at her own like it was bleeding. A shining malice rose from the depths of her pupils, and in a vicious outburst, she grabbed Tessa's arm and shoved her over the edge.

Tessa sat up in the tub, gripping the rim. She tried to blink her head clear, but nothing aired out the foggy feeling the girl had caused — if it was fair to blame her. Pharmacy bottles glinted on the windowsill. Tessa clinked her fingernail against one, its presence alone a balm for bad nerves. How soaked in barbital was her brain if she was seeing things? Now and then the flighty blue light reappeared, snagging her periphery. It drifted down the stairs or across the tablecloth, played along the tile or the wall. Tessa had tried to catch it, clapping down a mason jar, but it always swung back out the window.

The Wisp

If James were here, what would he think of this fresh unravelling?

But he was not there. Earlier, while refilling her sleep powders at the pharmacy, she had run into an old friend of James's, who explained that he had been gone for a week. "James left right after the Jacobs girl's funeral, selling dry goods to the county franchises," he said. "He was in a bad way, I think, being one of the few people who really knew her. Were you not there? At the funeral?"

The question stung with innocent accusation.

Tessa had considered attending the funeral. Deliberated it for hours. She had imagined standing at the edge, staring into an inexplicable black hole in the ground, her head filling with slippery whispers. But she had not, until now, considered how James might have needed her there with him. He had spent so many years being her and Sabrina's only other friend, ambling with them along the rocky riverbank to rescue frogs from fishermen and from the children who broke their legs. He read them grisly German folk tales, played games he had outgrown, made Sabrina the sugary pink lemonade she liked, the kind sold at the circus.

A cindery breeze swept through the window. It shivered over her shoulders and shook the pale haze of the wheat fields below. Tessa squinted against the sunset, piercing gold above the Hudson Valley maples. What had the girl meant? *There are things you couldn't possibly understand.* Spoken with an expression as serene and unflinching as a stopped clock.

Well. There were things the girl could not have understood, things Sabrina would never have shared. Though — Tessa recognized the slow twist of panic — Sabrina had never been so afraid of sharing.

The morning after the quarry — after black water had coiled like hundreds of eels around Tessa's limbs, after Sabrina dove in to fish her out and dragged her onto the dusty limestone shore, hands hysterical and voice scraped with panic — Tessa would not unlock the front door. It was only when Sabrina appeared on the porch roof, in her torn skirt, smacking the window, that Tessa relented. Sabrina had crawled through the window, cradling a record and her father's fine brandy. She hauled James's treasured record player into the bedroom and surprised Tessa with strange, slow-twanging love songs.

This was where Tessa's memory grew truly murky. As with dreams, she could only remember the midst, never the beginning. Warm, drunken breaths. Hands roaming, damp and hurried, beneath unbuttoned cotton. Sabrina's mouth burning against her ear.

Tessa stared into the bathwater. She brushed her numbed fingertips against a soap cloud. Her hair clawed down her shoulders and floated out against the white vacancy of the tub in streams so blood-rich, so red with life, they could almost stain the water pink, like a cherry thrown in with the laundry.

Had she come home to honour Sabrina or absolve herself, hear only what she wanted to hear?

Tomorrow would be Halloween, and the town would convene at the De Vries home for the annual harvest party. Hector would be there, as he always was. Certainly Alva would be with him, feeding off the weakened village like a devilish bark beetle.

She would get the girl alone, where Hector could not steal her away. She would ask whatever she needed to ask, and hear whatever she needed to hear. Did they not, both of them, owe Sabrina the threadbare decency of the truth?

The girl, with all her collected secrets. Sabrina's final confidante. Tessa had not wanted to admit that she believed Alva's claim to this role. In truth, Sabrina had stopped writing over a year ago. The ink of her last letter was as stringy and frail as the dark barbs of a feather. Her words seemed as though they might blow away before Tessa had the chance to read them.

The Wisp

✳

The harvest party was a golden, crackling affair, with children donning fantastic faces and stuffing spiced cake into their mouths. Despite the scarcity experienced by most, there were countless bowls of salted almonds and nut candies; the windowsills were decorated with elaborately carved jack-o'-lanterns, and everywhere wooden columns were wrapped in red velvet and hung with garlands of dark marigold, like burning maypoles. Soaked, happy faces bobbed for apples in the kitchen, where water splashed onto the windmills and tulips of the blue-and-white Dutch tiles.

Each year, Tessa and Sabrina had attended the party together. At sixteen, Sabrina spiked the punch and vomited in the prize rugosa roses, Tessa in the empty birdbath. As children, they dressed in starry cardboard crowns, their faces painted dolly white, with soft blue shadows under their cheeks. They hunted for their husbands' names in crabapple peels.

"Tessa will be my husband!" Sabrina once shouted. "Look, the peels say so!" She was so pleased that she did not understand the laughter circling the party, or was not bothered by it, until she saw the humiliation flaming across Tessa's face. Tessa locked herself inside a cabinet in the De Vrieses' kitchen for the rest of the evening, while the caterers pretended not to notice Sabrina sitting on the floor among the busy feet, dancing her fingertips against the cabinet door and singing quiet, sorry spells into the wood.

A boy with a ghoul-painted face stumbled into Tessa as she walked from room to room in search of Alva. Hector was playing medieval drinking games on the lawn, but the girl was not with him. Tessa ran over the journalist's instructions: *Know your questions. Don't fear persistence.* She opened the back door leading to the wrap-around porch, where women in Columbina masks were playing nine pins.

A Song for Wildcats

The half-remembered figures paused. Tessa swallowed her dread and asked if they had seen the ward. "The one who stays with Hector."

The frays in their masks and the worn patterns of their dresses were poorly hidden in the blackfly-sticky glow of the porch light. One woman, in a faded-rose mask, knelt and raised the wooden ball to her chin. Her eyes flicked up. "Aren't you Tessa Hemlock?"

The others were silent and glanced at one another.

"No — no, I'm from a paper, in the city," Tessa said, but their stares deepened with recognition. James said she had a habit of seeing old mockery in new faces, but she was sure they were looking at her strangely, their eyes filled with glassy curiosity and secret knowing, like crystal balls.

"Of course it's you — why, you look the same as ever." Another woman laughed as the pins clattered against the porch. "Where have you been hiding all these years?"

"We were such terrors to you in school," said another, reaching to remove her mask. "I've always wanted to —"

Tessa turned from them and hurried down the steps into the garden. Laughter from the house trailed after her as she wound through the wide yard and down the gravel lane, until a wispy silence fell like a snuffed flame.

If Alva had not come out with Hector, perhaps she was alone at the house. But when Tessa reached the pine-shadowed brick of the Hallamshire home and knocked on the door, nobody answered. She pressed her ear to the wood but heard no footsteps, called out and received no reply. She watched the windows. Waited for the tiny moon of Alva's face to appear, the dramatic illumination of her candle-like figure within the framed, unfettered darkness of the hall. But the darkness remained unchanged.

Tessa wandered. As she searched through the night, the roads began to belly and hum like musical saws. It was some time before

The Wisp

Tessa realized that she was standing in front of the pharmacy window, reading the products on display in mindless repetition. Lysol disinfectant. Bulgarian herb tea for influenza. Children's headache medicine with less strychnine than ever before. In the back end of the store was the cherry-flavoured soda fountain for making medicine more palatable. She had once pumped red syrup into her hand and smeared it over her face to make Sabrina think she had broken her nose.

Morning slowly blotted away the night. A car rolled by and its headlights swept across the window, Tessa's reflection flickering like a jumpy projector. When it settled, she was surprised to see it take the form of a grown woman in a shapeless yellow coat, rather than break apart into kaleidoscopic pieces of a little girl with a syrup-bloody face.

The blue light then appeared, blinking in the glass. Bright enough that she found it easily, floating by the church, when she turned around. Though it was surely nothing but a figment, she followed it to the church grounds, where it was silent except for the itchy buzz of flies. Stopping at the cemetery, Tessa wrapped her hands around the low iron rail. She did not know where in Mount Pleasant Sabrina was buried, would not let James tell her, and a pin of panic slid into her. A sharp puncture deep in her body.

Tessa's grip tightened around the iron rail. Cries came out almost tangible, as though she were ripping soaked rags from her lungs. *Where has everyone gone?* The world had emptied out. She took a long, strangled breath, and as she opened the gate, the light braided an excited ribbon of iridescence, like a blue ghost firefly. She wiped her eyes with her sleeve and followed it, rounding the corner of the church, where she found someone sitting in the centre of the toadstool ring.

The girl held her hands to the dawn, rinsing them in the clear pink light.

A Song for Wildcats

"Alva?" Tessa asked. "What are you doing?"

Alva's cheek was pulpy blue. She was barefoot, in only a cardigan with two buttons torn out and a skirt twisted all wrong around her waist. Before her lay several small, shining objects.

A light rain had started. Tessa pulled off her coat and held it out. Alva only stared, locked in some concussive dream, her eyes wide and unblinking as coins. Though she was clearly alive, Tessa found herself checking the girl's wrist for a mothy pulse.

"Did someone hurt you?" Tessa asked, examining the bruised cheek. "There must be someone we can call. Your family, where are they?"

"In the rainfall of the forest by the River Nid," Alva said.

Tessa thought the girl must be delirious. Alva looked as though she had grown out of the earth, covered in mud and grass, a twig sticking out from behind her ear like the last broken piece of dismantled antlers. She smelled of the wind on the waterfront, and honey, and new rain.

Helping her off the ground, Tessa caught the hardy gleam of Hector's ring on the girl's finger. "Why are you wearing this?"

Alva pulled her hand away. She looked about to run, but her gaze froze high over Tessa's shoulder. "Do you see it?" she asked, glancing eagerly between Tessa and the faint blue light. She smiled. "You see it, don't you?"

"Alva, why do you have Hector's ring?"

Alva's mouth hung open before words began spilling out like water. Not English, or Swedish, not any language Tessa recognized.

The objects sprawled over the grass finally registered. A small glass box, a thread of silver laced across its surface. Reverend Hallamshire's pocket watch, known to glint from its chain when he was not in his evergreen vestments. And between them, blinking at her with its cloudy green eye, the stolen jade pin Sabrina had sworn she returned. Their blood-oath pin, that broken cardinal promise.

148

The Wisp

The girl no longer needed to answer Tessa's questions. A soldering knowledge formed between them.

From each object in the grass rose a high, yearning sound as Alva dipped her fingertips against it. Her words lost shape, and yet somehow became clearer. *Home, home, home.* The compulsion to speak along with her was like a fetal hunger. When Alva looked at Tessa now, Tessa saw what she saw. A tunnel of soft grey lichen hanging from white pillars of trees and a sky of frozen lavender, binding two opposite seasons of time. Where Tessa stood, she felt the loose, rolling stream of minutes, while Alva drifted farther into a timeless place, where hours froze and hardened into wintered rivers, eternally preserved.

Alva reached out, drawing Tessa's hand to meet her own. *Come with me, come away.* Her voice obscured her mouth, like a mirage grafted to her face.

As their fingers touched, the blue light blinked wildly. Tessa could no longer see Alva, only the chilled place, the peaceful ice and untouched bark. Closing her eyes to it was like casting a net over static, but the relentless blue light only grew brighter, until it forced Tessa's eyes shut, bursting with the shrieking luminosity of a dying star.

The air fell dead. When Tessa opened her eyes, the girl and the little light were gone. As were the toadstools and stolen treasures. A cold curl of breath hung above the now empty spot in the grass before melting away in the breeze.

✳

The sun ripened and mounted the clouds as Tessa drifted on the wrong side of the curb.

"Miss Hemlock?" a man called.

Tessa stopped in front of Janssen's Hardware. The sound of her name struck the small of her back like a stone.

A Song for Wildcats

"Miss Hemlock, is that you?" the man continued. "It's Hessel Van Wyck."

She turned, cautiously, and found Mr. and Mrs. Van Wyck standing by their spoiled-cream car.

"We heard the news just now," Mr. Van Wyck said. He looked away, eyeing passing cars as if trying to recognize the drivers. "Awful sorry, Miss Hemlock, you have our condolences."

"Did you know Sabrina?" Tessa asked.

"Oh, dear," he said. "Saw you walking around so early like this and figured you knew." The hardened grey wax of his mouth flattened. "You know my brother, you know he works for the Rockefeller preserve, and he was out away by the bridge —"

"Hessel." Mrs. Van Wyck shifted a paper bag clutched in the crook of her arm. "This is hardly the place."

"Someone ought to tell her," he said.

Tessa's heart prickled. "Tell me what?"

"Someone was found. I'm sorry, dear. I'm afraid you knew him." The whites of Mrs. Van Wyck's eyes had a vinegary polish that matched her teeth. "You were sweethearts once, weren't you?"

Earlier that morning, according to the Van Wycks, Hector had been found with a cracked forehead on the forest-nestled bank of the Pocantico River. One of the groundskeepers, the younger brother of Mr. Van Wyck, came upon him lying among the fallen leaves and water-run rocks, the purple sheen of his scarf spotted out of reach, running over the edge of the stone bridge.

"So much terrible news these days. Someone's disturbed a spirit, you'd think." Mr. Van Wyck scratched the lacy pink rash on his cheek. "We know how much you meant to one another. Hector always said so."

Tessa recalled the gold flash of Hector's ring. "That girl," she managed to say, her knees guttering like candle wax. "The one who helped at your farm, who called your cows home for you."

150

The Wisp

An anchor was coming loose in her, with an onrush of roaring current. The Van Wycks mirrored her bewilderment.

"The mountain song," she stammered. "Alva, the Swedish girl."

Mrs. Van Wyck cast a glance at her husband. "We shut the farm down. We're just coming in from my sister's, up in Newark. Dear, are you quite all right?"

Their stares, fanged with pity, stalked her as she staggered down the road.

Little Tessa Hemlock. "Shut up," she said, holding her temples. *Mad and locked away.* "Stop it. *Please.*"

She was not mad. Was she? Hector had seen the girl too. But had her mind run loose, taken what was real and warped it into fantasy?

Tessa paced in a tight circle. Blew on her hands, marbled with chill. Dug them deep into her coat pockets, where she struck something cold and unfamiliar. Alva's lighter, glinting in her palm. She squeezed it and a pulse reverberated through her fingers, as though its ornamental fish had slipped from their gold binds, a gliding shoal now stirring her blood. She nearly dropped it. If her memory of the girl was misting with doubt, the sensation electrifying her hand was indisputable.

She had not imagined the girl vanishing, or the cold escape the girl had offered to her. She could trust — in this instance, and perhaps beyond it — her mind, her memories.

Tessa had the briefest notion: report a variant of the truth, that a murderous thief was slipping through towns in Westchester. Only, of course, to tell of this would be useless. The girl had gotten what she wanted, and Tessa knew that she would not see her again.

＊

In the years that followed, Alva's glass lighter would occasionally hum like the air between telephone rings. At night, or smoky twilight, it would compel Tessa from her bed, to the dresser, where she kept it hidden beneath papers and spools and magnifying glasses. She would pick it up and hold it to her ear, never sure what she was waiting for, what she could possibly hope to hear. She knew only that the firmness of its vibration kept the whispers at bay, and made the walls seem more solid, the sky more open.

Though the grief continued, absorbed into the low throb that had shadowed her heartbeat for so long, she often forgot it was there. Its familiarity somehow did not simplify it, and Sabrina's absence would hover beyond the realm of understanding. Tessa could not, would never, grab hold of it nor pin it down, any more than she could a flicker of light.

And for Hector, his death would be laid to rest as the tragic consequence of drunken revelry, a home-brewed morality tale. Children would dare one another to race to the edge of the riverbank and touch the rocks where the body had been found, though time lost track of the precise spot. And though the townspeople would spin their theories, and the children would teach one another their songs, it remained impossible to say why Hector had gone roaming alone that night. What might have drawn him away from his well-known course home, or compelled him to tread so carelessly along the rock-speared cascades.

*

Sabrina looked at her under the hot compress of the sky. Her ratty sweater was thrown over her nightgown, and her eyes were swollen and damp. She stood on the farmhouse steps with such bursting presence, Tessa knew she had run over with the intention of deciding what to say once she arrived, and now did not know where to start. It was nearly eighty degrees that day, the morning Tessa left home. They were eighteen and did not realize it was the last

The Wisp

time they would see each other. Sabrina itched at the wool sweater, swatted at the sweaty hair stuck to her neck. Panting hard over the suitcase between them.

That morning, all those years ago, felt close enough to step back inside. It was as if time had skipped directly from then to now, everything in between gutted out.

But time had filled the gap between her and Sabrina. Soon, most of Sabrina would disappear. What would be left of her? What carried on?

I wonder how long it would take me to become a tulip, Sabrina once said, comforted by how the body crumbles into the earth and feeds the flowers. Perhaps not realizing — Tessa thought — that *Sabrina*, as she understood herself, would probably not continue to exist. That her consciousness would not reside within the flowers her body fed, any more than in the hair shed onto her pillow, or the sweat spoiling her underclothes, or the memories of her that Tessa thumbed into the blue silk ribbon.

*

Feet moving in unconscious strides, Tessa wound her way home. The air was clean and rain soaked, and the farmhouse came into view across the tall grass fainting in the wind. It was so small that the entirety of her childhood could fit on the tip of her finger.

She breathed out, deep and tired. She would have made it right with Sabrina, one day, if that mattered at all.

As she walked the old cow path, round the field to the porch, she remembered what James had once told her. She had stumbled up the steps with a bloody foot, crying over what Sabrina had said at the pond, the moral code of wisps. James looked down at her with his hands on his hips, already as tall as their father. "Do you know what Ma told me when I was your age?" He knelt and pointed through the open back door to the garden, where their mother used to watch them hunt for fairy colonies. "She said even if I found a fairy creature, not to trust them. They're mischievous, apparently, and a little chaotic. Sweet if they're pleased with you, dangerous if they're not." He took the dishrag he had carried from the kitchen and wrapped it around her foot. "They have no moral judgment, and even if they did, who's got a better heart than you?"

Tessa was so steeped in the memory that for a moment she thought it had tumbled out of its proper sequence in time and landed right in front of her. There was James, on the porch. His jasper-red Ford was parked by the side of the house, the smooth indent of this habit fatally branding the grass.

"Kid," he called, rising from the bench. Musty maroon jacket and green-gold eyes. His hair, a dusty auburn like the dark side of a peach.

A rushing thaw of relief overtook her as she climbed the porch steps. "You came home," she said, nearly breathless.

"I could say the same to you." He held out an arm to scoop her against his side, where instantly she felt the vulnerable armour of his ribs. He smelled coppery, with discomforting notes of cologne, the one for important occasions.

"Long night?" she asked.

James looked at the car. Samples of Hemlock Brand dry goods and jarred fruit were stacked in the back seat. He scratched the side of his chin. "Long drive."

Tessa brushed cottonwood fleece from his jacket as it blew onto the porch. The tree, planted long before the house was built, exploded with feathery seeds through spring and summer. But unlike other poplars, the final traces of this strange, palpable mist continued shedding and shivering across their yard, until the frostbitten edges of fall.

The Wisp

Opening the front door, James paused and looked curiously back at the yard. Though the Hudson Valley maples bore their fiery autumn leaves, small spring-blue wildflowers bewitched the grass surrounding the house.

"I feel like she's here," Tessa said. "Sabrina."

James looked at her. "I've been worried about you."

Hand in her pocket, Tessa touched the lighter. Again, she felt its strange vibration — milder now, calming. She looked up at her brother with his warm, worried eyes, and at the family farmhouse that she was not so sure they could afford to keep, and she breathed in the old comfort and constancy of home. "I'm all right, James," she said. "We'll be all right."

A family of sparrows stabbed their flinty beaks at the oats thrown over the porch. Tessa shook out a little more from the jar that James had set out, and he grabbed his hat from the bench. Wisps of cottonwood seeds blew around their ankles, catching playfully on Tessa's skirt. She plucked one, thumbing it gently before tucking it into her pocket with the lighter, as she and her brother entered the house and left the door open behind them.

The Lyrebird's Bell

I.

LANGUAGE OF NEPTUNE

The woman lay tucked beneath a silvery spray of grass-tree. We were far enough into the forest and too worn to drag her any farther. There were trees enough to shield her from the sun; not much to be done about the snakes, of course — they would do with her as they pleased. The Australian bush was lush with mossy eucalyptus trees and loquat — not like the outback, which outsiders always expected: a dry, ruddy, cindery flatland.

I stepped back from the body, listened for the twig-crackle of footsteps. I heard only my own breaths, my frantic heartbeat, Annabelle's peculiar whispers to herself. She had told me she would not take a rock to her mother's head. She would not be vulgar. It would be done cleanly, befitting her mother's austere taste, though I had not seen how that was possible. Poison went down cleanly enough but made a frothing mess when it came back up.

A Song for Wildcats

The sky was deliriously blue, and mint and honey livened the air. I was surprised at the freshness of her mother's body. As much as I was able, given the circumstances, I had prepared my nerves for a sickening wave of foul odor. But Annabelle must have washed her in that strange, time-dripping hour she had me wait between the chipped-stone columns of her entryway while she and her mother were alone.

Sweat chilled my scalp and keen shivers ran up my arms. I could not take my eyes off Mrs. Chernova's hair. It floated about her head, tangled with insects and leaves and powdered pink with forest dust. Annabelle and I were only children, unable to carry her properly, and her finely pinned curls had been tugged out of place from us hauling her all the way from her parlour to the old snow gums where we now stood.

"Betsy? Do you think this spot is all right?" Annabelle was deeply flushed as she wiped her brow. The March heat gave her the mottled look of a pink ling fish, causing rosy, swollen patches beneath her freckles. She looked stunned as she stared at her mother. "She'll be safe here?"

I thought she could not be serious. After everything, did she still not understand what had been done?

"Nobody ever comes this far out." I swallowed, bile burning my throat. "She won't be bothered."

But I was not so sure. The breeze had been dead all morning, and the trees were so still it felt deliberate. Each one posed as stiff yet fluid as an ancient Greek sculpture, waiting to disorient us, to creep and twist behind our backs. My stomach continued the long, miserable drop that had begun the previous month.

Annabelle picked a beetle from her mother's knotted hair and set it carefully on the grass. She neatened her mother's dress, with its buttons like little glass bulbs of lemonade, swatted the dust from the scalloped collar, and tipped the black Wedgwood brooch in

The Lyrebird's Bell

place. Mrs. Chernova was white enough now to pass for stone, her dress the rich green of the wild. All we had to do was walk away and let the forest have her.

✳

My name is Elizabeth, though back then everyone called me Betsy — which I loathed, as nicknames tend to go. If we were going to reduce ourselves to nicknames at all, I was at the very least a *Liza*, like the genus of mullets from ancient Rome, or a *Beth*, like the poor March sister with scarlet fever. My mother had tossed the peachy *Betsy* across the room rather suddenly, years before, and it stuck to me like a rumour.

The first time we met, Annabelle agreed that it did not suit me. *It's far too darling a name for you.* She read my prickly temperament, my wily black hair and stern blue eyes. *You look like the Queen of the Crows.*

Our houses were the bones of Regency decadence, stout villas grown ashy with age. They had originally been built for two sisters exiled by scandal, long dead and buried under the red flowering gum. Annabelle had not lived here long — she and her mother had arrived a couple of years earlier, shortly after the war, in early '46, while I had never been outside Victoria. During the warmer months, I had an instructor who drove in from one of the little towns in the Shire of Macedon Ranges. Most recently, an uncompromising young woman of whom I drew, and burned, many lurid portraits. But I had not seen her in some time.

In the colder months, I had grown accustomed to seeing no one. I played alone on mossy stones and tangles of woody vines, and stared into the towering rock formations, which rose like a gravestone cavalcade along the Hanging Rock volcano.

A Song for Wildcats

Until, unannounced, Annabelle appeared. She strode up to me, holding a bouquet of dirty snapdragons, as naturally as though she had sprouted from the soil. A sheer blue kerchief was knotted around her neck, and a frothy underskirt lapped at her calves. She smiled with a slight, inviting overbite and handed me a snapdragon. With her warm gold hair, I thought she looked like sunlight glinting on the sea.

✳

One afternoon in February, Annabelle and I were studying among the wildflowers and silver-boned trees of her garden. I had taken up a disciplined home-schooling schedule. If she could be bribed with cheap candy bars, Annabelle would join and let me instruct her. Today was my Botanical Arts and Sciences class. It covered everything from floriography — particularly the daintily coded *language of flowers* once popular in my father's native London — to the morphology of sea spinach.

"They look innocent as anything," Annabelle said. She was reading a book on identifying toxic plants. Pulling up her knees, she rested the book on her lap. "Look at this one."

"*If ingested,*" I read, "*one could suffer slowed heart rate, fever, and death.*" I leaned over and took a bite out of her candy bar. "That's good to know."

She slumped against my shoulder. "Read the book to me like a story."

The air was itchy with mayflies, the breeze dirty with heat. I wrapped an arm around her. "Hydathodes," I began, sun sleepy as I trailed my finger down the index. "That can be the hero. Nectaries can be the nymph he murders —"

From the forest came the sudden ringing of a bell. We both straightened.

The Lyrebird's Bell

"Is there a bell tower nearby?" Annabelle asked.

"There's nothing nearby," I said.

We each tilted an ear toward the sky to catch the sound.

"Maybe a lyrebird being mischievous," Annabelle said.

I made a faint sound of agreement but continued listening. Nothing was only mischief in the bush. The closest townships lived as neighbours to the old-growth trees, and the wind carried both a primal, mystifying pulse and the sleepy hysteria found in any small community.

I looked up at the hazy light breaking through the leaves. The toll of the bell drifted over us, an adornment of passing time like a windblown pall. Such a cast-iron sound was misplaced out here in the true wild bush, more remote even than the local ghost towns and suffering goldfields.

"It's a dead bell warding off evil spirits," I said, running my fingertips up Annabelle's spine to make her jump. "There must be something wicked lurking in the woods."

She shivered, then laughed. "I almost believe you, this place is so odd. Did you know there are orchids here that grow only after a fire? They wait until everything else is dead and the smoke calls them out of the earth."

I pictured the smoke that covers graveyards in Bela Lugosi films.

"You're an orchid," I said, "whiling away until I come calling."

"I was born under the sign of the fish, so I'd be a water lily. My *babulya* told me so. She said I speak the language of Neptune and intuition."

Annabelle read the stars like tea leaves, charting her fortune with a tarot deck. She always asked to read mine; I told her no, it was pseudo-science, but that was not the reason. In truth, pseudo-science or not, I resented the unsolvable nature of its mystery, as though some beautiful, loving, empyrean secret meant to shove me away and leave me clawing at darkness in the scrubby bush that I had never left in all my life.

161

A Song for Wildcats

As she looked me over, I savoured the sugary tingle of her eyes on me. "I'm not sure what language you speak," she said.

One of smoky whispers. The cold breath carrying a wolf howl to the moon.

I said nothing and she groaned, grabbing my face in both hands. "One of these days I'm going to peel open your brain like a tangerine."

I poked her side, all in fun, and it was then that I felt her ribs. Her expression snapped and she stood, fretting clumsily with her dress and muttering at me not to play so rough.

"Why are you getting so thin?" I asked.

"Don't ask rude questions, Betsy," she said. "You're the one whose mother keeps forgetting to feed her."

I hitched up my shorts. They had faded from plum purple to minty violet and seemed to get bigger the older I grew. "Well, your mother's supposed to be home-schooling you, but you can't do basic maths."

"Maybe your mother will take a trip to the Americas and get sucked into the Bermuda Triangle," she said.

"Maybe your mother will spontaneously combust in her bed, and an orchid will grow out of the silhouette burned into the sheets."

She brushed a crumb of chocolate from her lip. "I can only hope."

We resumed our studies, but I could not help worrying. Was Annabelle not eating? I had heard of girls on diets, but we were only twelve. And besides, for whom would she be dieting? We had no playmates, hardly any family. My mother was always off in Melbourne, at some urban villa retreat or slenderizing salon, and my father was long gone. As far as I could tell, other than Annabelle's mother, we were all alone.

*

162

The Lyrebird's Bell

"You know how Betsy isn't your real name?" Annabelle asked the following day. She looked away and started twisting a loose button on her cardigan.

We were playing chess on the floor of her shady pavilion, using a folding chessboard my father had given me. Now and then, the breeze blew in whirling seed pods to catch in our clothes and skinny mozzies to suck our blood. It carried the scent of the fragrant camellias rounding the pavilion, which Annabelle had planted and meticulously groomed.

"You're mixing up the pieces," I said. I had hardly registered the shift in Annabelle's tone. We were using tin redcoat soldiers and *matryoshka* dolls painted like Easter eggs to replace the missing chess pieces. I was preoccupied with rearranging a doll the size of a kidney bean and a soldier brandishing a broken gun. "And Betsy's a version of my name, I guess."

"No, but I mean how it's a nickname. A variation." She paused, snagged by a thought. Then it all rushed out. "Annabelle Beaudrie isn't my real name either. My mother makes me say it is."

"Come off it." I could not tell if she was serious. "What do you mean it isn't your real name?"

She spun the button until it broke off. "The whole time we travelled, my mother said we were from Bordeaux. I wasn't allowed to speak. My last name is Chernova. But now I've told you, so you're not allowed to be angry that I lied."

I took the discarded button and placed it on the chessboard with the other mismatched pieces. "So you're *not* Annabelle?"

She put her finger to her lips. "Not so loud. My mother said she'd lock me in the cellar for twenty years if I ever told anyone."

"How would she know?" I widened my eyes in a spooked pantomime. "Is she *spying* on us?"

I waited for her to laugh, but she did not. Her gaze tunnelled down the path from the pavilion, between long, ruffled rows of chrysanthemums. It landed on one of the many shadowed windows of her house. There her mother stood between the shutters, watching us in a paisley dress and pearls.

It was true that Annabelle's origins were cosmopolitan and hard to distinguish. Along with its mild Soviet inflections, her accent was dappled with years of British schooling and summers in rural France. It had never occurred to me that she was anyone other than exactly who she claimed to be.

"Everything is different now. It all went away so quickly. You won't go away, though, will you?"

She was still looking toward her mother, so I crawled into their knotted line of vision.

"Last night I dreamed I stitched our souls together," I said, taking her hand. "And whatever happens to souls in dreams must be as true as what happens to our bodies when we're awake."

✳

At first, I teased Annabelle about her supposed real name, but soon it began to torment me — in a wormy, petty way — that she would withhold it from me, when I had been upfront about the whole *Betsy* mess. In its secrecy, her name writhed in my thoughts, pulsed on the tip of my tongue. I believed friendship to be a biological force. Primordial, burrowed into the bone. I knew it as I knew how to breathe that true friends told each other everything.

For days, I hammered away at Annabelle's secret, determined to crack it open. I guessed a hundred names to no avail. Daphne, for her wavelets of blond hair. Cecilia, for the butterscotch freckles over her nose and her cloudy green eyes. Loretta, for her fat strawberry mouth.

"What about Alice?" I asked. "You look like an Alice. Or something more Slavic than Annabelle. *Anastasia.*"

The Lyrebird's Bell

We were hiking toward the rippling green of Mount Macedon. Annabelle disliked venturing beyond the perimeter of what she called *our field*, stretched between our houses, and it was with reluctance that she let me guide her to my favourite haunts throughout the highlands.

She dug a finger under her training-bra strap, where a sore, red stripe had burned into her shoulder. "That's not how names work. You should know, *Betsy-bits*. It doesn't matter, anyhow."

"Doesn't matter? Don't you care what people call you?" I looked up from the grass, just off the dirt road, where I had stopped to inspect small, broken pieces of a folksy cornflower plate, perhaps lost on a picnic a hundred years back. "Shouldn't they know who you really are?"

She slapped the dust from her skirt. In her dirtied gingham, with her shiny rag-curled hair, she looked like a finely crafted doll that had been kicked around outside. "The old life is gone," she said. "I don't even remember my mother's eye colour."

"They're probably green like yours," I said.

"No, they've darkened over the years."

"Is that possible?" I held still as she brushed at the grass sticking to the back of my shorts. "I once read about a woman with a carved-gold eye, and ancients wearing painted clay over their sockets. Would you stop fussing? You're getting flustered."

Annabelle plunked herself onto the ground. She tore off a sleek white sandal to examine her blistered foot. Words fluttered inside her mouth, and I sensed the change in her breath. "That woman is *not* my mother. I just get used to her sometimes."

"Are you a changeling?" I sat down and slid onto my stomach in the warm grass, propping myself on my elbows. "Did fairies steal away with the real Annabelle?"

Her body stiffened. She drew closer to me and whispered, "*She's a spirit.*"

A Song for Wildcats

I gave her a hard look.

"You think you know so much?" she said.

I could hear my mother in Annabelle's tone, scolding me for being a derisive little know-it-all. Casting a dark cloud over my personality by saying I sounded just like my father.

"I know you need proper footwear, or you're going to be bitten by a snake one of these days. A poisonous one." I gave her calf a light pinch. "A pink-bellied, dog-fanged common death adder."

"I'm being serious, Betsy. She's a *likhoradka*. They're dangerous spirits who possess your body and fill you with sickness."

"Why are you so bleak today?" I asked.

"Why are you so difficult?" There was a reediness in her voice, like a dog's whimper. "I'm not making it up. I read everything in our library during the blockade, every book we had, trying to figure out what had changed her."

"Changed her from what?"

"From how she was before." Annabelle touched her ear, rounding it as if to tuck her hair away, though it was tied back with a ribbon. "Not sweet — but gentle."

I realized then that I had no solid impression of Mrs. Chernova. I saw her only in windows, gripping her cane and watching us like a lonely wraith.

"Maybe she's a Shivering Sheila," I said.

"What's that?" Annabelle asked.

I conjured an imaginary creature from memories of my mother, still as a corpse in her beach chair, beautifying and buried under glittering slices of cold grapefruit.

"Shivering Sheilas are spirits who haunt the creeks and rivers and billabongs they drowned in," I explained. "They come up out of the water, silvery like the Lady of the Lake, but they've been away from their bodies for too long, and it's made them wild, and when you look into their eyes, it's like stepping into a tomb, and when they speak,

The Lyrebird's Bell

it's like the click of a door locking behind you. And they're cold and wet and shivering all over, and *they try to drag you in by the ankle.*"

I snatched her ankle and she started.

"You're just making that up to scare me," she said, shaking her leg.

I raised my palms in acquiescence. "All right, fine — but if that's not really your mother, where did your mother go?"

"Starved to death, if you must know." Her voice was hot. "She was trying to save all the artwork in the Hermitage. Every day she sneaked the paintings off the walls while living in the museum cellars with Rubens and Raphael and all our favourites, eating nothing but crumbs and binding glue. And the spirit found her starved and took over her body."

Starvation, at least, did seem plausible. She had suffered the siege in Leningrad, and during the war, rations were ubiquitous the world over. Until my father took us in, my mother and I had lived in a boarding house in Woodend, where we ate rations and dandelion soup and cold, gummy peas on toast.

"But how could she carry everything all by herself?" I asked. "All those huge paintings and sculptures."

Annabelle threw me a moody squint. "Well … there were other people living there," she said. "Everybody coughing into the same dank space."

We were quiet for some time. It had to be a game, but even so, it frightened me, the possibility that she might be someone I did not recognize.

Evening fell over the surrounding fields, and the flittering chirps of magpies filled the trees. Annabelle looked across the waves of blue grass into the great eucalypt forest with such fixation that I grew anxious for her to speak.

"Betsy?" she said at last. "Do you really want to know what happened?"

I leaned in close, unblinking. "I want to know everything, always."

167

The spot of sun behind her, lowered to just above the trees beyond the field, lit her hair an icy gold. "My father was in the bathtub," she said. "He was singing something. I remember thinking how funny the song was, but I can't remember it now. And then there was this sound, like the world had blacked out. Everything froze, and the air tightened all around me like it wouldn't let me move."

"What sound?" I asked. She hesitated. I grabbed her elbow, shook it. "Annie, what did you hear?"

"I didn't know it came from inside," she said. "Not until later. Or maybe I did, but I didn't want to. There were a lot of gunshots back then, in the streets. How could I have known?"

"Someone shot him?" I asked.

Annabelle nodded. "He'd cracked my mother's face against the hutch the night before," she said, touching her mouth. "Chipped her tooth."

I did not know what to make of this. Another fabrication, perhaps, though I felt the chill in the air deepen.

"Was it your mother?" I asked. "Did she get in trouble?"

Annabelle sighed. "No — no, not really. Everyone knew how Papa treated her. And the siege had come by then." She spoke with a weathered resignation I had never heard in her before. "He was in the tub for a week before someone came to pull him out. I didn't know until after. Mama said she never left his side."

It was an appalling thought. What might happen to a mind left alone like that to stew in its own shock? Mrs. Chernova would have watched the body grow pulpy and pale in front of her, the stench of it mixing with the pink, soapy water.

"Bad spirits sneak into the hearts of wicked people," Annabelle said. "They use them as vessels to spread whispers of hell."

"But your mother was good," I said.

"A *likhoradka* mistook my mother's heart for wicked and flew into her. It must have seen her shoot Papa without knowing about

The Lyrebird's Bell

the chipped tooth." She spoke over the wind as it blew a husky dirge through the grass. "That's when she turned mean, drinking and always muttering how everyone we knew had failed us. How she hoped the fascists washed the city clean of all of them. That's why we had to run after the war ended. Because of her sympathizing."

Sympathizing. I figured this meant her mother had aided the Nazis, but it had been several years since the name hissed its way through the bush, and I did not want to be the one to bring it back.

Annabelle looked at me with an oddly tender intensity. A little breath jumped ahead of her, and she caught it. "Anita," she said. "So you can still call me Annie. She let me keep that."

I had not let go of her arm, as if simply holding her would prevent any distance growing between us.

"Were your mother and father ever cruel to you?" she asked.

"My father could be." I ran my thumb down the side of my hand, where the skin was smooth as plastic. "Once, he found my drawings of my instructor Isabelle, the Gisborne lady I told you about. He held my hand over a candle flame until it bubbled. The skin's all hard now. See? You can stick pins in and I won't feel it. I'm like a poppet doll."

We found ourselves laughing at this. I did not ask her any more questions, or show doubt in her story, whether I believed it or not. If my family had been so brutal, and I had lived such a sorry life, I would spin a story like straw into gold.

II.

A PROMISE

Annabelle and I were plucking witch hazel in her garden, collecting the scraggly yellow petals into a tea kettle. With our thirteenth

A Song for Wildcats

birthdays approaching, we were making home-brewed facial tonics for the bad skin she warned would soon befall us.

She had already washed her empty perfume bottles to hold these imagined tinctures. I thought to invite her to explore the flowers on my own property, but while her garden was violets and yellow roses, and sweet pink wildflowers coated in a haze of pollen, mine was filled with bat orchid and stormy smoke bush, and grew wild with neglect.

Lately she had seemed like two different people. The Annabelle I knew, and then this Anita, a pesky shadow inching its way between us. We had not discussed the *likhoradka* incident. I wanted to keep it that way, let it fade as a passing game I had not fully understood, but my own note of it as an *incident*, such a tiptoeing word, was evidence enough that something was wrong.

Annabelle busied herself with the shrubs while I drank Coca-Cola and read my mother's latest issue of *The Australian Women's Weekly*.

"Is that one of your mother's magazines?" she asked. "Are they profiling another poet?"

I nodded, but really I was poring over pictures of glamorous silhouettes. Women wearing dresses with sharp shoulders and cinched waists. Nothing had really filled in for me yet, figure wise, but I worried what would happen when it did. Whether I would resemble my mother in appearance alone, or perhaps take after her in more troubling ways. All the women in the magazine looked like her, even when they did not. They posed smiling and alone in kitchens, stood aimlessly on empty beachfronts, while the words *husband* and *wife* sat crabbed in the corner text like stubborn weeds, or hovered above their shoulders like flies.

I glanced up at Annabelle. "Look at you, so focused."

"I can concentrate when I want to," she said, nimbly picking the gangly shrub. "It helps when you're not trying to teach me maths."

The Lyrebird's Bell

Everything felt nearly right again, if I did not let my worry linger. She smelled of sweat, and I had a thrilling urge to press my hand, cold from the soda bottle, against her skin. Graze the hair coiling a damp, rusty blond against her temple.

"You have so many freckles," I said. It was my way of telling her that I loved the faint freckles on her nose. I was in the sort of mood that crept up on me, where I felt fizzy-brained around her. I wanted to ask her doting, weightless questions just to hear her answer, see her mouth shape itself around the words.

"You always smell like the forest," she said. "And you have sneaky eyes like that American actress." She lowered her voice to mimic Bacall's sultry playfulness in a movie we had watched, and told me to whistle for her.

A pressure beat against my lips. Pulsing yet empty, like hunger. I had felt it before, and in my daydreams it led to me giving her the lightest kiss, and her mouth melting, sticky and pink as candy, into mine.

Sweat greyed the armpits of my blouse. I pressed my arms to my sides so that Annabelle would not notice. She looked at me and sighed, pulling a twig from my hair, which earlier she had exhausted herself constraining in a long, neat braid. "Back home there's a saying about girls with unkempt hair. You're not even trying to keep it tidy."

"What's the saying?" I asked.

"I'm not telling you," she said. "It involves dangerous mermaids, and you'd enjoy it too much."

Dreamy from the sun, I began playing with the torn flowers in the kettle. I closed my eyes and imagined I was a witch three hundred years ago, surrounded by forbidden spices and herbs.

"Let's make potions with the flowers," I said. "Like Morgana. Something to protect us against evil."

Annabelle stared at me, alarmed. "What do you mean by that?"

"She's a sorceress from the Arthur legends," I said.

"No, about the potions."

"I didn't mean anything by it."

Her eyes wandered. She rested her arm on the empty flowerpot next to her and ran her fingers through the tiny dead leaves floating on old rainwater, warping her reflection. "If I show you something, you can't tell."

"Show me what?" Unease trickled into my stomach. Annabelle took my hand and tried to pull me up, but I drew back. "It's too hot. Let's just stay here."

"There's something else I haven't told you," she said. "Nobody knows about it. You're the only person I'd ever show."

For a moment, I did not move. My arm was extended, my hand in hers. I wanted to ease her back down onto the grass with me, the warm solidity of the ground, but she looked at me so imploringly that my voice evaporated. I let her lead me through the garden to a scuffed-up pantry door, hidden behind the leafy vines covering the side of her house.

"Annie, what are we doing?" I asked.

Without answering, she opened the door onto the pungent smells of souring apples and overflowing rhubarb stalks. Beyond the pantry, fruit flies speckled the kitchen ceiling and crawled over sticky spoons and fork tines clogged with food. We crossed into a narrow hall, and then a lounge room bright and busy with silver leaf and billowy valance. The couch was dimpled blue velvet, and sunlight swam through a glass chandelier, dappling the walls.

"Wait here, I'll be back in a minute," Annabelle said, hushing me when I argued. "I mean it, stay put."

She hurried from the room and up the staircase. Soon I heard her fretful footsteps through the ceiling.

I folded my arms and dropped into one of several finely embroidered chairs. I knocked the opulent wood of the armrest. In

The Lyrebird's Bell

my house, the fabric was frayed and snowed upon with dust, so that most rooms sat in a state of perennial winter. But people lived in Annabelle's house. She and her mother, however unpleasantly, shuffled about together, day to day. Ate together, talked with one another, breathed the same air. How could she have forgotten her mother's eye colour when their lives shared such close quarters?

Two years had passed since I last saw my father, yet I remembered everything about him. The pressurized prowl as he moved behind me, the click and peel of his shoes on the floor. His right hand, heavy as marble, hanging at his side and keeping order like a metronome.

I began fidgeting, restless for Annabelle to come back downstairs. Cigarettes littered the carpet under the tea table. From where I sat, I noticed a shattered ashtray lying below a dent in the wall. Annabelle had left her tarot cards on the table, and I looked at them to see what she had drawn. The devil card lay face up, goat-legged with broad, domineering horns. Something in his commanding posture taunted me — or perhaps was taunting Annabelle — to churn the unguarded idle hours into mischief and bad deeds.

I turned the card over and pushed away from the table.

Yelling and stumbling broke out overhead. I shot toward the stairs, but Annabelle was already spiralling down. She was clutching a spice tin to her chest and grabbed me so fiercely as she passed that I nearly tripped and fell.

Outside again, we ran all the way to the weeping cherry tree at the farthest edge of her garden. She clung to me until her panting wheeled into laughter.

"What's so funny?" I asked. "I thought we were in real trouble."

"Mama was angry that my noise woke her up," she said, shaking the spice tin up to her ear, "but she was angry about the wrong thing. Look."

A Song for Wildcats

She opened the small box. Inside were hard, browned discs, like dried mushroom caps.

I leaned over the tin and sniffed. "What are they?"

"Seeds from strychnine fruit," she said.

"Strychnine," I said, skeptically. "Where on earth did you find a strychnine tree?"

"In the northern parts, on our way to Victoria after we docked. One of the other lodgers warned me not to touch any of the poison trees, not even the bark. He said it would make me writhe around like a demon had got me."

I swallowed a sour knot of resentment at her having kept this from me all this time, but beneath it a bigger knot was tightening. "This isn't funny. Why would you take this with you?"

"For protection," she said. "Mama's always told me we aren't safe."

"But you're safe here," I said.

"Not from everyone."

"The seeds aren't to actually use," I said, in disbelief. "Not really."

"Elizabeth. Of course to use."

Syllables tried to leave my mouth but kept stopping before I formed a proper word.

"You're not being serious," I finally managed.

"Do you want a protection potion or not?"

"Who are you protecting?"

"Everyone," she said. "My mother from the bad spirit. You. Me."

I stared at her. "Have you gone completely mad?"

Annabelle's face fell. Then her eyes tightened. "Never mind. I can do it myself."

The tin snapped shut and she tucked it into her pocket. I reached for her, but she turned away, readjusting the ribbon holding back her hair. In lifting her arms, the frilled sleeves of her blouse slid

The Lyrebird's Bell

back, exposing a large bruise on her shoulder. It looked fresh, almost cloven, like a hoof had kicked her in the arm.

"Annie ..." The cherry tree's long tresses brushed my legs as I tried to think of what to say.

Her frame softened as she turned to face me again. She drew close, her fingertips grazing mine. "Swear you won't tell on me."

My guilt was sticky in my stomach. I had the queasy feeling that I really ought to tell someone, an adult, but it terrified me that she might never share with me again. Nobody had ever trusted me with something as precious as a secret.

"I swear I won't tell," I said.

Annabelle wrapped her arm around my waist and squeezed me close to her, leaving the warm stamp of her breath on my neck.

III.

ONLY THE RIVER ON THE WAY

"Does it hurt?" I asked, examining the bridge of Annabelle's nose.

"A little when I sniff." She looked disappointed and muttered a foreign expletive under her breath. "I didn't hear a crunch. Do you think it will still bruise?"

"We should call for a doctor," I said.

"I'm not allowed to call doctors. I told you, nobody knows we're here."

"But you might be really hurt."

"No doctors," she said firmly. "No matter how ill. Even if I break all my fingers and both my legs. That's the rule."

Moments ago, before tramping into my room, Annabelle had stood yelling at my window from the grass. One hand was clapped over her face, blood rolling down her chin and spattering her blouse. "I hit myself with a dictionary," she said plainly, breezing past me as

I opened the front door. When I did not follow, she paused on the stairs. She kept her back to me, feigning interest in the tapestry on the wall. "If I tell my mother she did it when she was drunk, she'll behave for a while."

She hopped onto my bed now, scattering the pieces of my father's rosewood chess set. The tea towel I had brought her was pressed to her nose. "You are the funny bird, *milaya*. Do you really play against yourself?"

"I'm playing against my father," I said.

"Isn't he dead or in London?"

"I assume so." The chessboard was all disordered. I settled it on the floor and steadied the pieces on their correct squares. With my finger hovering over the board, I traced my queen's eventual path to victory. "I know how he plays, though," I said. "Ezra cares too much about traps. It means he's predictable if you're prepared to be surprised. He's not scary at all if you think about it like that."

Annabelle made a muffled sound and nodded. She lowered the tea towel and considered the configuration of her blood.

Since showing me the spice tin a few days earlier, she had carried an air of buoyant distraction. Passive and polite, but only one ear attuned to the conversation. I knew what she wanted — for me to be the one to mention it first — and I was not going to give it to her.

Part of me wanted nothing more than to ring my mother and tell her everything. But my friendship with Annabelle felt perversely private, both a sacred and shameful secret. The disloyalty would be laid bare too; even if my mother could be trusted not to get Annabelle into trouble, was betraying a promise the sort of thing a person could forgive?

The bleeding eventually stopped, though Annabelle kept a bud of tissue up one of her nostrils. A bruise formed over her nose and winged beneath her eyes. It looked like a purple watercolour of a

The Lyrebird's Bell

bird taking flight. She glanced now and then into the mirror by my bed, looking pleased and poking the bruise until she winced.

We spent the morning sitting cross-legged on my bed, dabbing studs of nail polish onto the rims of bug-eye sunglasses. My mother had recently visited a resort near a small rainforest along the South Coast. She returned with a heap of plastic beachside accessories, along with a list some quack boyfriend had written, prescribing lens tints depending on one's desired mood.

Annabelle blew lightly on the painted sunglasses. "I'm annoyed with your mother."

"You barely know her," I said.

"Your shoes are too small." She nudged a raw patch on my foot with her toe. "They're always pinching your feet. And that T-shirt's had a hole in the armpit for ages."

"So what?" I said, grabbing the worn fabric, embarrassed.

"So why does your mother bring you fancy glasses?"

I wrapped my hand around my forearm, twisted the flesh until it burned. "It's not her fault."

"Then whose fault is it?" she asked.

"I don't know." I sent her a levelling look. "I guess it can be dangerous to live too in your head."

Her mouth shrank. My nails dug into the veins on the underside of my wrist.

"I shouldn't have said anything." She fell back onto the rumpled quilt. "Maybe your mother has her reasons."

The midmorning sun pinned us on our backs. Annabelle had gone silent. I could not tell if it was the heat or if she could read the worry swelling between my thoughts. She closed her eyes and I watched her breathe. Often I lay in bed, wanting to be near her in this way. I wished we had an invisible bridge leading from her small balcony to mine, or that I could pull her house closer by tugging the field like a rug. As I watched her, the stale sweetness of perfume in her hair caught in my throat. The desire to curl around her spread like a crack in my ribs.

She squirmed, pulled at her dampened clothes.

"What's wrong?" I asked.

"I can never remember anything," she said. "Is Morgana the adulterer in the Arthur stories? The one who sleeps with Lancelot."

"That's Guinevere," I said. "Morgana's an enchantress. She leads Arthur to Avalon."

A mystic psychopomp of sorts, a guide to the newly dead, in some iterations. A deviant and murderer in others.

Her chin shifted and relaxed on my shoulder. "I'm like Morgana, then."

"Just be Annie," I said.

As I faced her, our foreheads touched. My bed was too small, meant for a child half my age, with delicate white trim like cake fondant and a headboard patterned with black-and-gold bees. To fit we had to overlap our arms, let our skin stick together, tangle our raw-boned legs.

"I want you to be Arthur when he's young and just a boy king," she said. Her honeyed hair rolled with light. "I want you in a crown, or in a collar like a little *sobachka*, curled up at my feet."

"You look ridiculous." I pulled the tissue out of her nose and checked for bleeding. "Do you think you should be lying to your mother about something like this? Making her think she's hurt you?"

"She is hurting me. She won't stop drinking, and it feeds that *thing* inside her." She lifted her hips and pulled a lopsided cigarette and matchbox out from underneath her. She straightened the cigarette and lit it, then tossed the matchbox onto the floor.

"Did she give you the bruise on your arm?" I asked.

Annabelle blew at the smoke wafting overhead. "I just get them sometimes. You've got some on the back of your legs; I've seen them. They're from not eating right."

The Lyrebird's Bell

"That's not okay, Annie. She's your mother, she needs to take better care of you. Have you talked to her?"

Her hand, taloned by the lit stub, pointed to a framed photograph on the floor, propped against the wall. "You of all people know that's pointless."

The picture was of my mother at sixteen, taken by my father, who was then twenty-seven. As a present, he had enlarged it to the size of a movie poster: Josephine, pretty as a starlet, sitting in a rowboat, balancing on the tip of the bow. Her long, bare legs were dipped into the muddy water near the bank of the Yarra Yarra, a vital river drained and dammed so that picks could chisel at its gold.

"I talk to Mum," I said. "Sometimes."

Annabelle smoked the last of the cigarette. One of my mother's cocktail cigarettes, which we admired for their pastels and the pack's gold-lace letters, even though they made our lungs burn. "My lying isn't any worse than your vandalizing," she said with a shrug.

"I didn't say it was."

"You've drawn your own mother drifting through Hell."

In the photograph of my mother, in crude white chalk, I had scribbled writhing souls splashing through the water. "Not Hell," I said. "The Underworld, and only the river."

Annabelle sat up on her elbows, ticked her chin. "A whole shrine for your parents just so you can despise them."

Beside my mother's picture sat a twisted-wire frame holding the only photograph I owned of my father. A stack of books, too, which he had written on the ancient roots of modern psychopathology. In the photograph, he stood as a dark, featureless silhouette before an open doorway, looking onto a pale-skied country yard outside London on the day of his father's funeral.

I liked to shift the frame like a sundial, to face me, the window, the wall. My father in tolerable form: the colossus, shrunken and constrained.

A Song for Wildcats

"Or maybe it's that you miss them," Annabelle said. She sat up fully now, rejuvenated by a new idea. "How long has it been since you last saw your father? Two years, yes?"

I rolled over to squeeze my face into the pillow. "I'm not getting into it."

"You were just playing chess with him."

"Out of bounds, Annie."

"Nothing is out of bounds." She sprang up and straddled my back, pressing her hand against my head like she meant to suffocate me. "If you found a way to fix things with your father, I'd help you."

"Get off me," I said, irritated at such an obvious contortion of the conversation. "I don't want to talk about the stupid *likhoradka* again."

But I had done it, I had spoken the creature's name. Conjured it into my own bedroom.

Still sitting on me, Annabelle leaned her elbows onto my shoulders and propped her face in her hands. Now that she was free to speak, I could not shut her up. The *likhoradka* was feverish, she said. It broke out in sallow dew on her mother's skin. It slept most of the day now, when it was not shrivelling and vomiting. It could see through flesh and was observing Annabelle just as keenly. Peering not only through Mrs. Chernova's eyes but through her stomach, her knees, her fingertips.

I groaned. "*Enough*, Annie, just stop it. We're not playing at this anymore."

"Playing at what?" she asked, straightening. "This isn't a game. You believe me, you have to." She gathered my hair and absently pawed at it. "And I know you only joke that your father might be dead, so let's help each other. We can take care of our families, make things right again."

"He's *practising death*. That's what he told us." The lone letter he had sent after leaving explained *a pursuit of the mind and therefore*

180

The Lyrebird's Bell

the soul, a philosopher's desire to liberate the self from the material binds of marriage, the domestic banality of family.

"Remember my mother and I lived in London," Annabelle continued. "She always said she knew *people of influence*. I'll write to them, or get their telephone numbers. It will be easy to find your father."

I lifted my chin onto the pillow. The back of my neck was warm, and my hair was a sweaty web on my skin. I blinked at the sensible bees on my headboard before breaking into high, helium-headed laughter. From under Annabelle's weight, I wriggled onto my back and gawked at her. "You really have gone mad."

"My suffering isn't funny," she said.

I bit the side of my hand and laughed through my teeth. "Go on, then, rescue the colossus. Drag his body home across the bottom of the sea."

"And you say I talk nonsense." She stared down at me as if reading her reflection in a pond. "Do you really not understand?"

I swallowed the last bout of laughter. I became aware of how loudly we were breathing.

"You're starting to sound kind of scary, is all."

"Betsy, if we do this together, we'll always be part of each other. Isn't that what you want?" Her fingers, still tangled in my hair, tugged at my scalp. "Otherwise, we won't really know each other anymore. You'd see me differently. You're already starting to."

"Of course not, never," I said.

"It's not the kind of thing someone can help. Even if I'd never told you any of this, you'd know. I'd *change*."

I thumbed one of the coarse pleats of her skirt. My knuckles brushed her knee, but rather than the usual anaesthetizing effect of such soft, accidental contact, my fingers recoiled. "Annie, when you say *do this together* ... do you understand what you mean?"

"Do you?" she asked.

"I don't know."

"You could if you tried," she said. "I know you. I think you could glow in the dark if you wanted to."

My body burned underneath her. I gestured for her to get off, to let me breathe.

I knew this feeling. Interwoven one moment, then torn away thread by thread. Some nights I dreamed of my mother running ahead of me, just out of reach. Racing toward a bank of shadow before vanishing inside it like a child into the woods.

I sat up and planted my feet on the cool parquet. I stared at my toes, focused on the stillness of the floor. "When did you close the window?"

"I can't remember." Annabelle settled behind me. She rested her forehead in the curve by my neck, but I shouldered her off. "What's the matter? It's going to rain when the heat breaks."

"I like the rain coming in." I squeezed the side of the mattress. My bedroom felt far away yet fixed, as though I were existing in a memory. "I like knowing I could climb out."

I got off the bed and walked to the window. I jostled it open, breathed in the relief of fresh air. Annabelle's house sat across the field. I imagined I could locate, from this distance, the exact spot where the vines covered a crack in the brick. We had hidden the spice tin in that crack after she showed it to me in the garden. I had checked on it since then, the strychnine already pummelled into an odourless powder. It looked harmless, like the confectioners' sugar crusting in some musty cabinet in my kitchen.

Annabelle held out her arms, wiggling her fingers like a toddler. "You're not happy with me."

"That's not it." I shook my head and shrugged. "It's fine." Parts of me were speaking, my tongue and lips and throat, but not me. And they were not saying what I wanted them to say.

Promise me you won't disappear.

The Lyrebird's Bell

I knelt in front of her and folded my arms on her lap. "Everything is going to be okay. Do you believe me?"

"I always believe you." She tapped my left shoulder, then my right. "There, now you've been knighted. You're not allowed to lie."

My heart strained, bound in an elastic band.

"Let's go outside," I said. The air in my room was smoky, too stuffy to breathe. I had told Annabelle a dozen times not to smoke in the house, that the scent clung to the curtains, sank into the walls. "I left my skipping rope on the drive."

Heading down the steep drive in front of my house, we passed the plum trees along the terrace. Annabelle picked up one of the many swollen blue fruits that had fallen to the ground. The act, a habit of hers that I had always welcomed, now gnawed at me. The sound of each bite, a toothy squelch. My mother loved those battered plums, jarring them in syrup to turn into jam, the alchemy of sweetening the unpalatable.

✳

I peered into the hollowed fracture in the wall. It could not have run more than a few inches deep, enough to fit the spice tin, but it seemed like an endless tunnel, a rabbit hole into another world. I had the unnerving feeling that I could pry the brick wall apart like a scrim, whereupon I would find thousands of insects propping up the flimsy house like circus canvas.

Annabelle had left my house midafternoon. She would be having tea now. I kept listening for her voice or footsteps approaching from inside but heard only the rustle of the leafy vines. My hand shook as I tapped the strychnine into the empty matchbox she had tossed onto my floor, then replaced it with pinches of confectioners' sugar. I had taken the sugar from my cupboard and sat with it in the secrecy of the woods, arguing with myself for over an hour.

A Song for Wildcats

Now I had the strychnine, and I cupped it with care and caution, like an injured dragonfly. At home, I locked myself in the bathroom. All my breath bound itself in a tiny knot, pinned to the back of my throat. I strained my neck over the toilet bowl. Stared into its unwholesome eye and dim, draining pupil. If I flushed the poison, would it contaminate the puddles and ponds? And what if Annabelle could smell the difference, or read the microscopic change in texture? Who else would there be to blame but me?

A part of me was already turning back, unsure if it was my right to intervene, while another part held me firmly in place. I felt on the verge of floating from my body. Drifting high above myself, uprooted and immaterial. I smacked my hand against the edge of the sink. My fingers stiffened, petrified yet vibrating with mild convulsions. Then the pain rang through my body, reminding me of my nerves and bones, anchoring me to the ground.

At home there tarries like a lurking snake, biding its time ...

A radio drama was playing in the sitting room.

A wrath unreconciled, a wily watcher ...

I stuffed the matchbox into my pocket and opened the bathroom door. I checked the foyer window. My mother's candy-red convertible was not in the drive, but her presence left a trail down the hall. White vinyl suitcases with silver buckles, three cylindrical hat boxes stacked like a wedding cake. A package containing what appeared to be an extraterrestrial torture helmet called a Glamour Bonnet. My mother had chattered on about shipping one from California, how it would beautify her skin by lowering the atmospheric pressure around her head.

A drawer opened and shut with the clang of cutlery.

"Josephine?" I asked, following the sound. The shutters in the kitchen were thrown open, brightening the chilled lilac walls. A white glare broke through the wiry branches netting the windows. "You're back?"

184

The Lyrebird's Bell

My mother continued to smooth a rolling pin over a flat slab of dough. "Mummy. Mother. *Ma*. Any of these will do."

"You didn't call to say you'd be home."

"Shall I *leave*, then?" She looked over her shoulder and threw me a wry smile. A trick of sunlight made her eyes the same warm gingersnap-brown as her hair. "Go get Isabelle, darling. I need to speak with her, or has she left for the day?"

"Isabelle quit," I said. "A while ago. Remember?"

The rolling pin stopped. "I didn't think she was altogether serious. I spoke with her before my trip, I offered to pay her more ..."

I did not know what to say. After instructing me for several years, Isabelle had not explained to me her reason for quitting. "Did she say she'd come back?"

"Not in so many words, but I thought I was perfectly clear." My mother seemed to be speaking more to herself. "I assured her things would be different this time."

"What things?" I asked.

She waved off my question and opened the oven to check on what appeared to be a store-bought frozen casserole.

Beneath her cinched yellow apron, a loose white dress fell from her frame. Raindrops had once raced like glass vines over that dress, illuminated by the bracing headlights of downtown Melbourne. Whenever she wore it, I remembered sitting on a bench at a bus stop late at night. The sidewalk filled with black umbrellas, and my mother's luminous dress flickering in front of me like a white flame in the wind.

On the counter was a tiered stand holding plates of her favourite pastries. Pink coconut biscuits with raspberry drizzle, lemon tarts, spongy lamingtons.

"Did you bake those?" I asked, slightly stunned.

"Don't be silly." She let out a dry laugh. "They're from a bakery in the city. But some good old British scones are the real treat, and those I'm going to make myself. Go on and steal a pastry if you want. I won't look."

I had barely eaten in days, and yet the thought of food in my stomach made me queasy. I sniffed the nauseating scent of sugar clinging to the draft. "The kitchen door is open," I noted. "Did you open it?"

"Does it matter who opened it?" she asked. "We need to let in some fresh air. This place is appallingly stuffy."

We kept the kitchen door closed. It led outside to untamed grass and a stone well with dandelions sprouting through the cracks. With its high wooden roof and the heavy lid covering the hole, the well had the morbid look of a public gallows. My father had once threatened to shove my mother into the well; he bent her over the open mouth, the long drop into vacant shadow. He held one hand against the back of her head, the other pinning her wrists against her spine.

She carried on baking, airy as a bouncing spot of light. Cupboards slapped open as she shuffled sacks of stale flour, tins of coffee. "What have you done with the cinnamon?" She threw open the fridge and stared confounded at the glacially pristine shelves, the box of baking soda that had been here when we moved in.

"Why do you have all these desserts?" I asked, wishing Annabelle were here to see them. "Are you done with your diet? Are you eating?"

"Don't ask me that," she said. "I feel like a child when you ask me that. What was that funny creature you came up with back at our old place, the one who stole the veggies from the pantry and hid them under your bed?"

I gave a listless shrug.

"There's no point in talking to you when you're like this." She pressed her weight against the rolling pin. "How about *I missed you, Mummy*."

"You're the one who leaves," I said. My heart was beginning to pound. "You don't even take me with you."

The Lyrebird's Bell

"You wouldn't want to go with me, anyway. Wouldn't you miss your little friend? Annie, is it?"

Something in the utterance of Annabelle's name caused the bubble of our secret world to briefly dissolve. In that moment, I could have told my mother everything. I might have asked her to step in and help Annabelle in a way only an adult could have done. To put her hands under mine and take on some of the weight.

By the time I opened my mouth, she was humming to herself and examining her reflection in the small mirror on the wall. With one slender finger, she brushed the underside of a feathery false eyelash.

"Sure," I said, feeling so heavy I could have sunk through the floor. "I guess you're right."

My mother turned to face me, her eyes gleaming and impersonal as an owl's. "What do you want from me, Betsy? My trip took longer than expected." She smiled then, with her distant, starry warmth I could see but never feel. "Would you be happy if I apologized?"

"Just some food, maybe." I slumped into a chair at the table in the far corner, leaned my head against my raincoat hanging alone on its hook. "Please."

"That's it? Not a kiss, not a conversation."

I switched chairs, but the well outside followed me like a painting with wandering eyes. "I said please. Mum, I'm *hungry*."

She swept her hand toward the tiered tray. "What do you call this?"

"I mean *proper food*, Mum."

"The casserole will be ready soon enough. I think you'll survive."

"Will you eat some with me?" I knew how to measure my mother's waistline on sight. "Even just a plate?"

She slapped another plank of dough against the board. Flour flew up and powdered the air around her. My eyes fell to the floor, gauging the space either of us would have to cross to touch each other. The familiar Westminster chimes rang from the clock in the upstairs hall.

"Actually. On the matter of family dinners." She stepped toward the hall, only to turn around, her heels clipping against the tile. A wedding ring still noosed her finger. It glinted like my father's filling, seen when he yawned or laughed; it always looked to me as though light were magnetized to his molar and trying to peel itself free before his mouth snapped shut.

I wrung my hands under the table. "What's the matter?"

"I'm just a little winded by the past few days," she said. "Betsy. I know we've both missed your father."

I wanted to laugh. As if a puncture in one's life was the same as *missing*. "I haven't missed him. You shouldn't miss him, either. He was horrible to you."

"Darling, he's your father."

"Can a vampire *have* offspring?"

"Don't be smart." My mother's scarlet nails moved through the air with ribbony fluidity as she collected plates and glasses from the cupboards. "You've missed your father, and it will be good for you to have some structure in your life again."

"What's that supposed to mean?" I asked. She was inspecting the glasses, pacing back to the cupboard, exchanging them for finer ones. I followed her movements like a sunflower follows daylight. "Mum?"

"What do you think it means, Elizabeth?" She stopped moving, then covered her face with her hand. Her sobbing came sharp and sudden. "Why must you make this so difficult?"

My stomach squeezed. "I'll stop, Mum, I'm sorry."

Taking a deep breath, she shook her head and smiled. "Let's not ruin a perfectly lovely evening by arguing." She began fussing with a cardigan hanging from the knob of the open door. She folded it over her arm, then draped it over the back of the chair across from me. "It's all rather wonderful. Really wonderful, in a way, I think. It's just, so much excitement takes it out of me."

A shiver ran along the back of my neck. The cardigan had been a blur in my periphery. I had not recognized its vaguely familiar, fuzzy-blue wool until now. Or the almost indiscernible snag in the left elbow that I could not see but I knew was there.

"Darling, you do remember ..." My mother glanced toward the hall and lowered her voice. "You remember how to be careful, don't you?"

I sat utterly still, unable to speak.

She continued preening her tower of sweets, turning it and sprinkling more sugar over the tarts. She monitored the casserole, and I did not know how to break it to her that she had neglected to turn on the oven.

My throat stung as I swallowed, watching powdered sugar fall from her fingers. My hand tightened around the matchbox. From the sitting room came the patient page-turn of a newspaper.

✳

Classically handsome. Tall, and of trim but strong build, with ashy-blond hair, softly tanned skin, and pale brown eyes like tea crystal. Ezra Clarke, whose looks and charm were immaterial, he liked to say; his success had its roots in an astringent clinical intellect, as well as a steadfast and — as a psychiatrist, he had to admit — pathological need to dominate whatever passion to which he set his mind.

The day Ezra Clarke walked out on his family, he set a bowl of lemons on the dining-room table. They were purchased from the warm-faced fruit vendor who set up shop on the side of Brick Kiln Road. Ezra had stopped to buy them on his drive home the previous evening, in his flashy copper Buick, from either his clinic in downtown Melbourne (which I was allowed to know about), or his private apartment overlooking the beach along Port Phillip Bay (a rendezvous point for him and my revolving door of instructors — which I was not allowed to know about, but which of course I did).

Lemons were his preferred fruit. They were emblematic, he told me, of the elegant but acerbic tone he wished to instill in his family home. He placed them around the house, like watchful gold eyes, and instructed me to snack on them as a form of detox.

On the day he left, he placed the lemons in a bowl that had been passed down from one old pair of beringed and rheumatic hands to another, along the family line, and was pure-blue porcelain, inlaid with variegated shapes of chiselled ivory.

"Ivory comes from killing elephants," I told him, freshly eleven and horrified to learn of ivory's origins. To tease me, he said my teeth were sculpted of ivory and jabbed into my gums when I was born.

The bowl sat in the centre of the dining-room table, where the lemons radiated among plates of fried eggs and black pudding, bland beans and toast with marmalade, and other such components of a hearty English breakfast. My mother was drinking coffee from her favourite mug; it had a picture of a chintzy-dressed aristocrat falling off his horse, and we had picked it out together at a general store in Woodend. My father had set for himself a glass of ruby-black claret.

"*Conticuere omnes*," my father said, then waited. "Betsy?"

I was breathlessly piling food onto my plate. "*Intentique ... ora tenebant.*"

"*Inde toro Pater Aeneas sic orsus ...*"

Having forgotten what came next, I pretended to keep chewing after swallowing my toast. I stared at the wall in panic. The pattern of shimmery, viridian peacocks seemed to move. They marched

The Lyrebird's Bell

along the wallpaper, playful tails fanning hundreds of unblinking blue eyespots. Looking right at me, all of them, inviting me to join.

"*Ab ... ab ... alto ...*"

"That pronunciation of yours leaves something to be desired." Ezra glanced up from his newspaper. "Josephine, your Latin is beautiful. You ought to be helping her."

My mother nodded. She had not spoken since the night before, when she had gone crashing down the stairs. The fall had fractured her jaw, bruised it to a mottled blueberry stain, and left her inner cheeks raw with open wounds. She winced as she brought her hand to her mouth.

"Mum, don't eat the salty things," I reminded her. "Your cuts will sting."

My father ran his serviette hard over his mouth. He tossed it onto his plate, causing the silverware to rattle and scrape across the porcelain. "Don't simper."

"It's too *salty* for her," I said. "Why did you make her salt everything? She can't eat any of it."

"Enough, Elizabeth," he said.

"You don't even like salt," I muttered, making a deliberate racket with my utensils as I cut through my food.

My mother gave a smile like a crackling light bulb. "What shall I eat first?"

"Those lemons are fresh," he said.

The smile dissolved. She looked helpless, knife and fork poised over her plate.

My father's stare remained taut. His foot tapped beneath the table. As my mother reached toward the bowl, he sighed.

Her hand froze. "You told me —"

"You're not even going to distinguish one lemon from another?"

"Mum, you don't actually have to —"

"Hush, Betsy," she said.

191

A Song for Wildcats

I held my breath as she contemplated each lemon with care, her fingers following the tender mounds, never touching the skin. Once she had chosen one, she eased back into her chair, where she cupped the lemon to her chest like her own heart torn from her body. At my father's instruction, she dug her nails into the flesh and peeled it, exposing the swollen muscle, then broke the fruit apart into slices. Soon tiny lemon moons lay in a neat row. She placed each slice into the torn cavern of her mouth, like a hook she meant to pierce through her cheek.

I watched her eyes become pink and glassy. The hollowness falling over her face made her faraway and unfamiliar. I thought perhaps her spirit had slipped out and was circling her body, carrying a pain so potent that it would imprint itself on the air, like a cold spot forever occupying the room.

"Mum, *stop it*," I said. "You're hurting yourself."

"Elizabeth —"

"Tell her to *stop*."

My father folded his newspaper and rose from the table. He walked toward me and stood behind my chair, the full density of his presence like a marble statue tilting out of place. It was a habit of his to pinch the back of my neck with his full hand, and without him needing to do it now, a phantom spasm sprang through my nape. He placed both palms on my shoulders. His grip tightened. He bent low, his cheek next to mine, and his breath smelled of nothing.

Then he straightened, returned to his seat, and gave his newspaper a quick shake to sturdy it. "That's enough, Josephine, spit out the rest," he said, as though my mother were a child with an insect in her mouth.

IV.

TO CAPTURE A GOLD-HORNED DEER

A tectonic reshuffling of the world took place as I ran out the kitchen door.

When I had told my mother that she could not invite Ezra back, she continued rolling her pin, over and over, empty-eyed as an automaton. She offered a casual reconfiguring of the past. As if reality consisted of interchangeable properties, and old common sufferings could be remoulded, purified, made noble. The new truth was that my father had never disappeared. He had been travelling for research, with an obvious intention of returning. Everyone had understood that; my mother assured me that I had understood it too.

My legs moved independent of the rest of me, carrying me out the door and through the wild grass and dandelion ghosts surrounding the property. The sun beat down in sharp torrents until I reached the refuge of the forest.

Deeper than the bone-china eucalyptus trees was the largest of the old-growth stringybarks. Its huge trunk was plastered in mangy strips of sickly grey bark, like the feathers of a starving bird. I had slept some nights protected by its undergrowth. Squeezed among the roots that tumbled into the creek.

Leaning my cheek against the stringybark, I listened to the rhythmic rustle of the leaves overhead, the wind's soothing hush. A koala family was foraging in the trees of a nearby range. After we had first left Woodend, my mother liked to bring me here. We would sit in the dappled violet shade, sip minty gum-leaf tea, and pretend to talk like Ingrid Bergman.

"I won't ..." I said, an incomplete thought encompassing everything. There was no living in that house with my parents. No enduring the high-wire hesitancy of every move. My mother had once

A Song for Wildcats

understood; we had fled Ezra, she told me, when I was a toddler and she was eighteen. She had crept silently through the house, holding me and a single suitcase, too frightened to breathe. But eventually the war came. We needed food, a proper home; he offered the villa, stocked pantries, a fridge.

Leaves drifted across the creek, intricately veined scraps like a torn map. Maybe leaves were maps of the universe, and we were looking at them all wrong. Reality did not seem to have a reliable shape. Was it like water, did it exist in different and ever-changing forms? To go home would be to hand reality over to my mother and father, to let them twist and bend it into whatever they liked.

I grabbed two thick roots and held onto them like the sides of a careening wagon. Annabelle could hide me in her root cellar with the mushrooms and the wine. I would not be a bother. I was a quiet presence. Even moths were not disturbed by me.

I walked to the fringe of the woods. The field beyond it lay as reposeful as a lake. Halfway across stretched a low stone border overrun with centuries of moss and black grime. When I was younger, I thought of it as the gate to a medieval walled city, fortifying against invaders while locking the townspeople inside. The wall cut off at the forest, where a hollow log lay dead. In the cool soil of the log's shadow, I had buried a black purse like a doctor's bag, stolen from my mother's wardrobe. Inside were emergency necessities: cans of nonperishables, a coffee tin of rolled cash, and shiny, expensive trinkets my mother and I could sell.

I climbed over the border, which marked the exact point where I was closer to Annabelle's house than my own. Noisy, scraggy birds pecked at the moss-stained stone. They seemed to get louder the farther I walked. I could still hear them as I reached the staggered pickets of Annabelle's fence. It was open, the crooked branches of the tea trees hooking through the gaps.

194

The Lyrebird's Bell

The Chernova house had the look of an unpeeled anatomy in one of my father's gruesome medical books. Early dusk drained the pinkish stucco, giving it a clammy pallor, so that the climbing red vines resembled raw muscle. The door was unlocked. It was crowned in a blue arc of glass, with one dark panel like a peeking pupil that followed me as I entered the front hall. I looked into the parlour, where Annabelle liked to draw and read her cards.

"Annie," I said, once into each room.

Dull sunlight fell through the glass arc. None of the lights were turned on. As I walked up the stairs, I thought about how I had never seen these higher rooms. Annabelle kept the domestic scenery of her life to herself. We never argued on this matter.

What would she think of me roaming her house like a lost dust mote?

The wallpaper in the first room looked water spoiled, bubbling along the creases. There was a large hutch filled with long-necked wine bottles, and beside it a photograph of what I assumed was Annabelle's family. A man dressed as Grandfather Frost stood before a giant pine tree dripping with tinsel. He held a white costume beard in his hand, and the anchorage of a thick mustache weighed down his face. A younger Mrs. Chernova sat on the floor beneath a New Year's banner, surrounded by ribboned gifts, with Annabelle on her lap holding a toy teapot upside down. Snow, so foreign and enchanting, filled the lamplit street beyond their window.

"Annie," I whispered. "Wake up, it's me."

Annabelle and her mother lay in bed, asleep before sunset. Approaching the bedside, I felt like a child vampire about to pierce Annabelle's neck and vanish through the wall. The curtains were closed, and in the dimness I nearly tripped on a bank of clothes abandoned on the floor, my foot landing hard on a sharp-cornered bottle.

A Song for Wildcats

"Get up, Annie." I shook her shoulder, but she remained still. The way the sheet clung to her legs and spilled over the bedside gave her the shape of a beached mermaid. "Can you hear me?"

A sour whiff rose from the two bodies, mingling with the sweet, fermented stench already thick in the air. The buzz of vinegar flies vibrated around the ceiling. Annabelle's fist was bunched around the sleeve of her mother's robe. It made my own fingers ache, bundling empty air.

My voice sharpened as I said her name. An icy prickle spread over my skin. I lifted her arm, thumbed along her veins. There was no beat, and I was not sure I was doing it right. My mind emptied as I touched her throat, pressing into it until a soft pulse pumped against my fingers, and my heart eased back into place.

In my relief, I staggered backward, disturbing a tray on the nightstand. Glass clanged and tipped over. I quickly grabbed the tray to hold it still.

Nobody stirred. My eyes adjusted to the murkiness and swam around a jumble of empty liquor bottles.

"*Eto the* ..." Mrs. Chernova's voice strained from her mouth.

Startled, I began sputtering. "I'm sorry, I didn't think —"

Her stare rolled toward a glass of water soaking a ring into the nightstand wood. A stringy lemon floated in the water, waving its flesh like the fin of a dead goldfish.

I lifted the glass, and she nodded. It was immediately apparent that the glass was full of lukewarm spirits, the juniper punch of gin. I carried it to Mrs. Chernova in a loose daze. We had never been in the same room together. With her pale-orange hair, her jaundiced skin, and moony grey eyes, she brought to mind a mouldy peach.

"I'm Elizabeth," I said. "I know Annabelle."

She watched me with glazed curiosity. Mouth open, spittle crusting along the corners of her lips.

"Do you ..." I offered her the glass. "Do you need help?"

196

The Lyrebird's Bell

She let out a grimy cough, burying her mouth in her shoulder. When it stopped, blood clotted her robe. I stared at it like she was leaking oil.

Steadying her breaths, she cupped her throat, as if cradling an egg inside it. Something vulnerable that kept trying, with bloody flutters, to escape. "Drink ..." she said.

The back of her head was warm and sticky against my hand. I could smell the sting of alcohol rising from her skin. As she swallowed, the gratitude on her face made her sweat look weepy, like her pores were crying.

A deep soreness throbbed in my chest. "Do you need anything else?" I asked. "Are you hungry?"

Mrs. Chernova kept her eyes on me as she sipped. An unblinking severity settled in.

"Wicked ... vile spell on me ..."

She inched the glass away, clutching it with a look of contempt, as though I had tried to steal it.

"I didn't mean to upset you," I said, too nervous to move.

"*Malenkiyi ved'mi*," she hissed. She lay back and rested the bottom of the glass on her chest, holding it upright with both hands like a ceremonial candle. She closed her eyes. "Little witches."

✳

The field rolled under my feet, carrying me back to my familiar patch of forest. Away from Mrs. Chernova, whose life was sweating from her body. Her feet sticking out from under the covers, chubby as a baby's despite her gauntness — as if waterlogged, like she had drowned.

But in the middle of the field, a sound struck me. The honeyed strains of harp music, rippling overhead. The echoey static of a record player. I stopped and turned.

197

A Song for Wildcats

My father was standing on the terrace, one hand in his pocket, staring out into the mercurial twilight. The library doors were open behind him, letting out the music. His hair was the colour of dull champagne, the mild quiff unfastened by the wind. He looked as posh as ever in a sunny sport shirt, white Oxfords as clean as toothpaste.

My pulse thickened and pushed behind my eyes. In fleeing, I had run out into the open, where prey should never go.

✳

It was mid-March and Labour Day celebrations had begun. Local youth from around the Shire could be heard outside, having driven to the open plains for the glittering destruction of fireworks and bottle rockets.

By the time I arrived in the library, the music had stopped. My father was waiting between the dusty-green walls, with their pattern of pond birds and reed beds in chalky silhouettes, like children's stencils. He had known that I would follow him from the field. He never had to call for anybody; he simply appeared, then walked away with the cryptic cool of a ghost.

"Don't glare, dear. It unnerves people." He was sitting in a crushed-velvet armchair, one foot resting on his knee. He leaned forward and relaxed his wrist on the bony slope of his ankle, holding a glass of sparkling wine. "It's like a gloomy little hobgoblin is sneaking about."

Though he was directly in front of me, I felt his pull from all sides. An inescapable density at the centre of the room, a gravitational command.

He indicated a spot near the armchair, on the rug, and without thinking I sat at his feet and folded my hands on my lap. The rug had originally been a neatly woven mosaic, but I had tugged the threads, rather unconsciously, until they were as loose as cornsilk.

The Lyrebird's Bell

"Your stare hasn't softened any, I see," he said. "Still collecting secrets? Bartering with the dryads in the woods?"

"I suppose, sir," I said.

"Looking at you now, I can't quite find you. I'd forgotten that about you. Where do you go, I wonder?" He leaned back in the chair and smiled with meditative calm. "I see you're finally managing that hair of yours."

I touched the bobby pin above my ear. "Annie did it."

Remembering Annabelle made my breath swell in my ribs. I had told her that everything would be all right.

"Josephine was rabbiting on about how much you've taken to this friend of yours. Imagine my astonishment that you'd made a friend who wasn't a tree or a bullfrog."

The French doors onto the terrace were still open, letting in the breezy blue evening. On the field, drunken teenagers were arranging cheap pyrotechnics. Their laughter swept invitingly into the library, yet it seemed irretrievably remote, as though we lived in different strains of time.

"Where's Mum?" I asked.

The dining table was set across the hall, yet the lights were off.

My father held my gaze and extended his glass toward me. "Have a sip."

I recalled the inflexible machinery of these encounters, keeping my body rigid since sitting down. I reached cautiously for the glass. The wine was a fizzy coral and smelled of fresh strawberries. I dipped my nose over the rim and a cool, effervescent breath played against my skin.

As I started taking a sip, my father gave the glass a sharp tilt, and the wine went dribbling down my clothes. He clapped his hands together with a hard laugh.

"Oh, just to lighten the mood," he said, when he saw the shake in my lower lip. "Well, clean yourself up, you're not an infant."

A Song for Wildcats

I rushed my arm across my mouth, then patted my soaked shirt front.

"Your mother is upstairs having a rest." He pulled a kerchief from his pocket, unfolded it from its square, and handed it to me. "Apparently, you hurt her feelings earlier. It sent her into a mood, and we wound up exhausting one another."

"Is she okay?" My insides tightened into a coiled spring. In the time Ezra had been gone, my mother had regained some of the shape he had twisted out of her; I was not so sure that shape could hold. "Should I go check on her?"

My father paused. "Why would you need to do that?"

I gave a faint shrug, but my scalp prickled. "I didn't mean to upset her."

"I suppose you never do," he said. The muscles in my neck tensed as he reached out and brushed my cheek with the side of his hand. "It's a cycle, really. Your mother is invariably disappointing, but it hurts her to know we see it too."

"A cycle," I repeated.

"Don't echo, Elizabeth."

In the quiet, the first firework whistled high into the night. It erupted in a blazing red bloom.

My father set the emptied glass on the end table beside him. Rather than the marble surface, he placed it on my mother's antique edition of her most treasured book, where the wet base would warp the cover. "You're drawn to the illusory. What someone, or something, could be if you just gave more, and forgave everything. Trust me, if you look closely at your mother, there's nothing but cobweb."

I rose onto my knees and picked up the glass before any wine could drip all the way down the stem. "I can wash this," I said, but he shook his head and gently pulled the glass out of my grasp. "You're not angry with her, are you?"

200

He shifted in his chair. "Concern can often look like anger. But things will be better this time. We'll be a changed family, I promise."

Had he promised a *changed man*, I would have known that he was lying. But a *changed family* left the blame diffused and festering in the air.

"Mum will stay home more?" I asked.

"All the time," he said. "But you mustn't be a corrosive core, darling. Do you understand what that means? A child can rot the family from the inside without meaning to."

"I don't ..." My eyes stung, roaming the rug in a warm blur. "What did I do?"

His hand tightened around the curve of the armrest. I watched each subtle flex of his fingers. "Don't be tiresome. No daughter of mine is to be tiresome."

The scent of sulphur drifted in with the breeze. The fireworks mounted. With each crackling burst and messy round of howling, my father flinched.

My tongue pushed against the back of my teeth. I could feel my words ready to jump out of me. "Why did you even come back?" I said. "You don't like us. You hate it here."

He pressed his temples, as if a thread of electricity were spooling around his brain. "A manipulative little creature and her family were causing trouble for me in London," he said. "An absolute psychotic. There are worse women than your mother, I've learned. And far worse places to be."

I watched as the sounds outside nipped at his nerves. Nothing had ever flustered him so openly before, not that I had seen. There was a worn, pummelled quality to him, more than two years could explain.

It surprised me how compelled I felt to run to the medicine cabinet and get him some Aspirin, to close the doors against the

A Song for Wildcats

commotion, grab the ottoman for him to rest his feet. And yet I did not move. Twinges of pain cut across his face as the noise grew louder, sharper, more sporadic.

I once drew him split open on an anatomy slab, his insides composed of tunnelling lacunae, a body like a gutted beehive. No feeling, no blood, no warmth. It was almost worse to see him now. That he might suffer, as anyone else might suffer; that he might know how it felt, and have always known.

He flattened his palm on his chest and squinted against the lamplight. I imagined his hand sinking through his body, as though he were made of wet clay, and tangling in the empty net of his heart.

"Maybe you didn't have anywhere else to go," I said.

He looked at me as if staring into empty air. "Is that what you think?"

I said nothing, and held my breath until he looked away. After several minutes, I thought maybe that was the end of it. I moved my hands from my lap, hoping to leave, when the glass exploded next to me.

My father rubbed his hand over his face. "You *push*, Elizabeth."

The shock was numbing. I thought an ineffaceable spark from the fireworks had soared into the library. As I lifted myself up, my legs weakened. I saw that my calf had rolled into the shattered wine glass. Blood shivered from a deep gash onto the rug.

He glanced around the high corners of the room. His fist tightened, loosened. "You're touching on sensitive topics."

Pain spiked through my leg as I stepped backward, and my feet moved with the sense that the edge of a cliff might appear underneath them.

"Elizabeth, come back here at once." My father rose from the armchair and caught up with me in two easy steps. Taking my jaw, he pressed his thumb against my throat. "You're nearly a young woman. These outbursts of yours are no longer charming." I

202

The Lyrebird's Bell

squirmed, grabbed his forearm, clawed once at his face. "If this were an old tragedy, you'd end up with your tongue cut out."

Blood blinked at the corner of his mouth where I had scratched him. Senselessly, *vampire* played through my head, my own insult spitting back at me.

His hand slid over my mouth, and I drifted outside my body. Looking down, I could see a small, skinny girl in wrinkly cotton shorts, a T-shirt striped like a mime's. She had made it all the way to the open door before her father caught her. Though I was floating only as high as the ceiling, nestled in the corner like a wayward balloon, she seemed far below and unreachable, the act of carrying her away to safety as plausible as breaking through the barrier of a movie screen. I looked up at my mother's bedroom. No shadowy movement under the door, no sound.

A fierce grip somewhere inside me yielded, and I dropped back into my body. Searing, luminous feeling flowed through me, a radiant anger. For only a beat or two. Long enough to snap my teeth into the flesh of my father's palm, latching on like a wild animal.

His eyes squeezed shut. His expression tangled, then gradually smoothed, and when he opened his eyes again, they were bright and unblinking. With his hand still caught between my teeth, he knocked my head against the door frame.

"Never a bore, are you." He let out a cheerful laugh and sat back down in the armchair, casually toeing the glass debris. "You're wrong to say I dislike you. Of course I like you, darling. You're my daughter."

Crumpled on the floor, I thought first to play dead, but a twitchy new impulse took me. I blinked his image into focus and stared him down from across the room.

The terrace doubled and swayed. A ghostly sprawl of smoke hung in the sky like the pendulous wisps of a willow. The teenagers were barely visible in the hazy field, but their shouts rang clear and triumphant with the final gunshot pops of bottle rockets, like a purgatorial re-enactment of an old, unending battle.

*

Everyone knows not to enter the forbidden chamber.

Once, while my father was gardening, he cut his wrist on a frosty-flowered blackthorn. My mother laughed at him for being clumsy. He twisted her ear until she buckled onto the grass, and within the hour kissed her forehead.

The sorcerer had his bloody basin of maidens, the pirate his storeroom of murdered brides. My father's forbidden chamber hid only his reflection, bare and unflinching, which he, too, was not allowed to see.

After leaving him in the library, I locked myself in my room. I refused to open the door when my mother knocked and spoke to me through the cool white pine, where I rested my cheek. I cracked it open only when I heard her and my father gathering their things in the foyer.

At the bottom of the stairs, she fastened a waist-length coat above a pleated bloom of black skirt. Pearls were pinned to her hair like a strip of starry night draped over her head. My father straightened her scarf as she hand-combed his hairline. She beamed at him with vacant rapture. *This is what you meant. This is how it really happened.* I could almost hear it, whatever second-hand reality he had convinced her to accept. It was as though her brain were a camera obscura, with only a pinhole for her consciousness to peek through — and each day, through that pinhole, came Ezra's light, allowing impressions of the world to form.

They were off to Corio Bay for a two-night rest along the water-front. *A rest from what*, I thought. From my window, I watched them drive down the unpaved road, which soared off toward

The Lyrebird's Bell

broader roads and bigger towns, the moonlit silk of my mother's scarf waving up at me.

Pictures torn from travel guides crowded my walls, still colourful in the evening light. German Christmas markets, Mediterranean coasts with sea fennel and sand dunes and crystal-blue water. I sat on my bed and aimlessly rotated the small globe on my nightstand, feeling it spin against my fingertips. The pieces fit so simply, countries and continents puzzled together, one compact sphere of ocean. New Zealand, Indonesia, the Great Barrier Reef were all a thumbprint away.

What kept me here? Were loyalty, love, the same as choice? I feared that fate could be inherited, and I stayed because my mother stayed because Ezra stayed because ...

And what of Annabelle's inheritance? What were the genetic properties of possession? If she was correct in her beliefs, what had drawn the spirit to her mother, of all the vulnerable people it might have chosen? Perhaps she had a predisposition for possession, and it flowed through the family bloodline. Perhaps it began from childhood, from birth.

Knowing little of my father's childhood, I often fabricated possibilities: a boy who rescued tadpoles from shrinking puddles, left shiny milk caps on the doorstep for thieving magpies, and cried each winter over the death-melt of his snowmen. I wondered what might have happened to that boy, if someone long ago had drained him of something vital. If it was possible to be born unkind or careless, or if there was always a wound that might have been prevented, some other person he might otherwise have become.

He liked to say his own father's sole act of generosity was dying in his thirties. It could be that some uncanny cruelty burrowed into the Clarke men, deep into their core, as hereditary as high cholesterol.

I once came upon him sitting cross-legged like a child in the grass, wearing his saggy seersucker pyjamas and my mother's

205

plush terrycloth robe. He was red-eyed and smoking a thick, crude cigarette, and the smoke around him smelled sour and earthy. *Sometimes I think I'm nothing more than a revenant of my father,* he said. *My own insidious haunting. You look like Josephine, but I don't know if you're anything like her.* Looking at the stars, he took my hand and rested it on his shoulder. I could feel his pulse through his palm, and I tried to interpret his heartbeat. *I hope you never understand what I mean.*

V.

PSYCHOPOMP

That night, I could not sleep. Too much noise in the intensity of quiet. A common occurrence in an old, empty house with aching pipes and lonesome floorboards.

I paced my room, trying not to scratch the bandage I had stuck on my leg. The swollen mound on the side of my head released ripples of nausea when I touched it. I looked outside periodically; Annabelle's bedroom window glowed like a firefly. When it flicked off, the light in the upstairs hall replaced it, then the downstairs hall, then the kitchen, the firefly coursing through the house.

From my nightstand, the matchbox burned in my periphery.

I went to my mother's bedroom and began scrounging through her belongings. We would flee, as we had done before. We would take Annabelle with us. My mother would remember Ezra's nature soon enough, and when Annabelle saw how prepared I was, she would not be so afraid.

Over the years I had stolen enough to cobble together a fresh start, if ever needed. Other than the escape bag, I had hidden items throughout the house. Money stashed inside a hole in the wall behind the tumble dryer. One of Ezra's original sixteenth-century

The Lyrebird's Bell

woodcuts, wrapped in a tea towel and wedged under the foot of my mattress.

I had, at times, fantasized of running away on my own. A boy in my school in Woodend had told me that places existed for children in need, orphaned or not, and he would be sent to one if his father did not return from the fighting in New Guinea, and his mother could not stretch the rations among six sons. But how could I have left my mother alone? Outside of the danger, I could do nothing to protect her from it.

As I collected strings of pearls and crumpled cash, piling it all onto her bed, I took satisfaction in the vestigial clearings of dust on her bureaus, where once sat glossy Royal Doulton ladies and velvet jewellery boxes — none of which she noticed were missing — now stored in the cobwebby darkness under my bed.

Was stealing wrong if done for her benefit? It was an improvement over previous habits, futile efforts to keep her close. No longer did I feel the need to break her clocks and trick her into arriving late at the Macedon station. Or smash vases to weave tiny invisible traps for her feet in the powder-room rug. And it was not stunted by the victim never knowing, but nurtured by it, like a death cap mushroom growing in the dark.

Only once did I steal for the sheer satisfaction of the act. A silver quill-tipped pen, an antique my mother used for her most patrician correspondence. Bought in Vienna while on one of her adventures with some exquisite alcoholic who painted deathly cherubic portraits of her, who would surely take Ezra's place and open up the world for her. Whom one *must never insult with indifference, Betsy, never be rude to when he's over for dinner.* I had taken the box of dark chocolates he gave me, each one filled with dripping spiced cherry and shaped like Mozart's head. I squished them all over the windows in the parlour, so that it looked as though a brigade of magpies had blitzed themselves against the glass.

207

A Song for Wildcats

The clock on my mother's dresser read nearly midnight. I opened the top drawer, and the fresh scent of Ivory Snow detergent wafted out. Men's shirts and polo necks were folded inside. In the years since Ezra left, I had seen her wash and dry them, starch and iron them, fold them on her lap. From around the corner, I had watched her lower them with care into the drawer, like a mother easing her baby into a cot.

An enormous iron hand pressed down on me. I was sinking, the floor swallowing my ankles, while another part of me stood in the library below, watching my legs break through and dangle from the ceiling.

Across from my mother's bedroom, the door to Ezra's study was open. I found myself staring into it until I was somehow inside. I felt his presence instantly, as though he were keeping his heart chilled and beating in an icebox under the floor.

The study was drafty and scant of furniture. Across the walls flew a pattern of blue leaves that he had painted himself, each leaf caught in a gust and spinning its dainty apex toward his office chair. Small castings of deities lined the chimney-piece, over which hung a painting of nude nymphs with soft stomachs. They wore tiny pink rosebuds in their hair, and their flesh looked varicose with brittle cracks. Facing his desk, two blanched portraits of his parents seemed to float like disembodied spectres.

A forgotten tart sat on a plate, among the ledger papers cast across his desk. I looked down at it, unable to locate a particular feeling but rather every feeling, all at once, shrinking to a singular pierce in my chest.

The matchbox scuttled behind me in darting wisps like a centipede. I turned to catch it, but it was right where I had left it, perched and impassive on the nightstand. I touched the pulsing wound on my head. The hair covering it was crisp with dried blood. I felt light-headed, like I was a gentle current of air. I drifted again

The Lyrebird's Bell

to that liminal space, the dreamy barrier between me and my surroundings. I could see myself, as I had in the library. I was floating out of reach of my body, and I watched myself walk back to my room, emerge with the matchbox cradled in my hands.

Strychnine is so much softer than its name. Strange how the sensory impression of a word has nothing to do with the soul of its etymology. What we call things and what they are; what we think and what is true. Even *murderess* is too beautiful a word for what it means.

I stared into the open matchbox, shifting in and out of lucidity like a daydream. I was vanishing, particle by particle, until I was only the cold, sliding sensation in my stomach, the swift plummet into the dark.

Custard glinted on the plate, a pale leakage like an infected wound. How hard would it be to mix the powder into the tarts? A moment, a pinch of time.

And what would follow? I would rid the house of Ezra, and what then? He would be robbed of hope or redemption, in whatever meagre form it might come, and my mother would mourn. I wondered if she had ever held a letter opener to his throat as he slept, or eyeballed arsenic while stirring sugar cubes into his tea. Who did she blame for the pearly scar he had once kicked into my rib cage: him, herself, or me?

Sprinkle it into the custard. Nestle the pastry back into the cake tin, where my mother's tower had been condensed. Let it sit, be patient. My mother, terrified of food, would never dream of eating dessert.

I tipped the matchbox until the powder collected in the corner, inching toward the edge. I could solve everything — free my mother from my father, and my father from himself. Keep Annabelle from losing herself completely. And yet, what part of me would be lost? One brutal act could work its own kind of poison through the rest of my life. As lies do, as guilt and secrets do. Was that part of me not worth protecting too?

My legs shook. The pierce in my chest dislodged, and feeling began spinning through me — but it was dull and heavy, the whirling thump of a washing machine.

I slid the matchbox closed and put it back in my pocket; locked my hand tight around it, feeling its contours, its weight. I closed my eyes and breathed in and out, the same word filling my mouth and releasing into the air around me. *Enough. Enough.* When my breathing was so slow I could not hear it, and my tongue was cold and dry, I opened my eyes.

A glimmer reflected in the darkened window behind the desk. Two antlers — small, stunted, painted gold. I looked over my shoulder at the chimney-piece, where Artemis stood with her sacred deer. Stately and empowered, reaching for her arrow mid-stride. Goddess of the wilderness and its creatures, yet goddess of the hunt. *Which one is it, then? Protector or threat? Because you cannot be both.*

Perhaps I only meant to touch the deer. All its liveliness constrained, antlers still short enough to fit in Artemis's grip. But then the two conjoined figures were lying at my feet, cracked apart. Separated. Free. There was the memory of cool marble against my skin, the vibration of impact, the sound of Artemis smacking against hardwood. I picked up the pale little deer. I could not let it stay in this house. I knew it in a way that was deeper than knowledge, simpler than choice. An understanding, warm and intuitive as blood.

✳

A magpie's eyeshine blinked at me from the grubby stone wall as I worked handfuls of grass and bells of fallen heath into a nest. I

The Lyrebird's Bell

placed the deer inside and lowered the nest into the black purse I had dug up from the dirt. "You'll be safe here," I said. "I won't leave Victoria without you."

Hiking the purse onto my shoulder, I started across the field toward Annabelle's house.

The magpie cawed, and like a dishevelling of shadow, flew away.

The teenagers had driven off by now. The night was so quiet that when Annabelle slipped outside into her garden, the clang of the iron door latch flew clear above me. I paused, my feet bare in the scratchy grass and the thrum of gnats at my ear. I scanned the sky, following the jangling sound as it travelled into the clouds.

I found Annabelle crouched on the garden path, holding a rusty first aid kit. She looked faintly blue and luminescent in her white cotton nightgown. I watched from behind the cherry tree as she took pebbles from the kit and arranged them on the ground with delicate precision.

"Betsy, your foot's poking out," she said. "Why aren't you wearing any shoes?"

"I forgot," I said, shuffling over to her. The only sound was the scrape of my feet against the gravel. I had thrown on a jumper before leaving, and I pulled the sleeves over my hands, rubbed my arms. "Aren't you cold?"

"It's never cold here," she said. Her shadow was so dark and finely cut that there seemed to be two of her. When she moved, the shadow followed below with its own private intention.

"What are you doing?" I asked.

She settled onto her knees in front of the first aid kit, then opened the lid wider with a thin squeak. Inside were empty medicine bottles, a black candle and loose matches, a small pestle in a children's breakfast bowl filled with soaked groats. She had already removed the spice tin and placed it on the ground.

A Song for Wildcats

She picked up one of the pebbles and held it out to me. "It's a rune stone, like the Vikings used. My mother says 'rune' means *something hidden*."

"Your mother who's not your mother," I said.

She picked up the spice tin and held it tightly. "This will fix all of that. Look what I've done — the potion will take care of the body, while the spell takes care of the spirit. You see? I've worked it all out."

The mild chill was sharpened by the wind. I shivered and folded my arms for warmth. "There's a cold rain coming."

In one quick motion, Annabelle poured the white powder from the tin into the bowl. "I make her fresh porridge for breakfast," she said, grinding it into the groats with the wooden pestle. "It's the only thing she can stomach."

I felt heartsick watching her. The plastic bowl, baby-pink and swan patterned, the pebbles and their roughly etched symbols — the ritual, elaborate and arbitrary. A child playing make-believe. It might have been ridiculous if not for the severity of Annabelle's face. I sat down next to her. "Let's go inside and warm up."

"I thought you liked the rain," she said.

"You'll get sick out here in just your nightgown." I touched her wrist, and she stopped stirring. "We were only playing."

"You were only playing."

I pulled the purse off my shoulder and wrapped my arms around it. "Don't you want to see what I've brought? I've got thousands of pounds' worth to sell. More at home too. We can leave right now. Nobody would look for us."

"Why would we leave?" she asked, striking one of the matches against a rock. She shielded the candle and lit the wick. "This is the only safe place in the world."

"Not for me," I said.

She cupped my hand on her lap, toying with my fingers as if appraising the shape of my bones. "Don't say that."

212

The Lyrebird's Bell

"If we can get to the station, we can go anywhere," I said. "We can disappear."

Annabelle took the candle, lacquered in its own sweating wax. She held it between us. "The *likhoradka* celebrated all night when the siege came. Did I tell you that? The kitchen reeked of honey wine — she got so sloppy drunk she spilled it everywhere. *The city is alone now, myshka. Trapped. Nobody, nobody coming for them.*"

My stomach sank. I could not find her in that moment — only some remote embodiment, like holding onto someone's memory through a keepsake.

"You're not listening," I said.

"*You're* not listening." Her nose was running, a shine above her upper lip. "She wants me to do it. What choice is there?"

Her words hit a barrier in my mind — until the barrier cracked, clarity slowly leaking in. "What?" I asked. It was all I could think to say.

Annabelle sniffed and ran the side of her hand under her nose. I saw the tremble in her fingertips. "Sometimes I see her, a little part of my mother. She blames me. She says it's the way I look at her that's made her sick, and that I owe her peace. That I need to end her misery for her, she can't go through with it on her own. But you know I didn't make her sick, don't you?"

Understanding continued to wash over me. "Of course you didn't," I said.

The medicine bottles clinked together as she ran her fingers over them. She breathed a long stream of air and straightened her chin. "The *likhoradka* is done with her. She knows it. There's nothing more it can take."

I did not know my own decision until my hand was in my pocket. As I handed the matchbox to Annabelle, the sleeve of her nightgown brushed my fingertips. I tried to memorize the fabric down to the grain. The seep of rich perfume escaping from

213

beneath her cuff. Unfamiliar and more womanly than her sea salt and linden.

"I don't understand." She turned the matchbox over in her hands. When she slid it open, a calm confusion occupied her face, before her breath jumped. "Why do you have this?"

"I only meant ..." Shame burned the end of my thought before I could finish it. She was looking at me, wide-eyed and searching. "I don't know how to help you."

The candle flame whipped about in the drizzly wind. Annabelle's eyes narrowed. They seemed to cloud and darken, slowly from the edges, like blood moons. A flinch gathered inside me, and as she reached for me, I ducked behind my arm.

"Who did this?" she asked.

I looked out at her. "Did what?"

Her fingers hovered above the wound near my temple, springing back at the feel of hardened blood.

"Betsy, who did this to you? What happened?"

"Nobody," I said. "Nothing."

She swallowed, and we went quiet. Taking either side of my jaw, she held my face like it might blow away.

"You'll come home with me," she said, with the cautious tone of someone asking *how many fingers am I holding up.* "We'll wash your hair, and you can eat."

I nodded, hypnotized by the intensity of her care.

"You understand, yes?" she asked.

"I think so," I said, though a heavy fog had filled my head.

She flattened my hand against her chest, pressed it hard so that her pulse flitted against my palm. I focused on the steadiness of her heartbeat until my body melted in its rhythm, and I knew that she could see through me like I was nothing more than water.

I started crying, without knowing why. I thought then how she was not a fair-haired girl but, somewhere within, a ghost as soft

The Lyrebird's Bell

as seafoam. Whatever my ghost was, she saw, and in each other's company, we could be bodiless and free.

Water trickled from a fountain, somewhere behind the tall spires of cypress pines, into a small green pond. Annabelle hummed a funny tune, pausing now and then to correct the melody. She continued stirring, and I leaned my head on her shoulder. We held each other's hands, squeezing like we meant to braid our palm lines, sew them together like thread.

＊

It would be several weeks before I learned who was responsible for the plain green car rolling up the drive.

Birds sang clear and shrill through the kitchen window screen as Annabelle rinsed my hair over the sink. Her movements were rough, distracted, and my head stung from the Palmolive she had scrubbed into the wound. I had already thrown up the buttered toast she compelled me to eat. We had not spoken on the way back from the silver grass-tree where we left her mother. It had felt as though we had dragged her a great distance, our muscles straining, and Mrs. Chernova's shoe — part of the ensemble Annabelle insisted her mother be wearing — continuously falling off. But we were flimsy, hungry girls, and it could not have been that far.

When we heard the gravel crackle outside, we hurried out of the pantry into the garden, but Annabelle would go no farther. She seemed unable to pass an invisible threshold and instead huddled in the grass and shivering wet shrubs. I wrapped an arm around her and felt her bones tightening, the hum of her teeth clicking together. Even wearing my jumper, she would not stop shaking.

"That's not Mama," she said, like an accusation. A woman in drab brown plaid climbed out of the car in front of the house, and a man in bureaucratic tweed followed.

A Song for Wildcats

It shocked me, the ease with which they spotted us. I had imagined the garden to be an immense, harbouring shroud, but the
two strangers found us with no trouble at all.

I remember the man lifting me gruffly, his arm firm across my
torso, as I kicked and called out to Annabelle — but my limbs
were light and weak, like tattered fabric fighting the wind. The
woman pulled Annabelle by the arm, struggling as Annabelle dug
her sandals into the ground. Everything spun around me, and then
I was standing at the weathered white fence as the car drove away,
shrinking into a dot, a mark of finality.

I waited, but no letter arrived from Annabelle, no telephone
call. At the beauty parlour in town, I fidgeted on the sticky vinyl
seat, slapping through the pages of the local newspaper while my
mother showed the hairdresser glossy clippings from a magazine.
Still no mention of secret Soviets or a body in the woods.

Annabelle's house soon grew to be a distant fortress beyond
the stone wall, in a fallen kingdom I was not allowed to enter. It
looked desolate, with its door boarded up and its windows locked
and filthy. Woody vines and ramblers crawled unpruned around
the pillars. The pale mint bushes neatly dotting the property grew
ravenous, devouring distinction between beginning and end, destruction and growth.

My mother and father came and went like a battering wind-
storm. Josephine confessed — though, of course, she did not
understand it to be a confession — to having spoken of Annabelle
to Ezra. A little girl living without a father, and a mother so chron-
ically ill that she had never, in two years, accepted an invitation
to tea.

"An orphanage with a proper clinical staff," Ezra explained,
when I demanded to know where Annabelle had been taken. He
was rummaging through a bowl of keys in the hallway. "Where she
ought to be. Apparently, she's not a well girl."

The Lyrebird's Bell

"It's in a beachy little suburb, you'd adore it." My mother's hand rose to her chest. She made a tutting sound and shook her head. "Poor thing, simply abandoned like that, can you imagine."

"Annie's afraid of beaches," I said. "She thinks mermaids are real and swim around kidnapping people."

My mother laughed. "Trust me, dear, she'll be much happier where she can be taken care of."

"But I take care of her," I said.

"Darling, you're only a child." My mother stooped and licked her thumb, cleaned a smudge of breakfast jam from my chin. "Don't you want your little friend to be as loved as you are?"

One grey dawn in April, I sat by a nearby creek and listened to the stillness. Leaves shaken by the wind, the low murmur of oncoming rain. It was only me out here once more, and I saw no cause to speak, now or ever. A sound only floats away, as all things do. It seemed obvious to me now that no attempt to tether oneself to anything could last. One is always cut loose again by some stronger force and pulled into a more defeated isolation. A place where memories flash like mirrors and you are the only thing that will not leave you.

Sticky hoya climbers dripped nectar onto the soil next to me. Maybe every drip meant that an hour had passed, but there was no way of knowing. I had buried a watch out here somewhere, long ago. A gold cocktail watch that belonged to my mother, with a dour angular face like my father's, so was it my father's watch, then? Who had owned that unfriendly watch? I remembered only that its glass face was so cracked after I broke it that it looked like a spider's web.

Nectar landed on my hand. I ran the wax against my skirt, but that only spread it. I would have to dip my fingers into the creek to wash them clean.

It was peaceful across the creek. My mother used to walk with me along the bank, spotting lizards and paw prints, a lonely

A Song for Wildcats

bowerbird's collection of broken teacups and flowers. It reminded me of solid places. Baked earth underfoot and sturdy branches, familiar hands.

The surface of the creek was so fragile that it broke when I touched it. A reflection of floating rock faces and stringybark trees sprang outward in illusory ripples. Fallen reeds lay on the water and tangled over my feet. Or I was meant to think so, but I saw the bones forming from the long, grassy spires, the hand wrapping around my ankle. Rather than leave this place, I could sink into it completely, into its myths and stone, water and earth. I only had to let it take me, drag me to the bottom, where I had the strangest feeling I would find myself waiting.

Far in the distance, I thought I heard the singsong of a bell. A bird playing tricks, or a mourner sounding the end of a funeral. Some tune sent off into the sky, with little thought as to who might be listening, or how silent the world would fall once it was gone.

I surprised myself then, and drew back. Not entirely, one foot still submerged. It was the breeze that caught me, carrying honey and mint, a tinge of pine. This was my scent, what Annabelle must have meant when she said I smelled of forest. Outsiders marvelled at the sweetness of the trees, having only ever known of the bush as some perilous mystery. But I was no outsider. This place did not need to swallow me to claim me. It had long cradled my small life, its breath perfumed my skin.

Dawn began to lighten as I walked back to the villa. In my bedroom, I pulled out the black purse from behind the new peppermint-striped pinafore dresses and ruffle-trim skirts in my wardrobe. I clicked it open and looked inside at the marble deer. Part of Artemis's hand still clung to the stunted antler, but to break it off completely would be to lose a piece of the deer. I packed the one suitcase I had brought from Woodend and hauled my

The Lyrebird's Bell

belongings down the stairs, then outside and across the terrace, and down the slope to the side of the road.

For a long time, I sat on my suitcase and stared at the pebbles in the dirt. Nobody was stopping me, but rather than keep going, I fiddled with the suitcase's broken buckle, the strap of my shoe, the buttons on my coat.

Dark and obscure behind the fog, the nearby eucalypts appeared as shadow theatre. I looked back to where the fog tempered the villa's exacting lines; still, the verdurous leaves could be seen bursting through the brick. I had been enchanted with the villa when I first arrived in my mother's car. The wispy grass filling the cracks in a long flagstone path, the old well with its iron crank and rust-chewed chain. The pastoral decadence of fallen fruit scattered across the ground.

Was it still beautiful? Could I keep the comfort of its beauty, fixed and fundamental, or was beauty corruptible too? If beauty is corrupted, then it ceases to embody beauty; it takes on another form. Did that mean that beauty was incorruptible? What then of truth, goodness, love?

I lifted the hood of my coat over my hair. The sun broke through the horizon and doused away the fog. The leaves sharpened and gleamed. The distant blue mountains reappeared. As the sky broadened high above me, I felt the sunlight's warmth and nourishment, feeding me with such tenderness, as though I were the last blade of grass.

For many years, the horizon had enclosed my world, stretching its rigid border between me and elsewhere. *The world is home.* Deep breath, in, out. *I contain the world.*

I hoped that Annabelle was being cared for, and that we would see each other soon enough. I hoped that among the stone and ash that, little by little, heap up around one's life, my mother and father could each find those roaring bright sparks worth tending.

A Song for Wildcats

The suitcase kicked up a dusty brume behind me as I started down the road, my heart pecking wildly and a quiver through my legs. I would meet the horizon of my known world, and pass through it like an open gate.

Acknowledgements

My deepest gratitude to everyone at Dundurn Press for being so fantastic at what they do and for their incisive editorial insight, beautiful cover, and thorough team support. Thank you for giving my collection such a wonderful home.

I can't say thank you enough to Megan Beadle, my acquiring editor, for her enormous generosity in championing this collection and for how deeply she understood the beating heart of each story. Thank you, as well, to my agent, Julia Kim, for her warmth and enthusiasm and for seeing value in my work.

Thank you to everyone who read drafts of these stories and offered their unique editorial perspective, particularly my mother, Sandra, and my dear friend, poet Julie Cameron Gray. Thank you to Natasha Tsakiris, my fellow adventurer, for always sharing her breadth of industry savvy.

Thank you so much to anyone who's read this collection. There are so many books from which to choose, and I'm honoured that you cared to read mine. To those who also struggle with trauma, grief, and mental illness, please remember that you can always crawl between these pages and be held.

A Song for Wildcats

And of course, thank you to Ophelia, Allen, and Skits — the three wildcats who have steadied my heart.

About the Author

Caitlin Galway (she/they) is a queer author, editor, and instructor. Her debut novel, *Bonavere Howl*, was a spring pick by the *Globe and Mail*, and her work has appeared in *Best Canadian Stories 2025*, *EVENT*, Gloria Vanderbilt's *Carter V. Cooper Short Fiction Anthology*, House of Anansi's *The Broken Social Scene Story Project* (selected by Feist), *The Ex-Puritan* as the 2020 Thomas Morton Prize winner, and *Riddle Fence* as the 2011 Short Fiction Contest winner. It has also appeared on CBC Books as the Stranger than Fiction Prize winner (selected by Heather O'Neill). She is a passionate advocate for trauma survivors, the mad community, animal welfare, and social/environmental reform. She lives surrounded by haunted antiques with her tiny, thunderous panther, Allen Theodore, and her wistful little wolf, Ophelia Fflur.